Troubled Moon

Confessions of a Tarot Reader

*A Supernatural Journey Through
Reversed Major Arcana Cards for
Romantics, Mystics, and
the Magically Minded*

Kooch N. Daniels

ISBN: 978-0-578-55474-7

Printed in the United States of America
First Printing, 2019

Featured cover Tarot card illustration by Mikaila Beeler

Cover design by Mark Murphy, Murphy Designs
www.murphydesign.com

Dedication

This story is dedicated to the High Priestess awake in those who are daring enough to enter the maze of illusion and reality of occult mysteries. I also wish to pay tribute to lovers of the Tarot and the passion, tears, and fears that can sometimes accompany the meandering Fool's path.

Table of Contents

Chapter One: The Magician

Chapter Two: The High Priestess

Chapter Three: The Empress

Chapter Four: The Emperor

Chapter Five: The High Priest

Chapter Six: The Lovers

Chapter Seven: The Chariot

Chapter Eight: Strength

Chapter Nine: The Hermit

Chapter Ten: The Wheel of Fortune

Chapter Eleven: Justice

Chapter Twelve: The Hanged Man

Preface

If you're asking if this book is really a true confession, the answer is mostly yes. After all, life is stranger than fiction but this story combines life's realities with Tarot card interpretations.

Many Tarot books discuss history, symbols, and key thematic ideas to explain the cards. Most, however, leave out the exploration of the unpredictable worlds of potential realities and events that can accompany these underlying meanings. When I couldn't find a book combining real-life scenarios with card meanings, I was inspired to write about the true confessions of readers and experiences that can be associated with major Tarot card meanings.

Maybe you're a Tarot reader and you'll find the major arcana cards' keywords and themes woven into the fabric of each chapter. Perhaps this writing will enable you to recognize archetypes in the cards or view different dimensions and challenges they might represent. Perhaps you've picked up this book because you're interested in the Tarot or the supernatural, you love reading about romance, or you're hoping that these pages will inspire you to dance with your imagination. Whatever your reason, I hope you'll enjoy.

Acknowledgments

I'd like to thank Cris Wanzer and Nicola Scott Stupka for editing and giving feedback to my writing. I especially want to thank Lila Welchel for writing and mailing me her poem, which is presented in Chapter 18, "The Star." I should also thank the spirit of synchronicity that encouraged her to unknowingly send me this poem just when my storyline needed it. Also, I want to thank my husband, Victor, who critiqued each chapter after I wrote it and encouraged me to continue writing. I want to thank Jaen Murphy and her double-Gemini, Mercurial mindfulness for her prepublication insights; Smitty Wermuth for her wisdom about illusions and delusions; and Tara Daniels for her cups of tea and our walks together to help me stay centered on my path. Also, many thanks to Rob McNutt, who generously supplied some juicy details about drug challenges in the big city.

In addition, I want to thank NROOG and the Tarot teachers I first studied with in San Francisco in the early '70s, and my present-day Tarot community in the SF Bay Area, which includes the most awesome group of Tarot readers you'll ever be lucky enough to meet. Most especially, love and hugs to Stacey Haysler and the Tarot Media Company for producing the first version of this story. In this second edition, my writing has taken a slightly different direction and hopefully weaves the pages together with greater vitality.

Of course, I want to give a big thanks to all of you who are reading the words on these pages. From my heart to yours, sending you a big hug!

Chapter One

The Magician
Hermes, Be Our Guide

Carmella, whose stride showed unnerving confidence, had won Dylan's attention by flirting ferociously with him. Just thinking about the warmth in his glance and his larger-than-life smile made her grin. But now she resisted looking into his eyes, knowing that he was emotionally involved with someone else.

"Do you want to stop and take a short hike or go back to the city?" Carmella asked after they had been driving the Marin coast for nearly an hour, searching for a seemingly invisible address. In all of her twenty-six years of living the good life, she had never said no to adventure but because she was feeling a bit car sick from Dylan zipping around the zigzagging coastal curves on Highway 1, she would have been more than happy to turn around and go home.

Intuitively sensing Carmella's discomfort, Dylan frowned and replied, "It took us too long to get out here. I don't want to waste my time by giving up on finding this place."

The words had barely escaped his lips when he slammed on the brakes and made a sharp right into a driveway that was partially hidden by a decaying fence covered with overgrown foliage. He stopped for a minute and pulled his long, dark hair away from his eyes. He scanned the unfamiliar environment, then began to slowly maneuver down the long, bumpy, potholed dirt driveway. Excited but cautious, he lowered his speed to take in the eerie vista before them — an old Victorian farmhouse in visible need of repair. As if being pulled by a magnet, he felt guided to a patchwork of sidewalk and weeds that led to a barricaded entrance. He tried to ignore Carmella's pretty smile as he parked.

"Let's get going before it gets too dark," he said as he got out and moved around to her side of the car to open her door.

Eager to see the old house, Carmella promptly got out and followed Dylan. Walking two steps behind him, she continued up the path until she stopped to read a sign painted with barely recognizable, faded letters: *Condemned, Do Not Enter.* She felt the dampness of the fog that seemed to appear on cue at the sight of the sign and could hardly believe that Dylan was still proceeding forward at a brisk pace. Not wanting to be left behind, she took a deep breath of the cool ocean air and continued toward the front door, trying to match Dylan's swift stride.

Carmella, who had asked Dylan if she could tag along because of her interest in the supernatural, walked faster and faster, even though her common sense was telling her to go in the other direction. She wanted to make a good impression on her new friend so she decided not to complain or show her growing fear. Instead, she began to silently chant to the elephant-headed god, Ganesha, to protect her and remove their obstacles.

Dylan, who seemed excited to be on a mission to connect with some tangible part of a lost, departed soul, didn't waste any time. Within minutes, he had broken away the boards that blocked off the front door and was waving for Carmella to join him.

"It looks like we're entering a Grimm's fairy tale cottage in the woods," Carmella chirped as she joined him.

The ominous front door showed signs of better days. Carmella looked at the dirty but glorious antique stained-glass windows that portrayed dolphins dancing on the waves. The door creaked as Dylan pushed it open, then fell from its rotting hinges, almost hitting him on the head as it tore away from its frame.

Without hesitation, they propped the door open and entered the dimly lit old house. Each began to gingerly walk through its empty rooms, all filled with cobwebs, empty beer cans, cigarette butts, and shattered glass. The rotting wooden floorboards creaked loudly in response to their steps, as if warning them that they didn't belong there. Carmella could hear her heart pounding as they came to a long, circular staircase that led to the second floor.

"So far, I don't feel anything strange or supernatural," Dylan said. "Let's go upstairs and see if we can find anything out of the ordinary. Do you see anything weird, Carmella?"

Carmella stepped over to an old dresser that sat near the base of the staircase and began pulling open its drawers. "Just some broken jewelry in this dilapidated chest of drawers, filled with the dust of ages," she said as each drawer creaked when she opened it.

She spied a small, blue triangular-shaped stone that seemed to be shining from a crack in a backboard of the chest. To reward herself for facing sinister shadows instead of running from the approaching darkness, she gave in to her love of bright, shiny things. Carmella reached for the stone, which fit perfectly in her palm. She saw that it was engraved with the golden Egyptian eye of Horus. *How cool is this?* she thought and put it in her pocket. "No, I'm not having any luck seeing anything except for disgusting cobwebs, dirt, and little stones," Carmella whispered. *And Dylan,* she thought, who was so cute that she would follow him into an eerie old house. Thank God it was late afternoon and not midnight, or she would have run.

As they began to navigate the decaying stairs, she took a deep breath and consciously relaxed the muscles in her legs, which seemed to be protesting the climb. Not wanting to disappoint Dylan, she stopped herself from telling him that she preferred to study what it means to truly be alive instead of investigating the shadowy ruins of the departed.

Breathe, she told herself. If she wanted to understand the meaning of the Great Mystery and the Tree of Life, she shouldn't be afraid to search for truth under the crumbling compost of the nature of existence.

Moving slowly, lost in a sense of dread, Carmella forced herself to follow Dylan. *He sure has a cute behind,* she thought, trying to distract herself from her expanding sense of fear.

The first upstairs room they entered was just like

the rooms downstairs. Cobwebs, beer bottles, a dead bird, bat guano, and a few ugly pieces of broken furniture were visible between walls that seemed to come together without symmetry. But when they entered the most distant room at the end of the long, dim hallway, it had an otherworldly silence that felt dreary and strangely unnatural.

Carmella couldn't help herself and said, "This feels creepy..."

Completely empty, without any telltale signs of anything from the past — even dust — the room seemed to express the deviant silence of the painful agony of someone left alone with the devil in the dark. A weird symbol that looked like something you might see in a B-grade horror movie to mark the doorway to hell was drawn in red paint on one of the blackened walls.

"Do you hear that?" Dylan questioned with a look of anticipation.

"I feel the hair on the back of my head crawling toward the ceiling but I don't hear anything. Can we leave now?" Carmella inquired, trying to muffle her sense of alarm.

"No...I thought I heard some scratching inside this wall," Dylan answered, paying no attention to Carmella's visible anxiety. He looked forward to communicating with spirits who roamed the outer edge of waking reality and this environment had just the right qualities for making it happen. "Do you see anything in the corner?" he asked, pointing to an area that had unusual marks on the floor and a rusty chain hanging from a large meat hook mounted on the wall.

Not wanting him to notice that she was starting to panic, Carmella answered calmly, "Some strange marks.

Maybe they're saying 'Turn left to exit.'" Carmella noticed her hands were beginning to tremble.

"Are you kidding? Those marks, if you turn them upside down, look identical to magical symbols used for calling elemental spirits. This room could be an opening between the worlds of the visible and the invisible. It looks perfect for doing a séance," Dylan said with excitement. "Let's sit down on the floor and try to open communications with the spirits of eternal night who might be using this room as a dwelling place."

Trying not to appear unnerved, Carmella took out her cell phone to take a few pictures. Because her hands wouldn't stop shaking, even her camera seemed to shudder with fear as she tried to capture the room's cryptic images on her phone.

Except for the sounds of deep inhaling, Dylan had become quiet as he went into his meditative, trance-like mood. But soon Carmella heard him talking with some invisible presence that only he perceived.

"Where do you come from?" he inquired earnestly. "How old are you?"

The closed window in the room suddenly opened with a rusty moan, then quickly slammed shut. Carmella's adrenaline bolted as she perceived an indecipherable stream of words shoot like warring arrows above her head. Then she heard a sinister demand: "Give me my rabbit back!" The nearby window opened and slammed shut several more times in rhythm with the sad groaning of the aging glass encasements.

"Dylan, I want to leave," Carmella said in a panic while tugging at her motionless friend's shirt.

A hound started barking from somewhere outside

the room. As cold chills covered her arms, Carmella ran to the door, expecting to see a dog, but there was nothing there.

"Dylan, please! This house feels so creepy. Can we leave?" she prodded, wishing she hadn't decided to spend her afternoon getting to know Dylan better. She rubbed her eyes in disbelief but she couldn't deny seeing a flickering light swirling in a circle above Dylan's head.

As if in a daze, Dylan, seemingly disoriented, stood up and stumbled out of the room. A crimson trail of blood dripped from his wrist. "I was attacked by something with sharp teeth. Let's get out of here!" he yelled as he dashed down the stairs.

"Wait for me!" Carmella shrieked, her voice breaking from the release of high-intensity fright as she rushed to follow him.

The weary trespassers couldn't leave the dilapidated dwelling fast enough. As Dylan and Carmella ran like frightened school children outside into the seemingly normal world, the sound of their relieved sighs was echoed by the strong coastal winds. Chilled to the bone, they rushed to return to Dylan's unlocked car and jumped inside. The sound of their car doors closing triggered a returning rational sense of personal safety. As they sat in a familiar haven, safe and away from the previous uncertainties, they turned and looked at one another.

"You're bleeding!" Carmella said as she saw his bloodstained hand. She began to search for something she could use to bind Dylan's wrist. The only thing she could find was her favorite tie-dyed hanky, decorated with a peace sign, which was wrapped around the Tarot cards she'd left sitting on the car's floorboards.

"Goddess, bless me and my cards," she murmured as she removed the cloth from the cards and began to swathe Dylan's curious wound.

"Ouch! Go...easy...on...me..." Dylan complained in a series of painful notes, sounding an SOS as she pushed on his wrist to staunch the bleeding.

"Sorry, I'm just trying to help."

"Yes, I know, but please, can you be little more gentle?" he asked, wincing with noticeable discomfort.

Carmella, realizing that her nerves were still trying to recover from their recent adventure, relaxed her grasp on Dylan's arm. "Yes...OK," she said. "Just tell me how I can do this so I don't hurt you."

"If you really want to help, you can start talking to me about the 49ers. Talking about sports always helps me get back into my normal, everyday reality. Once I'm more grounded, I'll be able to drive without my mind going into another dimension and us flying off the road," Dylan replied. His voice carried a disjointed but purposeful tone that made it obvious his recent, nimble rush out of the house hadn't totally pulled him from his out-of-body, trance-like state.

"OK, OK," Carmella replied, even though she knew nothing about sports and hated the competitive gladiator qualities of athletic games. She still remembered the humiliation and embarrassment of always having been the last one chosen to play on any team when she was a teenager in high school, and she still tried to avoid sports. The only thing she could think of in relation to the 49ers was Joe Montana. Her dad had talked about him all the time when she was growing up. "What do you know about Joe Montana?" she asked awkwardly while trying to appear calm and relaxed.

She watched Dylan trying desperately to find

where to put the key in the ignition. It became obvious that he was partly in this world and somewhere else far away. It seemed that his wrist hadn't sustained serious damage as he no longer appeared to notice his wound.

"Well, he has a beautiful wife," Dylan muttered almost inaudibly as his key found the starter and the choking ignition made it known that the car was ready to leave. Dylan put the car into reverse, slowly backed out of the driveway, and barely missed going into a ditch before he turned the car around to begin the journey home.

Carmella couldn't get Dylan to talk with her. He fell into complete silence. Feeling frazzled and a bit inept as a ghostbuster, she looked at the Tarot cards she held in her lap.

"My auntie would give me card readings all the time when I was a teenager," she said, trying to get a conversation going. "When I got older, before I went to college and when she thought I was becoming someone much like her own self, she taught me how to use them. She told me that instead of me calling her all the time to ask her to draw cards to answer my questions, I would know how to use the cards to answer my own questions."

Carmella might have worried about Dylan's lack of response but luckily he seemed to be driving with an attitude of alertness. At present, he was navigating the curves slowly and smoothly without the reckless impatience he had shown earlier that evening. Truthfully, she was happy that she had been able to witness Dylan acting as a psychic investigator, and even felt proud that she had overcome her initial fears and had entered the old house.

As if on autopilot, she began shuffling her cards.

"Dylan, I'm going to pull a card for you," she said, once again trying to engage him in conversation.

Carmella stopped her shuffle and intuitively turned over the card that felt like it had the most influence, then sat it on top of the deck. "This card represents you in the present moment," she said, looking to see the front of the card she had overturned.

She grinned as she saw the image of the Magician, one of his hands pointing toward the heavens and the other aiming at the earth. "As above, so below!" she declared, trying to get Dylan to talk. "What's the connection between the micro and the macrocosms? Do you think the Caduceus, the universal, curative wand of the Mercurial Magician, can heal the broken heart or does it solely reflect the strength of will of the subconscious mind? Can there be any emotional cures without agreement with the law of karma?" she asked, seeking Dylan's insights.

Dylan didn't answer except to say, "Know thyself."

Carmella reflected on his answer and decided it might be best if she echoed his silence and didn't ask any more questions. Lost in deep thought, they quietly made their way back to San Francisco, tracking the bizarre events at the old house in the seclusion of their own minds.

Chapter Two

The High Priestess
Touching The Sacred

A few days later, Carmella was happy to be near the coast in the countryside again. Smiling and carefree, she gingerly hiked the winding trail that led to the top of Mt. Tam but stopped suddenly when the gathering in the large meadow came into view. It was hard for Carmella to believe that most of the people she viewed in the distance were "skyclad" — a word used by pagans to refer to being naked in a magical circle.

To overcome her mounting anxiety, Carmella took a moment to slowly inhale the invigorating sea air. She dropped her heavy backpack, took a moment to relax, and rubbed the new stone in her pocket that she had recently found while exploring the old house with Dylan. Its smooth surface seemed to warm her hand with a subtle electric current that made her hope it would bring good luck.

Soon lost in thought about the recent, unexpected change in her career, she walked toward the circle, eager to carry out her freelance assignment of writing an article on the present-day practices of witchcraft. She tried to distract herself from the uncomfortable thought of taking off her clothes in public by musing about the most probable theme for her writing project. Without showing any signs of nervousness, she walked into a group of about thirty people, all in different stages of undress, who were gathering at early dusk to celebrate the lunar eclipse.

Trying not to appear odd, Carmella bravely took off her clothes, placed them nearby under the branches of a mighty oak, and joined the circle of friendly, smiling folk. To her surprise, both her modesty and her writing assignment drifted into indifference as she began moving in the revolving human spiral, kissing the cheeks of all who danced childlike in front of her. By the look in their eyes, the line of merry-makers seemed to silently agree that they were celebrating something timeless, beyond intellectual measure. Swaying in unison, they moved to form an unbroken circle in rhythm to the silent command of an infinite voice.

Daggers, wands, silver chalices, food, and wine played an alluring role in the ritual that was being performed in the center of the circle by three cantaloupe-breasted women whose bellies revealed the rippled swells of past pregnancies and too much indulgence in the good life.

The presiding priest of the circle, who looked like a scrawny rag doll with flowers in his braided beard, wore nothing more than a mask, a crown headdress of horns and feathers, and a magnificent sword that dangled from his star-studded belt. He appeared to be hypnotized as he followed behind the priestesses, handing them magical artifacts when they needed them as their voices mingled with a seductive appeal to become one with the goddess. Carmella couldn't stop looking at the size of his penis, which was growing larger than any she had previously witnessed. *No wonder he's the lord of the circle*, she chuckled silently to herself.

In accord with ceremonial etiquette, Carmella bowed to a priestess who was blessing each person with smoldering sage as she rhythmically strolled around the human ring. When this part of ritual neared its end, it was time for an experience that one of the high priestesses identified as "calling down the goddess." With her sword pointed to the sky, she commanded everyone to lie down on the ground with his or her head toward the center of the circle and open their hearts to receive Mother Nature's cosmic blessing.

"She is one, She is all!" the priestesses bellowed.

"Love is the only law!" everyone replied.

As Carmella became more comfortable lying on the cool ground, her entire body began to feel enveloped in the underlying energy of the earth. The voices of the priest and priestesses faded into the distance. Effortlessly, Carmella went into an altered state of consciousness, where dreams and reality seemed to merge in euphoria. Through a repetitive rhythm from which she was not separate, she began to recognize a soundless, pulsing beat of life, death, and rebirth, constant and transcendent. As she listened through a mental haze, the world around her was transformed into a resounding melody that included muffled voices of people whispering, women and men shouting, and bodies moving with roused emotion. Confused yet fascinated, she soundlessly asked, *What is happening to me?*

Instead of hearing an answer, Carmella felt someone tap her shoulder. "You're going to get stepped on if you don't move. Do you need help getting up?"

It was Dylan.

Reaching for her hand, he gently said, "You looked like you were sound asleep. If you want to truly be awake in this moment, I know where we should go. It's a wondrous spot where the magic of this special place becomes more alive. You'll be able to see the sun setting over the western waves and the moon rising in the east. Can I take you there?"

Roused from her reverie, Carmella lost touch with the subtle voices that were filling her mind. Smiling, yet overwhelmed by her shyness at sitting completely naked in front of Dylan, who was completely dressed, she quickly went from her sublime *Alice In Wonderland* experience to being a mainstream tourist in a foreign land. Her sense of embarrassment eased as she reminded herself that she was on a mission — her writing assignment.

"Oh...of course. I'd like to see the moon rising," she replied, feeling vulnerable and strangely breathless. She tried to stop herself from hoping that this would turn into a perfect make-out opportunity but she couldn't control her emerging desires.

Dylan's strong but gentle arms pulled her upright. He looked deeply into her eyes and dusted a few leaves from her hair. When he started to speak, Carmella turned away and ran to retrieve her clothes. *What good fortune to be invited to spend more time with Dylan,* she thought. She decided to leave her cumbersome backpack behind so that it wouldn't distract her as they walked. Soon she was back by his side, dressed, with a modest air of schoolgirl charm.

Without talking, they began walking away from the circle toward a jagged cliff decorated with windblown junipers bent sideways with the telltale signs of time. Inwardly, Carmella watched herself move farther away from what seemed like a remarkable and unusually intimate connection to the spirit of Oneness. Even though she was happy to be with Dylan, she had just experienced something other-worldly and was reluctant to leave the dream-like state of the previous moment. Never before had she felt like she could reach out and touch the infinite mystery of creation. But now that feeling was gone.

Her mind kept slipping into feelings of joy at her unplanned meeting with Dylan. Out of control, her emotions felt an undeniable longing to hold him in her arms, to feel his lips press against hers...but since he was presently in a relationship, that feeling wasn't welcome and didn't make any sense. Still, she couldn't help but wonder if their souls had called one another to meet once again.

Even though she was becoming absorbed in the natural beauty of their surroundings, she couldn't help but notice how handsome Dylan was, with the wind blowing through his hair and his taut, muscular body climbing with almost a feminine grace. Astounded by getting to spend unexpected time with Dylan, her mind raced, thinking about what she might say. Perhaps she could confide in him and tell him how devastated she felt about losing her job on the editing staff of *Vanity Fair*. She scrunched her shoulders to release the ensuing tension in her neck when she realized that she didn't want to discuss something that felt like an embarrassment. Or maybe this would be a good time to tell him about the rock that she had put in her pocket while they were together in the old house. It was different from any rock she had ever held as it seemed to leave a heat impression on her hand.

Instead of discussing anything that could distract them from enjoying the surrounding beauty, Carmella dismissed these thoughts and simply said, "I didn't see you when I looked around the circle."

"I arrived late. Everyone was lying on the ground with their eyes closed when I got here," he replied as he led her down the well-worn path on the bluff.

"Oh..." Carmella said, suddenly recalling her original purpose for attending the ritual. She remembered her cell phone with its great little camera and reached into her pocket to grab it, but it wasn't there.

Oh no, she thought, *I must have left it in my backpack under the tree.*

It baffled her that she could be so forgetful to leave it behind. If she could get one good picture of the witchery circle before it completely disappeared, she was sure she'd be paid extra for her article. She exhaled a heavy sigh when she realized that leaving her camera behind meant she had lost all possibilities for taking photos. Still, she couldn't help but smile as Dylan took her hand to help her scale a high rock leading to a stone perch on the sea-cliff wall. Her heart jumped as she followed his vertical ascent to a balcony seat high above the crashing ocean waves.

In spite of their unplanned meeting, both Dylan and Carmella were obviously happy to have found private time to be together. Lost in the perfection of the moment, they sat with their feet dangling free over the cliff, enjoying each other's company. While others nearby in the woodlands were howling like a pack of wolves, they both sat silently, spellbound in awe of the brilliant, crimson-red light of the setting sun and the misty illumination of the rising moon. Carmella started to feel an unfamiliar happiness that made her wonder if she was going love crazy as she looked into Dylan's eyes. She looked away, breaking the magical spell of the moment from his magnetic stare toward the horizon, where the sea and sky blended into one. In her timeless reverie, she thought of a new title for her article. "The Revolving Wheel of a Sacred Circle" effortlessly came to her mind.

Just then, as if some invisible force had ordained a change in their encounter, one of the three priestesses who had led the circle giggled her way into their private meeting. She spoke with a British accent.

"You've found the best seat in nature's amphitheater." She fumbled with her cape to cover her naked body before sitting close to Carmella.

Luna's wild, curly red hair was not the only prelude to her ability to draw attention to herself and her bold, dominating personality. Carmella felt her strength. Clearly, there was something peculiar about her angelic voice. It seemed almost hypnotic and amplified the intensity of her words. As she joined their conversation, she quickly inspired Carmella to feel as though they were three entwined beings searching as one soul for answers to transcendent questions that reached beyond the known boundaries of time and space.

Chattering incessantly, Luna confessed that while walking, she had been intuitively drawn to the beautiful moon-watching couple and their glowing auras, and felt inclined to risk the rocky climb to meet them. "I love mysticism," she exclaimed, then professed herself to be a channel for the voice of the invisible masters who wanted the world to hear their wisdom. "The earth is running out of time. At a certain time, you run out of time. The right time interfaces with the wrong time. Timeless, timely, or untimely, only now is the correct or proper time," she spoke, her words dancing in rhythm to the crashing waves below their roost.

Suddenly, with a peculiar look on her face, Luna took off one of her beaded necklaces, which had a pendant of Isis, the Egyptian mother goddess of the Nile, and handed it to Carmella. "Dear me, you should never join our circle without a necklace," she said without skipping a beat.

"Thank you," Carmella replied, hesitant to take the gift. She felt a blush cover her cheeks as she reached for it.

Sensing Carmella's unease, Luna said, "Don't worry, I made the necklace myself and blessed it during a new moon using crystal pyramid power. The amulet of Isis is for your protection. Let me help you with the clasp." She gently put her hands on Carmella's back. "It's good luck if someone puts it around your neck the first time you wear it. It helps you remember its value. Promise me that you'll wear it."

"OK," Carmella giggled, feeling a bit anxious at Luna's gentle stroke of her hair.

As Luna's hands touched her shoulders, they seemed to send a jolt of electricity throughout her body. Carmella quickly moved back from Luna's see-mingly too-familiar caress.

Without mentioning the obviously awkward moment, and bubbling over with enthusiasm at their meeting, Luna started to channel a moon meditation.

She guided Carmella and Dylan to open their inward, intuitive eyes and see within the invisible, golden light of the lines of psychic energy created in the sacred circle they had joined.

"Let's see what you can find within. If you draw on the energy of our circle, you can go back in time," she stated matter-of-factly. "When you walk psychic power lines, you can channel their light and create a power grid that can intensify the healing energy of the earth. Our sacred circle can be used to recharge the healing properties of our ailing planet."

Two ravens flew overhead, sounding a cry that seemed to emphasize a sense of urgency to see the healing light within.

Dylan added his own explanation and discussed working in harmony with the earth's power grids. "When you assist in this process, your mind automatically shifts to a higher level of understanding of these naturally occurring currents of invisible power. With practice, you can learn to use your intuition as an instrument to accelerate the evolution of humanity."

Even though Luna nodded her head in agreement, her attention seemed to be directed at Carmella. Luna wasn't sure what it was about Carmella that made her look so naïve and innocent but she was drawn to her. She was also very curious as to why Carmella's right hand was abnormally illuminated with a dazzling, deep-blue aura.

As Carmella felt Luna's gaze, she became filled with a strange sensation that went beyond logic and recognized it as something akin to sensuality and seduction. Was it only in her imagination that Luna seemed to be attracted to her? Why did she keep staring at her?

Without offering any clue about what might lie beneath the surface of her smile, Luna continued talking to her new friends about "otherworldly" knowledge associated with vortexes, psychic realms, and invisible dimensions hidden behind the veil of Maya, or illusion.

Dylan agreed with Luna. "Our higher purpose is to offer ourselves as vessels to heal the planet and offer care to those in need. The more of this work you do, the more you realize how important it is."

"You sound like you're the voice for the High Priestess card," Carmella responded with a smile. She wondered if Dylan knew her words were dancing in the ether for him alone.

Dylan wondered what he should be feeling about the connection between himself and Carmella. He wasn't sure.

As the three new friends continued to talk, nimble fingers of fog began reaching the coastline, leaving behind murky shadows rising and falling on the rolling sea. The light of the early evening was beginning to fade.

"Your words are very wise but I'm getting cold," Carmella said. "Maybe we should get back before it's too dark to see where we're going. And I need to be heading back to town soon. My dog's been in my apartment all day and he usually gets into trouble if I leave him alone for too long."

"Yes, it's that time of day when we all need to find warmth or freeze to death," Luna replied with a noticeable shiver. "Perhaps we'll find an excuse to speak again. When we get back to the circle, I'll give you my business card with my number. If you're interested, call me and I can give you more information about my work and connecting with the lines of energy in the vortexes."

Carmella instantly thought of asking Luna for an interview. *It will give my article more depth and interest,* she thought in response to Luna's offer. "That's great. I look forward to meeting you again and learning about invisible energies."

With no more than a smiling nod from Dylan, they all got up and started walking back toward the sacred circle. Dylan wasn't sure what kind of energy he was sensing from Luna. It wasn't really bad but his intuition told him he was confronting a rival.

"Luna, how long have you been a priestess?" Dylan asked, trying to overcome his sense of being excluded from what was beginning to be a girls-only conversation.

"Initiation things are only for initiates to know," she replied, ignoring his request for information.

With a quick smile, Dylan hid his disappointment in response to her refusal to share information. *Women are so strange,* he thought, deciding to become meditative and quiet.

Luckily, the moon rose higher in the sky, casting its lunar glow to illuminate a safe way to traverse the rocky path. With each passing moment, the cool wind became more savage, prompting the three hikers to move quickly down the trail, which seemed painfully long in the encroaching darkness.

Even though her body was chilled, by the time Carmella could see a bonfire in a clearing in the woods, crackling a warm, welcoming hello, she could feel her energy being recharged, uplifted, and more aligned with a higher sense of purpose. Perhaps the magical circle truly was magical, she thought as she followed close behind Dylan.

Chapter Three

The Empress
Touching The Girdle Of Venus

"Dylan, you're raiding my cookie jar," his mother declared while walking briskly into her newly remodeled kitchen. "Did you come to visit me because you want to eat all my chocolate chip cookies? And who are you calling on the phone? It wouldn't be Lisa, would it?"

"Well, it doesn't matter, does it?" replied Dylan with an undertone of disapproval. "She's not home anyway." He hung up the phone and quickly walked to where his mother, Rowan, stood, and gave her a distracting squeeze while loudly chewing a cookie in her ear.

Rowan pretended that she wanted to smack him. Dylan responded by jumping out of her way. Her self-assurance made her seem sizeable even though she only stood as tall as Dylan's shoulders. Not willing to let go of her question, she snapped, "You should give her up. A married woman isn't going to bring you happiness. I don't like my handsome son hanging around with an older woman, especially when she's involved with someone else. All you get from Lisa is what's left over after she satisfies her husband. Besides, you're already married to a very sweet woman who's committed to giving you a hundred percent of her love."

Dylan cringed as he heard his mother's remark about his wife, Stella. Rowan didn't have a clue about what was going on in their relationship, and most embarrassing, what was not. Stella's secret affair with a younger man was cruel-hearted but Dylan was too intimidated by his mother's expectations for his perfect marriage to explain his current, unsettling emotional situation. Instead, he snapped, "Mom! Get off my back. Stop acting like I'm a little kid. I'm an adult and I know what's right for me. Besides, I'm happy when I'm with Lisa."

He frowned, knowing that his mother would continue to bug him about Lisa for as long as his relationship with her lasted. Why had he confided in her? In the past, she'd always been supportive of his endeavors to find love. It irritated him that his open-minded, new-age, "hip" mother had surprised him with a lecture on family values when he'd told her about his clandestine love affair with Lisa. It was even more irritating when she started lecturing him on the merits of loyalty after he told her that he treasured Lisa more than any woman he had ever known. He wouldn't even attempt to explain to his mom that he'd recently found an attractive, new lady friend, Carmella. Or had she found him? Whatever. Looking at the expression on his mother's face, it was evident that it would be better not to mention Carmella.

"Just because you're six-foot-two doesn't mean that I can't tell you to be a good son. Don't expect me to stop yelling at you until you stop screwing around with some married woman who isn't your wife. Think about your karma," Rowan declared, rubbing the rose quartz heart pendant that hung on a thick gold chain over her heart. "Those sad eyes! You look like I've mortally wounded you. Stop fretting. I don't have time to talk about your personal affairs right now anyway. Moe is coming over soon and I'm going to need you to leave so we can have our privacy."

His mother's criticizing tone hastened his departure. He could only hope for her sake that her mood would improve by the time her new boyfriend walked through the door. "Mom, I'll leave as soon as I get a drink. Stop stressing about my love life. If you want to look at making bad choices, think about your ex-husband. Remember the days when you were always crying 'I can't live with your father anymore. His womanizing is driving me crazy.'"

"You shouldn't talk to me like this. I'm your mother and I worry about you because I love you. When I left your father, it was because I was frantic about what your future and mine would hold. I did what I had to do to stop being vulnerable to Mark's lies and abuse. And I didn't want you to live with that immoral jerk as your daily role model."

The water he was about to swallow seemed to freeze in his mouth. "Truce, Mom. Let's not start talking about the past again. When are you going to realize that I've already heard you complain about Dad way too much? I grew up thinking the sky was going to fall because of the crazy stuff you said he was doing behind closed doors. At this point, do me a favor and don't make matters worse by complaining about Dad or my romantic choices." Dylan turned away from his mother's glare and grabbed a handful of cookies before moving toward the door.

"Is there something you're not telling me?" Rowan implored. "I can feel that something isn't right. Something weird is going on in your head but I don't have time to pull it from you, like this cookie," she said as she stole one from his hand. "Being married and then getting involved with a married woman is going to be bad for somebody, and I'm hoping that somebody isn't you. People can become violent when they find out they are being betrayed. What do you think will happen if her husband finds out? And even though it might do you some good to talk to me about this, it's time for you to go. I hear Moe coming up the driveway."

"OK, I'm getting out of here. But kindly do yourself a favor and stop worrying about me. I ride my own waves and have fun doing it. Besides, you'll always be my number one, the grand Empress herself. Oh, before I forget, I want to tell you about the strangest dream I had the other night. I dreamed that Dad was crawling on his knees, begging you to take him back."

"That doesn't sound like your father. Now get out of here!" Rowan howled as she pushed him lovingly toward the front door.

Dylan was relieved that the conversation about his father had ended quickly. The knot in his stomach told him he wasn't happy to be talking with his mother about his topsy-turvy love life either. She was an expert at meddling with his emotions and had an uncanny knack for prying into his private affairs. He was happy she had given him an excuse to leave before their conversation escalated into an argument. As he walked toward his car, he gave a friendly nod to Moe, who was hurrying toward the house carrying a large bouquet of red roses. An obvious showman of love or not, there was something about the guy that Dylan didn't trust. He wished his mother had better taste in boyfriends. He was sadly aware that his dear, sweet mom, who his dad had bitterly nicknamed the "vagina vampire," always required a boyfriend to distract her from recurring dark moods and their antidote, a handful of depression meds. Dylan couldn't remember a time when Rowan's medicine cabinet wasn't filled with little golden bottles of prescription downers, uppers, and weight-loss pills.

She's been on too many diets and taken too many drugs for her to complain about the wisdom of my choices, he reflected. He wasn't too far from the door to hear his mom say in her sweetest voice, "Come in, Moe. I'm so glad you're here."

Rowan, wearing a long, flowing green gown, smiled as she stood at the entrance of her apartment to greet her foreign friend who brought the flavor of the exotic into her life. She was happy that Dylan had left so she could be alone with Moe, who had brought her a beautiful gift of flowers.

Although he walked in with a smile, Mohammed wasn't sure that he like being called Moe. But he wasn't going to complain. He didn't want to upset his chances of being invited into Rowan's bed. After all, he was getting used to his new American name and she, unlike some of the others, was willing to shave herself in the forbidden zone so that he could be comfortable having sex with her. Priorities needed to be recognized, and since she was more than happy to oblige him, he felt a little indebted to her for her favors.

"Yes, I'm happy too," Moe replied with a crooked grin as he walked into the living room. "Who was that young man that just left?"

"My son, Dylan. He's such a sweetheart but sometimes he acts like he's my father, always trying to tell me what to do."

"Grown children can be like that."

"Yes," Rowan answered while thinking that lovers were more often that way than sons. "Thank you for my lovely roses. They're a treasure and oh so appreciated!" she said as she put them in a rose-colored vase.

Waiting impatiently for her to finish arranging the flowers, and moving like an awkward teddy bear, Moe reached for Rowan and began hugging her. Smiling, he took her hand and walked her toward her Valentine-red sofa. Without hesitation, he pulled her to sit down with him. "You're my Aphrodite, so beautiful..."

"You're very sweet, Moe. Are you sure you're not lying to me?"

"No! What a foolish question. I think you look radiant. I want to hold you in my arms," Moe answered before kissing her reverently.

"Wait a minute, Moe. Let's talk a little before we go any further. I need to ask you a few questions about our last phone conversation. Do you *really* want to marry me?"

"My sweet Rowan, I'm not in the mood to talk about this question right now. Maybe after we make love I'll be in a better state of mind for such a serious conversation."

Rowan felt her body tighten. The line felt disturbingly familiar. First make love, then talk, had been the motto of too many men she had known both before and after her marriage to Dylan's father. She tried to shift her body to gain more physical distance from Moe. "But I'm in the mood to talk for a little while. I was wondering if you truly love me or merely want to use me to get your green card."

"Don't talk like that. Don't disrespect my feelings!" Moe exclaimed. "I've just arrived at your home and you're already making me feel unwelcome."

"I'm not trying to be insensitive but I need to know more about what you're feeling. I'm flattered that you've asked me to marry you but we've only known each other for a couple of months. Perhaps I'm a little insecure because I have a cousin who married a man who left her shortly after he got his citizenship papers. Seriously, Moe, do you really think of me as someone you want to live your life with, or are you looking at me as an easy ticket to citizenship? Be honest." Since her divorce from Mark, the man of her dreams who turned into a nightmare, she wasn't letting any man dictate who she was or what she was supposed to say or do.

"*Mon amour*, I'm wanting to make love to you and you're talking about things that are so difficult to discuss. Why would I bring you flowers? I see you as the most beautiful woman in the world. I want you in my arms right now!"

Rowan was happy for Moe's compliment and his kisses excited her. But he had talked about marriage on the phone and it felt like he was rushing things. She did hope to get married again but she didn't want to become a victim to any man's wrongdoing. "Well, you seem very loving. You don't think I need to lose weight? I have a hard time believing I'm beautiful when I look at my big belly," she said, rubbing her stomach playfully. *I really need to go on a diet again*, she thought, noticing for a quick second that Moe looked disdainfully at her belly.

In truth, Moe perceived Rowan as a cougar, his favorite American term for an attractive, mature woman, and he didn't want to fall prey to discussing her bulges. He knew from past experience that this subject was taboo for romance. He wanted only one thing and didn't feel like extending this ego-busting topic as he knew it would spoil her mood. Disappointed that he had not been able to have sex for the last two weeks, his lustful desire was urgent. He reached to turn off the nearby light.

"Rowan," he said pensively while rubbing her inner thighs, "let's forget all this nonsense. I only have a little time to be with you today and I'd really love to take advantage of it. We can continue this conversation on the phone later tonight after I get home from work, but let's use our time together to hold one another. I want to make love to you."

Pulling her to be near him, he unzipped his pants and moved on top of Rowan, who began giggling like a teenager.

"Your kisses are so delicious," Moe said, kissing her neck and moving his hand inside her blouse to rub her breast.

But at that moment, as if by divine intervention, the phone rang and Rowan wiggled out of his heated grasp to answer her nearby cell phone.

"Hello. What? Today? Really?" she said into the receiver. "Are they crazy? Why, yes of course, I'd love to go. I can get ready almost immediately. I have a friend visiting but he's getting ready to leave soon. Yes,

I'll be ready. Bye." She tried to hide the look of relief that might reveal how happy she was to have an excuse to escape from her emotional confusion and Moe's assertive grasp.

"Oh dear me, I'm so sorry," whined Rowan as she moved her body away from his. "I have an activist friend who wants me to join the fight for the rights of endangered trees and the spotted owls who live in them. Some developer wants to cut down an old grove of trees in order to plant a vineyard. If I have anything to say about it, he'll have to bulldoze my screaming body before I'll let that happen. Just because redwoods exist on his property, he thinks he can cut them down to make a few bucks. These ancient trees have lived for hundreds of years before he and his greed were even born. Concerned people are getting ready to rally and I want to be one of them. My friend's coming to give me a ride to the gathering and he's going to be here soon. He wants me to add to the voices of those who want to protect the redwoods."

"Someone calls and you push me away and want to end our date?" Moe asked with a flash of anger in his eyes. "Now I see where I stand with you. Do you think I'm a moron?"

"Moe, this cause is so very important. My heart feels pain when I think about someone killing those mighty giants. I'd like to stay here and be with you but I have a chance to help save an old-growth forest. There aren't many of those left. My friend just found out about the rally. Don't be mad at me but I want — no, I *need* — to help. I'm sorry but I can't tell you how excited I am to do something of real value. You must understand how important this is, not only to me but also for our future generations. And I'll be getting to spend time with people who are actively involved in the green movement and creating positive changes — working to heal our planet."

Rowan consciously stopped herself from being too eager to talk about her friend who was picking her up in his red convertible sports car. She didn't want to tell Moe how excited she was to have a chance to be with someone who was motivating her to rise to a higher sense of purpose to make something of her life.

"So your affection for trees is more important than making love with me? It's insulting that you want me to leave when I only arrived fifteen minutes ago."

"Moe, I'll call you when I get home and you can come back later."

"Well, don't expect me to come back because I don't feel like visiting you anytime in the near future. That's for sure."

"Moe, give me a kiss. If you really love me, you shouldn't mind that I have a chance to make important changes and help protect our planet. Don't get stuck in negative thinking. Inflexibility drives me crazy."

"And if you're so flexible, you shouldn't mind calling me Mohammed," Moe said indignantly as he gathered his pride, zipped up his pants, and moved rigidly away from her. He walked toward the door without saying another word.

"I love you, Moe! I mean...Mohammed!" Rowan called out in a voice as sweet as candy. "Don't be angry. Mother Nature needs me more than you do right now. Please understand. Call me later so we can talk," she pleaded softly as she heard the door slam.

Chapter Four

The Emperor
Vintage Swagger

Mesmerized by memories of his own grandeur, Mark lay on his comfy couch wishing his youth hadn't passed so quickly. Not that he minded being older. On his better days, he even imagined that he'd become a better person because of all the craziness he'd survived earlier in his life. But he longed for the return of the days when it was easier to meet pretty chicks and he could always count on having someone eager to play in his bed.

Trying to shake off the fatigue of the haunting reminiscence of good times long gone, Mark sat up, took a vial out of his shirt pocket, opened it, and poured a thick line of white powder on a mirror that was conveniently placed on the nearby coffee table. Half smiling, he inhaled the crystals into his nostrils through a tightly rolled dollar bill as fast as he could, waiting for the euphoria that he knew would soon follow. As his mind started to soar, he watched his imagined destiny arise from shadows in the room, as if it were an actor playing a sublime role in the drama called *Mark Wins Again.* "I'm ready for this," he whispered with a smile.

Forgetting that his left hand was bandaged, he reached for the nearby remote. Pain shot through his finger like a raging fire when he moved his hand. As his agony intensified, he was jolted into remembering that he was still recovering from a scorpion bite. Like a hammer, the strike from its sting was pounding the exact spot where he had once worn his wedding ring. "I'm surprised it didn't kill me," he mumbled out loud. "I should never have agreed to watch my teenage daughter and sleep at Rowan's house — my old, so-familiar home sweet home — especially on a full-moon night. I must have been drunk to agree to that witch's demands," he mused, trying to push the lingering pain out of his mind.

Why am I still trying to prove to her that I'm a good guy? he thought, feeling sorry for himself. Even twelve years after their divorce, he and his ex could still find time to argue about their two kids and her insatiable requests for money to pay the bills. Rubbing his throbbing finger, he imagined the pain to be like his angry heart that pounded fast and furious whenever they exchanged unkind words. It offended him that Rowan always had to be acknowledged as being in the right if they were to reach any truce and he wouldn't be forced into acting like a crazed villain. Hadn't he already paid dearly for her emotional traumas caused by his unfaithfulness? After all, the divorce judge had awarded her their home and way too much of his paycheck. Getting married a second time was obviously a big mistake. He should have known after divorcing his first wife that a woman's tears have bargaining power in divorce court.

His mind continued to spin. *Two failed marriages, two spiteful wives, two prying kids, and two prime real estate investments now belonging to my ex-significant others should be reason enough to keep me happily renting my bachelor pad for the rest of my life*, he told himself. But Mark knew that even after all this time, he was still having trouble forgetting the delicious smell of musk in Rowan's perfumed hair.

The unexpected knock on his front door vibrated like a helicopter flying overhead. Preoccupied with thoughts of his past, it seemed to echo in haunting rhythm with his self-proclaimed injustices and possessed the hazy quality of a foreboding dream from which he could not awaken.

An eternity seemed to pass as he made his way to the door. He looked through the peephole and saw Mary fixing her hair in the dim porch light. *Hmm...maybe I'm going to get some love tonight*, Mark imagined as he opened the door. *She may be a little plump but she isn't shy about giving me what I like*, he thought. He invited her into his love den.

"Mark, I was hoping I could borrow a little cash. I'm waiting for my paycheck to come in the mail and of course, it's a little late." Mary knew that if she looked him straight in the eyes she had a better chance of getting him to say yes than if she called on the phone. To help her appear trustworthy, she had gone to the extra trouble of putting on her nicest dress, black lace pantyhose, and her Sunday church heels.

"How much do you want?"

"If I can borrow a hundred that should help me get by," Mary replied shyly while trying to hide the anxiety she felt.

"Is that all you want?"

Mary looked surprised.

"I mean, would you also like a glass of wine? I've got some really good Merlot," he replied, rubbing his nostrils.

Mary scanned his large, expensive apartment and thought that he might be more willing to comply with her request if she agreed. "Sure, I'll have a glass," she said, putting on a cheerful face, although the look of despair in her eyes revealed that she had serious concerns.

The doorway to Mark's rational mind swung open with anticipation of what might come next as the prospects for a night of lustful enjoyment appeared to be improving. Smiling, he handed Mary a tall glass of wine and invited her to sit next to him on the couch. Just as they both started to get close and comfortable, his doorbell rang again. "I must be in Grand Central Station," he said with an annoyed laugh. "I'd better see who's at the door."

"And who is this?" Mark questioned as he opened the door. "Norman, my man! Come on in."

Mark's attention instantly fastened on the attractive woman who was standing next to his friend. A young Mediterranean beauty with high cheekbones and rosebud lips looked back at Mark with large dark eyes. Her smile ignited Mark's libido without her needing to say one word.

"Mark, I'd like you to meet Carmella, my new friend. She's recently moved to the Bay Area from New York City," Norman said, showing relief that they were being invited out of the cold of the night.

Mark, who felt an overpowering sense of attraction, couldn't take his eyes from her. "So glad you could come by. If they have women as beautiful as you in New York, maybe I should move to the East Coast," he added, watching her closely as she appeared to float effortlessly into the room. She wore purple velvet tights and a sheer top that highlighted her curves.

Without paying attention to Mark's comment, Norman put out his cigarette in a nearby ashtray and continued, "I'm wondering if we can stay here tonight. I just smashed my car. Tonight's damn fog was so thick I couldn't see two feet in front of me. As I was going around a curve, all of a sudden I hit something and it turned out to be a street sign. We're OK but the front end of my car is wrecked. Carmella's really shaken and I've had too many drinks to get us home safe tonight."

Great, thought Mark, *my luck keeps improving every minute.* Trying not to give away his delight at having more time to get to know Carmella, he shot a stoic, sympathetic look at his intoxicated friend while his mind conjured visions of Norman's gal pal naked in his bedroom. Expressing concern, he replied without hesitation, "Sure, you both can stay here. I've got an extra room. Sorry for your accident but you both seem to be OK. Perhaps the looming hand of fog grabbed you to conjure our meeting tonight."

"Maybe...but I feel victimized by the weather and we barely missed hitting another car," Norman whined. "You're psychic, so you must know that I have another reason for knocking on your door. Dylan told me that you wanted to buy some of my Maui Wowie."

"Really? Do you have some with you?"

"Yes." Norman pulled a pound of weed out of his backpack and handed it to Mark. "I didn't want to leave this in my car while it's being towed to a garage. If you don't have the money right now I can front it to you. It's not like you were expecting me to knock on your door tonight. Besides, I trust you because your son's one of my best buddies and it makes us kind of like family. Dylan's one cool dude."

"Yeah, he's one of a kind," replied Mark, grabbing the shoebox-sized package and slyly smelling the contents. "I'm happy Dylan told you that I need this 'cause I definitely do. And my friends will also be happy that I have enough to share," he added, placing his new acquisition on a bookshelf as they walked into the living room. Noticing the bewildered look on Mary's face, Mark realized that he needed to make an introduction. "Oh…this is my neighbor, Mary. She just stopped by for a few minutes to visit."

Norman looked curiously at Mary. "I know this is crazy to ask," he whispered to Mark after instantly judging Mary as uptight, "but she has the vibe of a nun. Is Mary as cold as she looks?"

"Yeah, she's cold…except in bed," Mark quietly replied with a crooked grin on his face that only Norman could see.

After taking a seat across from her, the young man stared at Mary with an intense, strange curiosity. "Nice meeting ya. Hope we're not disturbing you," Norman said with an artificial smile. Then, as if he were a member of Sergeant Pepper's Lonely Hearts Club, he looked into his backpack and pulled out his foot long bong. "Hey Mary, do you smoke pot?" Norman thought the middle-aged woman seemed to be a bit more conservative looking than most of his friends, but if she was visiting Mark, she must be all right.

"Sometimes," she replied, sipping her wine, not wanting Norman to suspect that she was starting to feel uncomfortable with his little beady eyes focused on her. She couldn't help but think that Mark was acting like a cad, continually looking at the young lady who had captivated his attention as soon as she sat down in his favorite chair. And Norman, even if he was wearing an expensive sports jacket, was being a bit too presumptuous for her comfort. She could feel knots tightening in her neck. To counteract her tension and the arising sense of insecurity resulting from the younger woman taking a seat close to Mark, she tried making a joke. "Mostly I like watching global warming from the bottom of my wine glass," she said in a tone similar to funeral chatter.

"All right! Let's get this party started. Too bad Dylan isn't here," Norman replied, lighting his pot-filled pipe. "Mary, do you want the first toke?" he asked, becoming aware that her voice and her expression seemed a little pained.

"You can let Carmella go first," Mark interjected, feeling like a lone wolf nearing his alpha mate. "Company first and Mary's not company. She lives right around the block. Carmella, are you ready for some of Maui's best? You got it from Greg, didn't you?"

"Hey man, don't get personal. I can't tell where I got it but I can tell ya it's really good," Norman replied while giving Carmella the lit pipe so that she could get the first taste of what he believed to be instant paradise.

Although quiet, Carmella was obviously pleased to take the first turn. Trying not to look distraught from her recent encounter with a street sign, which had resulted in a three-block, uphill hike in the cold night, she inhaled and smiled with her eyes closed until her energy seemed to fill the room.

She looks like a statue of Artemis I saw in a museum in Greece, Mark mused, wishing Mary would leave. He didn't want her to get in the way of making himself more available to Carmella, and surely playboy Norman wouldn't mind if he took a little time to talk with her.

Without saying another word, Mark took his turn on the pipe. After a long toke, his mind seemed to whirl out of control. Without success, he tried to remember how much crystal he had just snorted. Even though he was doing his best to act normal, he no longer felt connected to his body and knew it would be to his advantage to withdraw from the living room.

Mary, trying to fit in, wasn't going to let everyone get high and not give it a try. With an awkward smile, she took her turn and inhaled from the pipe Norman handed her. As she did, she noticed Mark staring at Carmella.

"Hey, Mark. What's up? Your eyes look like they're swimming in lava," chuckled Mary anxiously.

"Maybe it's because I just got back from a trip to Hawaii," Mark responded, sounding as though he was half asleep. "Hey Norman, do you think you could keep Mary busy while I talk with Carmella for a few minutes in private? I have some questions for her and I'm going to show her your room for the night."

"But Mark," Mary whined in protest, "we need you to keep us entertained."

"You can amuse yourself for a few minutes," Mark said while assertively taking Carmella's hand and pulling her to her feet. "Maybe you and Norman can get to know each other a little better while I'm talking with Carmella. I just need to check out a personal dream that seems to be a déjà vu communication involving her."

"I don't want to be here if you're going to go off with Carmella," Mary stated coldly.

"OK, OK. Get over yourself, Mary. Just hang out for a couple of minutes with Norman. He won't bite you," Mark said as he escorted Carmella down the hallway toward the back bedroom, leaving Mary and Norman with no other choice.

Once they entered the bedroom, Mark closed the door. Carmella couldn't get her Tarot cards out of her purse fast enough. She wasn't sure that she wanted to be alone with a stranger and it made her feel more secure to be able to ask the oracle what she should make of this night's craziness. Hoping for good luck, she also brought out her new acquisition — the stone she had recently found. She blew on it, made a wish, and put it on the table near her cards.

"What kind of stone is that?" asked Mark. "Its color is amazing." He reached out and picked it up. It sparkled like a large diamond and filled him with an instant desire to take it from Carmella.

Carmella didn't want him to touch it and her stomach knotted as she tried to stop him. "Mark, give that to me. It's my magical stone," she said in protest. She didn't know why but a current of fear shot through her body. At that same moment, the electricity went out and the room became completely dark. "Give me my stone," she repeated.

Dancing shadows filled the room from a glow that emanated from the stone in Mark's hand. Its shape seemed to shift into what appeared to be the head of a sphinx with luminous eyes that penetrated the darkness.

"Wow, it glows in the dark," Mark said. "Is it some

kind of crystal or is it plastic? Where did you get this thing?" Mark strained his eyes to find her hand in the dark. "Oh, crap! It feels like fire ants are biting my palm. Here, take it before I drop it."

Just as the rock slipped back into Carmella's hand, she pulled away from Mark's touch and the electricity went back on.

"I found it in an old abandoned house," she replied, feeling relieved to be able to see again. She pushed the rock into her pocket. With renewed composure, she awkwardly smiled at Mark and started to shuffle the cards.

The first card she cut from her deck was intended to represent her strange companion, the straight-arrow-looking man who had insisted on calling her to this mysterious meeting. The card she chose to represent him seemed to jump from her hands. It was the Emperor reversed.

"Yes, that seems a perfect fit for me," Mark said egotistically as he examined the image of a powerful-looking man wearing a crown. "That's because I usually do anything I set my mind to do. I honestly believe that the gods watch out for me and give me opportunities to make quantum decisions that will promote healthy change in society. I've made my fortune in life promoting spirituality and investing in reciprocity."

Now that she heard Mark talking, Carmella could relate to his blatant sense of authority and controlling manner with a little more understanding. But she wondered if he had any spiritual sense at all.

"Really? That sounds impressive. The Emperor, Aleister Crowley claims, is 'the male fiery energy of the universe.' He sits on his throne as a charismatic, successful leader. Perhaps this card also represents your son, Dylan…like father, like son. By the way, do you know I'm friends with him? He's amazing," Carmella said, trying to transform their private meeting into a discussion about Dylan.

Mark was disappointed that she was talking about his son instead of him. He didn't know how to answer. Instead of speaking, he stared blankly and nodded his head.

"But let's focus on the present," continued Carmella. "Do you know that Mary longs for you to hold her hand?"

"What?" replied Mark in disbelief.

"Yes, it's true. I felt her silently asking you."

"Oh...and you're an intuitive?" Mark asked.

"Yes, sometimes. I keep my mind open to using my sixth sense. Part of the reason she likes you is because you're one of the few men she can talk with. She never got to know her father or a father's love. He left her and her mother when she was a little baby and vanished completely from their lives."

"Are you making this stuff up? You just want me to cozy up with Mary, so you're trying to make me think she likes me," Mark spoke, disbelieving what he was being told. "You've got a wild imagination for someone who is so anxious about a stupid stone."

Outside of the bedroom, at the other end of the apartment, Mark's closed door seemed to create a communication gridlock. Getting more stoned and trying to be casual about the unexpected social arrangement, Norman reached over and touched Mary's leg. "Are you Mark's lover?"

"Well, lately when I've made love it's been with Mark, so I'm not too happy about him going into the bedroom with your friend," Mary chirped loudly, brushing his hand away from her knee. It wasn't the first time she'd been ditched because of another woman and anger was easier to express than the pain of her jealousy. "I'm really pissed at him right now," she added, and then, to make sure Mark heard her, she repeated in a loud, shrill pitch, "I'm *really* pissed at him right now!"

The bedroom door swung open and Mark came out of the room with the energy of a charging ram. "What is the matter with you? What's all the commotion? You're being too loud. You want the neighbors to complain?"

Carmella, after quietly closing the bedroom door, walked slowly, as if in a trance, back to the living room.

"Your friend was just wishing that you were out here with us," Norman said. He had felt the hot sting of Mary's touch when she pushed his hand from her leg and wasn't sure what else he could say. Even though he was open-minded about bedroom situations when he was lucky enough to play musical beds, he felt a bit annoyed at Mark for assuming that he could have private time with juicy Carmella while leaving him to sit with a lifeless fish. Knowing that Mark was one horny dude, Norman wasn't sure whether he'd made the right choice by asking if they could stay with him. But he didn't know of anywhere else they could go when he wasn't able to walk straight this late at night.

Moving gingerly toward Mary, with no regard to her obvious upset emotions, Mark's fiery nature began to show. "Come on, Mary. Stop being so uptight. Can't you handle having some alone time with Norman while I simply talk with Carmella for a little while?" He looked at Mary without really seeing her. He put his hands on her shoulders, trying to create a lack of distance between them. "You're frickin' hilarious, being so uptight."

"Mark, you're being a prick! We were making love three days ago and now you're telling me to relax while you're taking someone else into the bedroom. And you want me to hang out getting stoned with someone I don't even know," complained Mary. "I can't handle it."

"And you're ruining my high," Mark said in a tone that made everyone aware of his underlying anger. "Get with it! I thought you liked having fun."

"I do like having fun," Mary replied with disgust in her voice. "But this is no fun for me."

"Do you want another hit of weed or a little more wine?" Mark asked, ignoring Norman and Carmella. "Would that make you happy?"

"No. I want you to act like you did three days ago when we were together," she replied with a look of sorrow.

"Well, let me tell you what really happened in the bedroom and maybe you'll stop acting like a possessive bitch," Mark hissed.

"Oh, now I'm possessive? That is so stupid. But OK, what happened?"

"Carmella told me that you want me to hold your hand."

"So? That could be true when you're not treating me like a puppet on a string," Mary said with a little pout, somewhat stunned by the truth of his words.

"And she said that you lost your father when you were a baby and you don't feel comfortable with most men because of not having any relationship with him.

Is that true?" he earnestly inquired.

"What? She said that? I never tell anyone about my father. How could she know?" Mary muttered. She gave Carmella a fearful stare. Was Carmella the devil in disguise?

"How could you not tell me that?" Mark asked while reaching for his wine glass. "So...maybe right now I should forgive you for acting like a wet blanket on a chilly night."

"I thought you had integrity but you're acting like an ass," Mary replied.

"Why don't you just get out of here? Maybe it's *you* who is acting like an ass," Mark responded.

"Fuck your party!" Mary blurted, tears stinging her eyes.

"I could throw you out but it's late!" Mark shouted. "Let's get over this hump and talk about what's important. Maybe everything that's wrong in your life is because you never had a dad."

"I don't want to be here!" Mary screeched, jumping to her feet. "I'm leaving!"

"You're so defensive when you aren't being offensive. Didn't you ask me if you could borrow some money? If you're mean to me, you won't get it. Come on, Mary, stop fretting. Let's go talk."

Mark wolf-howled while grabbing Mary's hand. He pulled her toward his bedroom.

"You're a bastard, Mark!"

"You love me, Mary. Admit it," he replied with a smile while remembering the affection they had shared during their previous passionate time together.

Mary felt a cold wind wrap around her as if she were outside. What was happening? Perhaps her imagination was spiraling out of control. But what could she do about anything that was happening this night? Should she love or hate Mark? It didn't seem to matter what she thought. She felt an emotional yearning to be in his arms.

Mark, releasing the adrenaline of recently being in a power struggle with one more woman striving to control him, knew that things were lining up in his favor. "Mary, you're number one on my lover list," he said, turning the doorknob to enter his bedroom.

"You're number one on my shit list," she replied, trying to dismiss her tears. Could she let go of her anger? Would he lend her the money she desperately needed?

Her wrath slowly gave way to desire as she realized that she was falling into the arms of a generous man who could help her feel secure in this solitary moment. Her painful sense of rejection began to fade as Mark's kisses opened the door to feelings of immense pleasure. As he dimmed the lights and began taking off her clothes, the hunger in her heart began beating in a rhythm of celebration. Inwardly, she sensed him enveloping her entire being and chuckled to herself that she became one with a manly love machine.

Chapter Five

The High Priest
The Invincible Truth

We'll turn two hundred dollars into twenty thousand in no time, Taylor said to himself while envisioning stacks of hundred-dollar bills sliding into his wallet. *What that idiot doesn't know, and hopefully what he isn't going to find out, won't hurt his bank account too much,* he thought with a mischievous smile.

Taylor, king of the gypsies, loved his family — not just because he got most of the earnings from their spiritual work but because they lived to love and to be happy. And making money made them all happy.

Destiny, his twenty-two-year-old daughter, had large, smiling, dark eyes and luscious full lips. She was amazingly good at using her feminine wiles to sweet-talk him. At times, too good. By the time she was a teen, she had figured out how to wrap him around her little finger and get his generosity flowing so that he'd give her more than her fair share of their family's earnings.

She's so beautiful, it's hard to tell her no, Taylor mused as he looked in his bedroom mirror, twirling the tips of his freshly dyed, midnight-black mustache.

And then there was Angel, his fifteen-year-old, first introduced to him by the frantic words of his wife when she cried out "just an accidental pregnancy." But now, after the arguments concerning her arrival had long passed, he was thankful that she had come into his life. "She certainly is getting ripe," he muttered to himself, envisioning her breasts to be like firm grapefruits. *But damn,* he thought, *she's the only virgin left in our family who can work our ancestral rites. If someone takes her to bed, she'll lose her opportunity to be initiated into our secret order — and the ancient scrolls revealing how to become the master of timeless space will forever be beyond my reach.* Looking into the mirror while towel-drying his hair, he saw his facial muscles tighten into a frown. *Her innocence will not be consummated before she's astral traveled the subtle cosmic planes,* he vowed to himself. He'd make sure of that.

Taylor didn't mind playing guard dog to keep Angel out of love's alluring danger zone. His bullish efforts would be well rewarded once she was initiated as a vestal virgin and allowed the privilege of leading the sacred rite in his fraternal circle. He knew that she would need his help to guide her untrained spirit consciousness to float out of her body and journey to the juncture of alpha and omega, accessible only to the pure of heart. Reaching this invisible summit of success would be worth whatever measures he needed to take to avert any danger and assure her safety. If her initiation strengthened the power of the veiled forces, she would be able to remove the ancestral curse placed on his family hundreds of years ago. He was confident that her caring nature would cause her to agree to whatever he deemed necessary to ensure this possibility. So what if those less resolute had lost their sanity while crossing the shrouded sea of dreams? If needed, he had a talisman that could turn adversity into benefit, and he could invoke the power to unleash a psychic shield of unwavering protection for an innocent heart.

Without being deceptive, he could avoid sensitive issues about her risk of diving into the space beyond time that led to wandering the endless maze of death-provoking mysteries. After all, he was willing to do whatever he must to have an opportunity to see the sacred formulas for conjuring the eternal fountain of youth, which would be in her hands after her ordination and successful journey into the cosmic conundrum. As long as he didn't discuss matters that were better left unmentioned, surely Angel would approve of his plans for her.

Actually, he had no idea of the true advantages the ancient scrolls might offer. He had lost his first chance to gain access to their secrets when Destiny, his oldest, had managed to sneak off the month before her intended initiation with her then-boyfriend, Dylan. If it hadn't been for that bastard, Destiny, who was smarter than her younger siblings, would have been the ideal virgin to perform their ancestral rites. Knowing from his own past mistakes that he must stay vigilant, Taylor was doing everything possible to make certain that the same fate didn't befall Angel. However, he would be glad when he could stop worrying about her chastity. *That time will be coming with the next full moon, when she can first perform the Hecate ritual,* he thought as he murmured a silent invocation. "Heavenly maiden, mother, crone, keep my youngest safe and chaste."

As he combed his long, dark, graying hair, Taylor continued to reflect on his family and each person's unique value. After putting some Tantric love oil on his skin, he walked over to his desk and turned his thoughts to another important matter — making money. Did those pretentious fools really think his family's talent came so cheap? Before someone had the last drink at the upcoming socialite coming-out party, he'd have more money in his pocket than he could count in an hour. He was confident of that. His family had the best training in the art of using fortune-telling to weave people's problems into high finance. Knowing how proficient his wife and her sisters were at building their business, Visionary Pathways to Prosperity, it was difficult to not count their money before they worked as party psychics for the event.

Certainly, no one had ever learned to take advantage of people's fears more than his wife, Naomi, or "Know-Me" as she liked everyone to call her. Once again, Naomi, who bounced around like a youth even though she was in her mid-fifties, had just finished buying his entire family new clothes. It was reassuring to know that even a woman could wield power over CEO executives like Mr. Deep Pockets himself, Richard Jones. Poor guy! He had really believed Naomi could bring his dead wife back from the grave. Perhaps he wouldn't have been so vulnerable if he hadn't been seeking forgiveness for his untimely act of making love to another woman at the exact same time his wife was gasping her final breath. When he found his wife's body, it was obvious she had not died with a smile on her face. Poor Mr. Jones had come home late, his car's headlights shining on the love of his life who was lying in the driveway staring blindly at the moon with her eyes frozen in a sorrowful, soulless glare. Her rigid body, cold as stone, seemed to recoil in rejection to his immoral touch. She had choked on a bite of peach plucked from a tree they had planted together in the early days of their relationship, when they were transforming their yard into a Garden of Eden. Hopefully, the $40,000 he had recently paid Naomi for communicating with his wife's dead spirit, channeling a plea for forgiveness, would bring some relief to his relentless torment. Taylor looked down at his new shoes. *I hope so*, he thought with a smirk, knowing how the pain of guilt always brought top dollar.

His thoughts were interrupted as Angel knocked on the door and let herself into his room. "Dad," she announced with an exaggerated moan, "I can't be in your ritual. I'm afraid."

Once again, Taylor's smiling face contorted into a frown. "What?"

"I've been chatting with Dylan and he's been telling me that some people get lost and never come back from taking an astral trip to the other dimension. That scares me."

"Doubt is the voice of self-destruction. You must believe that you can do it. When you believe you can do something, nothing can harm you, especially when you have been anointed with the sacred serum your grandfather brought back from the caves in the Himalayas when he was a young man. It's an elixir made using an alchemical spell that binds salt crystals dug from a hidden quarry, millions of years old, with your own DNA. Your grandpa went where the power of magic is stronger than what any modern day person can imagine. And I've told you before, Dylan can't be trusted. Look how he broke your sister's heart! It's good to be suspicious of anything he tells you."

"Well, if the elixir is so powerful, why did Grandpa disappear?" she asked, ignoring the mean-spirited comments about her friend Dylan. "And why don't we know what happened to him?" Angel sounded as though she had spent a long time rehearsing her argument.

"When you get a bit older, I'll be glad to tell you about what happened to your grandfather. Right now, you must trust me," Taylor said while reaching out to hug his young daughter. "You have this one chance in your lifetime to visit a land where miracles are commonplace. You'll see a light so bright that its radiance spreads to the farthest orbits in the universe. You won't be tethered to the earth. Your spirit will be free. Don't let Dylan talk you out of becoming one with powers that are rooted in mysteries so profound that they can't be understood by the majority of humankind."

"It's easy for you to tell me not to worry, Dad, but Dylan said that I have to drink a potion that can kill the faint-hearted. I don't know if that means me or not. And he said that I'll see disembodied spirits and that one might try to take over my body." There was worry in Angel's eyes. Too often she'd had a hard time talking to her dad, but this time she was going to stand her ground. She moved her tense body farther away from her father.

"What does he know? He's just a puppy coming out of the kennel, thriving on hearsay," retorted Taylor, his anger rising. "He's done an exorcism or two and he finds weirdos to talk to who say they've astral traveled. No wonder he's scared and warning you of a power he'll never understand. Perhaps he should listen to his own advice and stop hanging around people who are half crazy." Then, sensing her unease, he let his anger subside and said in a caring, concerned tone, "However, since you've brought up the possibility of unknown forces, it might be useful for you to learn some practical psychic self-defense. Do you have time for a little lesson?"

"Right now? I don't know..."

Angel, trying not to react to her father's authoritarian attitude, felt like giving him the middle finger. She held back her impulse, figuring that he was still angry with Dylan for the pain he had caused her older sister when he walked away from their relationship. But she was having a hard time not being angry with her dad for always telling her what to do. She sensed that, like always, he wouldn't let her have her own way, even if she was almost sixteen years old. *When is he going to realize that I'm old enough to make my own decisions?* she wondered.

"Let me assure you, Angel, I would never let anything or anyone harm you. You can learn to create a magic circle of protection so that wherever you go, in this world or beyond, you will be safe. If you have a little time, we can get started right now."

"Now? I don't want to listen to your magical mojo right now. I have homework I need to finish. Besides, if you're really such an important high priest like Mom says, can't you just beam me up, like they do in *Star Trek?*"

"Sure, of course I can," he replied, looking straight into her eyes, "but it takes cooperation on your part to let me be 'the revealer of sacred things.'" Ignoring her resistance to practicing magic at that moment, he said, "Let's do a little experiment. For just one minute, close your eyes. I want you to look through your third eye—the one that sits inside the middle of your forehead. Just do this for one minute. Please."

She sighed and rolled her eyes. "OK, Dad, but only for one minute."

"Once you have your eyes closed, look inward and tell me, do you see a white bird or a blackbird flying through the space in your mind?"

"Neither one. I see a hippopotamus," she said with her eyes closed.

"Angel, please take this seriously. Slow your mind chatter, breathe deeply, and look inside. Tell me what you see, a blackbird or a white bird?"

After a few moments of silence, she replied, "Well, it looks kind of like a magpie and a vulture, all in one large bird shape. It's white and black and it keeps flying higher and higher. Now I can't see it anymore."

"Great! That's a good omen. Open your eyes, Angel. You have proven you can use your inner sight. If you would have seen a blackbird, it would have been a symbol of dark times, black magic, and potential difficulties. But you saw a black-and-white bird, a symbol of the middle path and protection. If your bird had been all white or all black, you would have a hard time harmonizing the forces of duality that keep the mind locked in a battle between evil and good. The mixture of colors is a sign of your innate power to master duality and negative forces."

"OK..." Angel looked around the room, where light and dark shadows appeared and disappeared through the torn curtains. "I'm not sure about all this mumbo jumbo. But you're obviously trying to make me feel good about taking part in your ritual."

"Sweetie, I want you to do this ritual because, for a

singular moment, you will become queen of the heavens. The ceremony can only be done when you're young. It only lasts a little while and I'll be by your side the whole time. You'll be richly rewarded for your efforts because you'll know more about magic than adepts who are fifty years older than yourself. You'll have access to the Akashic records and be free to read the sacred texts of our ancestral lineage. Things will be revealed to you that no one else knows. No one will ever be able to lie to you without you knowing."

"Dad, I understand what you want. You make all this weird stuff sound easy but I still have to think about what I want. I'm the one who has to drink the elixir. I still need to think about it." Angel looked away from her father's penetrating glare.

"You're the only one in our family who can do this ritual."

"Will I have more power than my oldest sister?" she asked, with what sounded to Taylor like a surge of interest.

"Yes."

"Does that mean you'll give me more money than her?"

"You'll get more than money from participating in this ritual. You'll be able to hear a higher wisdom and be united with the strength of the gods who watch over our clan."

"OK. I'm all for having the strength of the gods. Does that mean I can have all the boyfriends I want? Hmm, maybe I should do this...well...I guess...well, maybe...most likely, I'll do it. But I'm done talking. You can explain to me later how I'm going to learn to astral travel. For now, I've got a date with someone who wants to chat online. I'm out of here. Besides, I've got to think about what boy I'm going to use my future powers on. See ya later, Dad." With that, she turned and walked out of the room.

"Don't worry about using your powers until after the ritual," Taylor replied with a sigh of relief. He felt in his heart that his youngest would honor the intended fight-and-flight soul mission he was planning for her. Not having any desire to bring attention to details that could generate fear, he decided not to discuss the dark forces. He didn't want her to have any doubts or second thoughts. After all, her purity was her refuge, and he, the high priest, would be her bodyguard in both the physical and ethereal sides of reality. He had tricks up his sleeve, passed down from generation to generation, and their magical traditions would protect her.

Whether Angel would choose to fearlessly drink from Hecate's fountain of love or Draccon's cauldron of evil was a choice only she could make at the exact timeless moment when her spirit would be called to capture the nectar of the moon. Would she be able to make the distinction between benevolent but veiled truth and the malevolence disguised as virtue that mocks the soul's integrity? Luckily, the power of her purity was the best remedy for the menacing choice she would need to make.

Perhaps it was time for him to tell Naomi, his wife, that Angel had agreed to take the role of rightful successor in their secret order. But really, the motivation to guide her spiritual evolution wasn't his choice. He was only following the decree of Hecate that was written with invisible ink on the fraying, time-worn parchment of the ancients.

Chapter Six

The Lovers
Fooling Around With Love

*A*s he breathed in the crisp smell of the ocean mist, Dylan felt lucky to live close enough to the beach to go there whenever he needed to clear his mind. Before the sun sank beneath the sea's horizon, the sky became a kaleidoscope of mesmerizing, golden colors. Most people were leaving as it became dusk and this was the perfect time to climb the sand dunes in solitude and let the sound of the crashing waves wake up his muted, feel-good mood. Giving in to the temptation of possibly connecting with Lisa, Dylan took out his cell phone to call her. It's not that he was obsessing over her...but he had to try calling one more time.

"Damn, why isn't she answering?" he muttered to himself after dialing her number again and being directed to her voicemail.

Before the day was over, Dylan hoped to see Lisa, his clandestine girlfriend for the last several months. Since the last time they were together, four long days ago, he couldn't stop thinking about her and his hunger for her body was growing with her memory. He reflected with amazement how their unexpected liaison while waiting in line at a coffee shop had quickly become intimate. But unfortunately, their bond was stressed by an unspoken complexity. How were they to know, when their eyes first locked in an electric embrace, that they would feel a magnetizing sense of being soul mates, even though they each were already married to someone else?

Lisa, who was twelve years older, turned him on like crazy. Despite what felt to him like judgmental glances from onlookers when they were together, he didn't mind their age difference as much as the fact that she was married to someone the same age as his father. Even so, he longed to be with her, otherwise, he wasn't sure he wanted to be in a sexual relationship with any woman right now. His own wife, Stella, had sliced through his heart with words as sharp as a razor's edge when she told him that she was making love with someone new. The shock of being betrayed by the woman who had sworn her undying love to him, and whom he had trusted to share his life, had come as a brutal awakening. He was still recovering from a sense of emotional numbness because of her frequent snubs in their bedroom.

In general, since Stella's rejection, women and their fickle nature turned Dylan off. At least, that's how it was until he met Lisa, his part-time lover, who proved to him that his wounded heart could still fall in love. Being aroused by her made him forget the anxiety and shame he felt from his wife's rejection and helped him feel more like the guy his father, Mark, the charismatic ladies' man, expected him to be.

Lisa's husband, David, was an executive who

worked in the financial district. He put in long hours. Getting ahead in his business was his primary obsession and Dylan had been told in confidence that Lisa struggled with being left alone and feeling like she was second in line for his time. Even when he took her out, it was obvious that David was more comfortable with his computer than conversing with her friends. And it secretly hurt Lisa's feelings that he wouldn't visit her family, who he hadn't made an effort to see in the last six years. She had given up trying to make excuses for why he wasn't available to visit with them, and his obvious avoidance of her kin had created a rift. Everyone in her family believed that their father's first and only argument with David, right after their expensive wedding, had put him in an unforgiving mood from which he refused to recover. The old man should never have accused his new son-in-law of using Lisa as a trophy wife, but once said, it couldn't be retracted.

Lisa told Dylan that as their marriage became more routine, it also became less exciting for her. She complained with an unsolvable frustration that David was rarely interested in her sexually. With her Christian upbringing, she hadn't intended to cheat on her husband but her good-girl values couldn't combat his frequent coldness in their bedroom. Becoming involved with Dylan was unplanned, yet even her guilt-ridden mind couldn't ignore the heated connection between them.

It's my good fortune that they're sexually mismatched, Dylan thought while feeling a surge of heat through his entire being as he imagined her naked and wrapped in his arms. Their special longing for one another felt naturally delicious, even though neither one of them dared to talk about plans for their future.

In truth, for Dylan, part of their relationship was pleasure and the other part was a test of patience. Something unexplainable happened to him when he was with her. When he came within four feet of her, he became like a dog in heat. Nevertheless, his biggest challenge seemed to be not giving in to the aggravation of waiting for her to make time to be with him. He was impatient and it was easy for him to become annoyed as he waited endlessly for her calls. And when she was at home, she didn't want him to call as she was afraid David might overhear their private conversations.

Dylan, trying to be a pragmatist, wasn't sure how long their relationship would last, but he couldn't deny what he felt. He knew that the chemistry between them triggered a joyful feeling that he didn't experience with any other woman and he had a craving to be with Lisa, whatever the obstacles. Even if she was married to someone else, their attraction was too strong to resist and his worries about the logic of choosing the right partner didn't compete with the irresistible sorcery of her lovemaking. Intellectually, he could list all the reasons why she wasn't the right partner for him. Bt that didn't stop him from dialing her number one more time.

After not getting an answer once again, Dylan decided to call Norman, who was next on his list of calls needing to be made. It was time for him to start thinking about someone besides Lisa and he knew he could count on his good friend Norman to distract him.

Dylan dialed and heard Norman answer the phone with his typical cocky attitude. "I can hear in your voice that you're ready for some Maui Wowie. Come on over. I've got some flowering buds waiting for you."

"OK. I'm on my way," Dylan replied while watching the fog roll across the waves toward the shore—a sign that it would soon be too cold to stay at Ocean Beach.

"I forgot to tell you, I've got a little company," Norman chirped. "Hopefully, I'll have her in bed with me by the time you get here. If I do, just wait in my living room and help yourself to anything at the bar. Amazing good luck for you, there's another little chickie who's also at my house who can use some of your attention. Her name's Jodi and she has a cross tattooed on her ass, so I call her Hot Cross Buns. See ya soon, buddy!"

The prospect of having primo weed and a fun evening being distracted from his emotional concerns cheered up Dylan. Giving up the thought of seeing Lisa for the moment, he moved in long strides toward his car. He mentally outlined a map to Norman's house and calculated the fastest route heading north from San Francisco toward Stinson Beach. The tail end of rush hour was a bad time to cross the clogged Golden Gate Bridge, but he had no other choice if he wanted to visit Norman soon. He jumped into his car, turned the ignition, and started to drive.

In just a little more than an hour of dodging sluggish traffic, Dylan was turning his wheel and going up a country dirt road pitted with potholes. The sweetness of the fresh air and the unaccustomed quiet made him think that maybe he should move from the city and its ceaseless noise of sirens and horns...except he was certain he wouldn't enjoy driving these curving roads every morning to get to his job in San Francisco.

For this moment, he was happy to be out of the city and watching the fog sweep across the hills like a legion of silent ghosts coming from the sea. If he let his imagination have its way, it appeared as though he was driving through a shadowy, soul-enveloping matrix on a moonless, alien planet.

An oncoming, speeding car jolted him back reality. Blinded by its headlights, his mind swiftly adjusted to the one-lane road and the eerie darkness settling over the terrain, which grew more murky with every turn.

As he neared Norman's home, he was relieved to smell the sweetness of the earth as he passed a grove of giant redwoods. He slowed his car to ensure that its wheels would securely follow the drive on the steep embankment rising high above a narrow ravine. In the distance, Dylan could see bright lights beckoning him to come out of the crypt of darkness.

This place is ideal for the life Norman likes to lead, thought Dylan. *It's tucked away from the world where he can keep his life private, and no one's around to watch his drug-dealing affairs.*

Dylan parked in a clearing, got out of his car, and crossed a small bridge that creaked under his hurried footsteps. Anxious to get out of the damp, cool wind, he walked hastily toward the light shining from Norman's old farmhouse, which looked like it sat in the middle of an oasis filled with the echo of mating calls from lovestruck owls. The sound of his own approaching steps announced that he was about to knock on Norman's door.

A voluptuous young woman answered. "Hi. You must be Dylan. Norman said you were coming."

Dylan's heart jumped an unexpected beat.

Her warm smile was inviting.

"My name's Jodi. Would you like a drink?" she continued as he let himself into the dimly lit room.

"Sure," Dylan said. "That would be great."

"Norman's talking privately with Carmella for a little while," Jodi said with a crooked smile. "Well, actually, it may be a little more than that."

Dylan thought her expression covered an embarrassment that she was too sophisticated to willingly show. And he needed to exercise his self-control to hide his surprise at hearing that Carmella was in bed with Norman. Recently, he had noticed his two friends talking together at a mutual friend's birthday party, but he hadn't realized that they were interested in dating one another.

Blinded by his obsession with his own emotional dilemma, Dylan wasn't sure whether he was happy or bothered that Carmella seemed to be dating Norman, but he felt a twinge of unexpected jealousy. He reached for his drink as Jodi handed it to him, and then uncomfortably tried to start a conversation. He felt her eyes looking through him and wondered what she was thinking. As he listened to her rambling, "...the pig doesn't own me. I can go where I want..." he wasn't really sure what she was saying. Dylan sensed that she was in a world of her own.

Feeling a sense of distance, even though she stood near him, he wondered if Jodi was one of Norman's party girls who stayed near him to benefit from his openly generous drug dealings. He watched her movements. Her feet barely touched the ground as she walked. *She must be really stoned*, he thought.

As if reading his thoughts, Jodi said, "I like to get high. Do you?"

"Some," Dylan answered, not feeling comfortable

talking about his personal habits with a stranger.

"I've got a pipe almost ready to light," she said while putting some pot into its bowl. "Norman won't mind."

"Sure," Dylan replied, searching for his matches. Secretly, he was hoping that getting stoned with Jodi might break her icy exterior and that he might meet her on a more comfortable level.

As Dylan inhaled his first hit, he heard Norman's rough voice, "What's going on in here?"

Although Dylan jumped slightly, he relaxed when he saw the grin on Norman's face. It was obvious that his question was more of a joke than a demand for an answer.

"Look at you two, getting stoned without me. If you want to get high, let's all get high together. Come on up to my room. You can join Carmella and me. We're talking on my bed." Norman started gently pulling on Jodi's arm, moving her toward the steps that led upstairs. "Good thing you're here, Dylan," Norman squeaked. "I want you to do your psychic thing and tune in to me and Carmella, and tell me what you think about our connection."

The red-and-black upstairs hallway was poorly lit. It was hard to see where he was going but Dylan, led by the smell of sandalwood incense and the chattering of Norman's voice, followed him down the corridor, wondering what he had gotten himself into. He was sure he didn't want to do a reading on the energy between Norman and Carmella.

Norman's bedroom was candlelit and mirrors covered the walls and ceiling. "You know Carmella," he said to Dylan. "Come on, sit down on the water bed with us. Take your shoes off and get comfortable."

Dylan agreed but retreated from the bed as he looked at Carmella's nearly bare breasts and the hint of anger in her eyes. *How weird to see her voluptuous body popping out toward me twice within the recent past,* he thought, remembering their recent meetings. Both times she still had her underpants on, but otherwise, she was mostly naked. *How beautiful her body looks in the candlelight,* he thought, feeling uncomfortable and wishing he was somewhere—anywhere—else.

Jodi looked at Dylan and noticed his eyes watching Carmella. Nonverbally searching for clues as to what he was thinking, Jodi reached for his hand and pulled him to join everyone on the bed. Playfully, she moved like a carefree child, making the waterbed bounce the intimate group up and down as if they were riding waves on the surf.

"Stop moving around so much, Jodi," Norman demanded. "Or we'll all be seasick."

In defiance, Jodi jumped a couple of feet closer to Norman on the bed, causing Carmella to spring up and down as if she were a frog hopping on a lily pad. Dylan, finding it a little difficult to enjoy his unexpected, present circumstances, inched his way toward the edge of the bed. He couldn't ever remember feeling possessive with his female friends until now, and felt awkwardly confused and torn by his unanticipated stirrings of lust for Carmella.

"Open this bag," Norman requested, handing Dylan a brown grocery bag.

Dylan reached in and to everyone's surprise, pulled out a green plastic dildo in the shape of a dragon.

"Damn! Wrong bag," Norman chuckled. "Here's the bag I want you to open," he said, and reached under his nightstand to grab another bag.

After seeing the contents of the previous bag, Dylan wasn't sure he wanted to know what was inside this one, but with a naive curiosity, he peeked inside. His eyes widened as he saw a large, clear, cellophane envelope filled with white powder. He looked at Norman.

"Let's get high," Norman said as he pulled a tray-shaped glass mirror from under the nightstand. After taking the bag from Dylan, he proudly poured the white powder onto the mirror and deftly divided the crystals into eight thin lines. After making sure the lines were in tidy, equal rows, he handed the tray to Dylan along with a small silver straw, and said, "Have the first toot, buddy."

Dylan had expected weed but...*well, sometimes you just take whatever life offers,* he thought, trying to look surprised. He momentarily considered his oversensitivity to drugs and what he needed to do the next day. *No worries,* he told himself. He'd be OK if he only took a little.

The others waited patiently for Dylan to snort his lines, then each took their turn. Before Jodi, the last in line, had finished, Norman's hands were rubbing Carmella's thighs and he began whispering mischievously in her ear. Giggling, she tried to embrace him by wrapping her legs around his middle while turning her back toward the others.

Even if the bed hadn't been making him bounce around, it was hard for Dylan to sit still and watch the lovebirds embracing. His mind raced back to when he and Carmella were checking out the haunted house, then to when he had seen her at the full-moon ceremony. At those times, he hadn't thought about her in a sexual way but now he felt an unanticipated attraction toward her. And worse yet, with her arms wrapped around Norman, his spirit wilted into an icy shroud of an all-too-familiar growing sense of aloneness.

Dylan began to realize that he was too stoned for his own comfort. Through his mental haze, he knew he needed to be moving or doing something but he wasn't sure where he should go or what he should be doing. He became like an underwater video camera filming *Lost at Sea* while his body floated in space. He knew he was within touching distance of three aliens but they were blurred from recognition.

"Hey, buddy, why don't you give Jodi a massage? I know she'll like it..."

Dylan heard Norman, the wild child in his own circle of friends, through a jumbled echo chamber in his mind.

"And can you dim the lights?"

"Who says I'd like a massage?" Jodi snarled, her body tensing.

"Come on, baby. Relax! Dylan's one of my best friends and I know he can give you a great rub," Norman replied, pulling up one of Jodi's feet and lifting her toes toward his mouth. He stuck his tongue between her two largest toes and started licking them, making Jodi squeal and move about like a tiger on a chain.

Everyone on the bed began to roll uncontrollably from the frantic tsunami waves that were unlocked from inside the mattress.

Carmella, feeling jealous of Norman's advances toward Jodi, started to move away but Norman grabbed her with his other hand and put his arm around her shoulder, holding her tight and caressing her breast as if she was the mother and he was her child.

"Dylan, what do you think of these two babes? They come around here and I get them high and look how they treat me. It sure would be nice if you'd help me keep my lady friends happy."

Overwhelmed, Dylan knew that he had snorted too much of the white powder, whatever it was. Trying to intellectually access this situation, he dismissed his confused feelings for Carmella and pushed Jodi into complete insignificance in his view. Even stoned out of his mind, he knew he didn't want to play an amourous role on the impromptu stage of Norman's bedroom playground. He liked intimate moments but he couldn't be happy being part of this foursome, no matter how high he might be. Admittedly, seeing Carmella nearly naked was getting him physically aroused, and that was something he hadn't anticipated, especially since his heart had been beating in unswerving rhythm to his thoughts about Lisa. Nor had he expected Norman's sexual openness with his lady friends to transmit a tantalizing heat across the bed. Dylan couldn't deny feeling turned on but he could still say no to becoming involved in a sexual entanglement. He didn't want to tell the group that he believed sex was a sacred act and he didn't want anyone to know that he was sweating profusely, as if he were chained to a bed in Hades. He just wanted to hide under the covers.

"Dylan, buddy, why are you sitting so far away? You look lonely. Come over here by my Jodi," Norman coerced.

"OK," Dylan replied robotically, frozen in place.

Jodi, quick as a hummingbird, jumped up and moved to turn off the light. Then, without a word, she scampered out of the candlelit room.

"No, Dylan, don't get up," Norman complained in a rough voice while pointing to Carmella, who was coyly staying silent.

Dylan felt anxiety rolling inside his belly. He wasn't sure about this ménage à trois. Previously, he hadn't been turned on by Carmella even a little bit but now he was feeling territorial toward her and wanted her to leave Norman's side. "Norman, I think this isn't the kind of meeting I had planned tonight. I'm feeling a little gun shy being around your two lovers," Dylan managed to sputter as he started to get off the bed.

Before his feet were planted solidly on the floor, he was knocked off balance by Carmella, who lunged at him and pulled him toward her with unending giggles. Dylan let his body go limp while trying to surrender to her grasp as she held him close—so close that he could smell her sweet perfume and feel the softness of her firm, inviting breasts. Norman moved his body to physically intertwine with them and together they all rolled about as if they were stones in a tumbler. Norman, growling like an animal in heat, was creating a wild spectacle from which Dylan wanted to escape.

Suddenly, Carmella screamed, "Stop it!" and in a tantrum, hit Norman with her fist.

Dylan jumped from the bed and tried to pull the frantic Carmella away from Norman. She reached to slap Norman's face. Even in the dim candlelight, Dylan could see their faces become frozen in anger. Dylan held her back far enough from Norman so that she could no longer hit her target.

"Namaste! Namaste! Relax!" Dylan said as he

looked Carmella in the eyes and tried to calm her down.

Norman sprang up from the bed and headed for the bathroom. "What's biting you?" he shrieked, walking out like a wounded wolf sadly leaving his pack.

Dylan, alone with Carmella, couldn't believe how quickly this crazy situation had materialized. "Carmella, please stop crying and pull yourself together. Come on, what's wrong? We can just leave if you want. Stop crying," he whispered tenderly, holding her shaking body.

"That bastard bit me really hard. I just want to punch him," she replied, her arms crossed over her chest.

"Norman's high. He's not thinking right. Drugs can make people act crazy. You'll be all right," Dylan said, stroking her hair and relaxing his hold on her tense arms.

She started to sob hysterically, then grabbed a corner of the sheet to stop the bleeding from the bite on her breast.

"Oh, shit..." Dylan was horrified to see blood oozing from her nipple.

As if Dylan was in the middle of an x-rated video, at that moment Norman came running back into the room wearing nothing but chaps and a Zorro mask. While cracking a long black whip, he wailed, "I'm ready to make love to ya, baby! Come and get me! I love you, my precious!"

"I need to get out of this room," Dylan muttered with a tone of urgency.

He wasn't sure whether it was the right choice to leave Carmella but he couldn't think of anything else to do to assuage his unpleasant emotions. He was getting angry and was unaccustomed to these surging feelings he couldn't control. Why wasn't Carmella making any effort to leave? Frustrated by a feeling of helplessness, he hoped that she was smart enough to take care of herself.

Looking at Norman and seeing him butt naked in black leather chaps turned the moment into a comedy of errors. Dylan couldn't believe what he was seeing. He couldn't rush to the door fast enough. He refrained from making insults about Norman's cellulite-ridden bare ass, even though he considered it to be the perfect thing to do. Instead, he quoted Aleister Crowley as he walked out the door.

"Love is the law—love under will."

It was obviously going to be a long night.

Chapter Seven

The Chariot
Wheels Spinning In The Mud

"I'm getting out of here. I need to clear my head," Dylan told Jodi, who was sitting in Norman's living room with her head buried in her hands. "Want to come along? Some fresh air will make you feel better. We can go get coffee or something. And please stop moaning. It gives me the creeps."

Jodi moved her head slowly as she turned toward Dylan, then stared at him. Dylan felt uncomfortable seeing her small, half-naked body and handed her some clothes from the couch, hoping they might belong to her.

She pulled a sweatshirt on over her head, smoothed her hair, then said weakly, "I took too much of that shit. I thought it was going to be coke but now my body is telling me it was crystal meth. I hate that stuff. It makes me feel like I'm about to die."

"It might help if you stop playing with your hair, stand up, and move. Even taking a few steps will help you feel better." He took her trembling hand and pulled her to her feet, hoping that she would be all right.

"Let's go outside. The night air will breathe some life into you."

"I'm an Indigo child and no one tells me what to do," she said, sounding irritated. She pulled her hand away. "I've been criticized enough times to know that I don't have to listen to *anyone* telling me what to do. I'll do what I want, when I want."

"I'm not telling you what to do, I just know that if you choose to go outside, you'll feel better." Secretly, Dylan wondered whether he'd made a mistake inviting her to go with him. Why did he feel the need to rescue people? Considering his present condition, he didn't have the mental strength to take care of anyone besides himself.

As soon as Jodi had finished dressing, Dylan grabbed what he hoped was her shoes and led her toward the exit.

"I don't like to wear shoes," she complained when she saw them in his hand. "Besides, those aren't mine."

"OK," he said, leading her out the door while trying not to feel annoyed. "Hopefully your indigo aura keeps your bare feet from stepping on any sharp rocks or thorny vines."

He thought he detected a slight smile and was relieved that she wasn't too stoned to follow his lead down the steps. As they walked close together, he felt like they were two disgruntled lovers trying not to touch. Dylan had keen night vision and guessed that he was better at seeing in the dark than his new acquaintance. He moved slowly to make sure she could find her footing on the narrow path leading to the parking area and his car.

Just as they started across the old wooden-plank bridge, Dylan stopped walking. He sensed an aura glowing in the dark. In a distressed voice, he whispered, "Do you see that?"

Jodi froze. Anxiety rushed through her body and she tensely asked, "See what?"

"That pulsing light across the bridge..."

"What light?"

"That blue-green cloud of haze. I haven't seen anything like that since I was fifteen."

"What are you looking at?" Jodi inquired, squinting as she tried to see whatever Dylan saw.

"It's a Seega!" he managed to say in spite of feeling frozen to his core.

"What? Are you hallucinating?"

"The Seega! It's a spirit tethered to the earth by ancient rites for wrongs they committed when they were alive. Their souls are damned and their ghostly forms are imprisoned in solitude as punishment for their crimes." He felt himself growing in stature as he conveyed this important information to her. "The neighboring water elementals of the creek, the Waktcexi, their supernatural caretakers, watch over them as their perpetual guardians."

"You're bullshitting me. I don't see anything," Jodi said in a skeptical tone. "And I thought I was having problems. You must be really stoned...or just nuts."

"I thought Indigo children were supposed to be psychic. You don't have to believe me," Dylan replied. "But I see it. Luckily, they have a difficult time crossing water. So if it tries to bother us, we can go back across the bridge and the creek below will block it from crossing our path. But right now, it's far enough away. Let's hurry to my car." He pulled her to quicken the pace.

Before they could reach the car, Jodi screamed. "I

just felt something cold on my neck! I'm scared!"

They broke into a run and headed for Dylan's car.

"Let's get out of here," Dylan said breathlessly while he struggled to unlock the passenger's door. As soon as it was open, Jodi jumped inside. Dylan then rushed around the back of the car to the driver's side. He too could feel icy hands. They shook his neck as if he were a rag doll. It took all of his strength to stay upright and not run while he fumbled with the keys. "Go to the light!" he shrilled. "Back away, spirit of the dark!"

Even though his adrenaline was clearing the fog and fear from his mind, he dropped his keys.

"Jodi, open the damn door!" he commanded while searching in the dark for the keys on the cold, rocky ground. He couldn't believe Jodi was so dumb that she didn't know to unlock his door from the inside.

As his hands touched upon the keys, Dylan glanced over his shoulder. He felt a familiar chill and in a frenzy, his shaking hand tried in vain to fit the wrong key into the locked door. He could see Jodi crying and sinking down in her seat with fright, as if trying to become invisible. At that point, Dylan realized that even if she tried to help, she would only get in his way. Summoning all his energy, he found the right key and managed to unlock his door. His mother always said that he could be depended on in an emergency, and most of the time she was right.

Relief spread through his drained body when his door opened. He dashed inside, slammed the door closed behind him, and felt the safety of his familiar seat. With sweat dripping from his forehead, he was ready to be finished with his current venture. Moments seemed to stretch into eternity but finally, he turned on his headlights, started the ignition, and gunned the engine.

"What was that?" sobbed Jodi, talking through her tears.

"It's an entity associated with turbulent powers and evil forces. Only the water spirits can withstand their foul temper. They work as etheric guards to keep them from doing harm," Dylan said while trying to restore his mental equilibrium as they sped away.

"Well, I felt its cold hands on me and the water spirits didn't protect me," Jodi pouted.

"Maybe the water spirits didn't move fast enough to stop it in time. We don't really know what happened. Perhaps they stopped it from hurting you or doing physical harm."

"Why didn't it attack you like it did me?" she asked, sounding a bit more relaxed as they zoomed farther away from their uninvited excitement.

"It did but I psychically called on my totem to protect me and to stop the Seega from harming me," Dylan answered, consciously trying to calm his breath.

"What's a totem?"

"How old are you? You haven't heard of a totem?" Dylan noticed that his voice sounded incredulous.

"And you're such a smart-assed big shot because you know what a totem is?" Jodi promptly confronted him. "It sounds like you think a little too highly of your stupid self. You're putting me down and you don't even know me."

Her attitude hit him like a left-cross to his jaw.

"We don't have to fight about what I know or you don't. A totem is a spirit animal you call on for protection. For example, I just called my raven friends to come to my rescue. Black as coal, they're invisible in the dark and they can peck out someone's eyes if needed. The Seega couldn't even see them coming."

Dylan wondered what he was going to do with Jodi, who seemed more and more naïve and unpleasant to be around.

Restraining his combative impulses, he added, "Native Americans say that if you want a totem, you have to find what animal is attracted to your energy and which one you feel a kinship with—or at least, discover one you can communicate with on some inner level. I've spent a long time calling raven energy into my life. I've searched for their habitats, collected lots of their feathers, and have taken hundreds of photos of them. I've even created a sacred space to represent their nest in my room and I can make sounds that are identical to their calls."

"Well, Birdbrain, what animal can make my head feel better? That's the totem I want right now. I have a headache," Jodi whined.

Dylan held his anger in check. "Dolphins play a significant role in healing physical problems. Maybe you can call on a dolphin to help you and ask if it wants to become your totem. And yes, healing is important to both of us right now. I'm feeling on a bit of a jagged edge from the powder we inhaled. That was some pretty rough stuff. Hopefully, a cup of something warm will help."

Dylan's cell phone rang but before he could answer, it went dead. "Damn! My signal's gone. Good thing we're almost to town," he said to Jodi, who turned away and looked out the window.

They remained in cold silence as Dylan sped down the highway in what he jokingly called his "golden chariot." He began to wonder what he was going to do with his annoying new acquaintance. She couldn't hold an intelligent conversation and she wasn't even trying to be nice. Although she was cute, he wasn't attracted to her, not even a little bit, and his interest in rescuing her from Norman's crazy drug scene was waning.

He soon saw the lighted signs for an all-night café and was happy to see an absence of cars in its parking lot. Wrapping himself in his warm Peruvian poncho, he got out of the car and breathed the cool ocean air. He forced himself to be the gentleman his mother taught him to be and walked around the car to open Jodi's door. With a little frown, she got out of her seat. Without looking at him, she moved slowly toward the well-lit door that featured a sign that read, "We don't serve grumps."

As he shut her car door, Dylan gritted his teeth, thinking about his current predicament. He hurried to catch up with her and they entered the café together. In the dimly lit rooms in Norman's home, he hadn't realized how young Jodi was but now, as she stood under the café's bright lights, Dylan could see that she was much younger than what he had first guessed.

Jesus! She's jailbait, he thought.

"Hey Jodi, how old are you anyway?" Dylan tried to sound nonchalant as he looked for the right table.

Jodi looked at him with wide eyes and smiled. "How old do you think I am?"

"Seventeen," he guessed, taking a seat in a black, worn-leather booth in the back of the restaurant.

"Nope. Guess again," she answered coyly as she moved to sit across the table from him.

"Oh great. We're going to play a guessing game. Are you nineteen?"

"No. I'm almost sixteen," Jodi replied as if she

couldn't care less about her age.

"No way! What are you doing hanging around with Norman? He's twice your age." Dylan asked, trying to hide his surprise by looking at the menu.

"I met him one night in San Francisco when I was panhandling on Broadway, and we went out and got high together. When he found out I was homeless, he told me I could stay with him."

"And so you went home with him?"

"Of course! I'm not as stupid as you think, and besides, Norman's one cool dude," Jodi replied. Her girlish smile reminded him of a mischievous child waiting to steal candy from a bowl.

The waitress appeared and took their orders, then made a hasty departure back to the kitchen.

"How long had you been living on the streets?" Dylan inquired, feeling a knot tightening in his stomach. He had walked by too many sleeping, homeless women on the cold sidewalks in the city and it wasn't a pretty sight.

"About six weird months. Right after I got to the city I met this guy, Simon, who took me home with him to get high. At first, we were just having fun but then he started pushing me out the door to make money for us by selling my body. He'd beat me till I'd bleed if I refused. After a couple of beatings, I knew the only way I could survive was to stay high and work the streets to make him money. I wanted to get away and plotted what I could do. When he realized I was getting ready to leave, he followed me everywhere. He once held a blade to my face and threatened to slice me from my vagina to my nose if I didn't come home. And he said he'd know where to find me." She sighed. "One night after I worked about twelve tricks and Simon was stoned asleep, I took all my money and got on a bus to visit a friend who lived in Daly City. I knew Simon wouldn't know to look for me there. I'd met this nice guy through my work who wanted to help me get out of my business even though he was one of my repeat customers. He was young, tall, and good-looking, and he told me he could get me a job working as a waitress at the Fairmont Hotel where I could make lots of money legally."

Jodi paused for a breath.

"I couldn't figure out why he had to buy love. Maybe because he was raised a strict Catholic and he didn't feel like he fit into the San Francisco dating scene. And he complained about living at home with his mother, who couldn't speak of anything but the fear of God. He was an adult yet she kept telling him not to have girlfriends because if he could be tempted to have sex with them, he would lose his special God-given gifts. To keep her happy, he never told her about his private life. He joined a singles club where he paid hundreds of dollars just to meet lots of nice women but he hated the match-making parties. He said it made him feel like a piece of meat on display at the butcher shop.

"We got along really well. He didn't mind paying me for my services and trusted me enough to give me his phone number. He said I could call if I needed him. That night when I was running from Simon, I took him up on his offer and called him for help. Since he couldn't take me home because of his mother, he rented a room for us to share at a friend's place who had a spare." She grabbed a napkin and rubbed her dripping nose.

Both Jodi and Dylan were so lost in her story, they

didn't notice the waitress hovering over them. The older woman looked at the couple dubiously, dropped off their order of fries, tea, and milk, then disappeared, shaking her head.

"So...you went from living with one man to living with another," Dylan said, trying not to show that he was disturbed by her story. He had heard about teenage runaways surviving on the streets but couldn't believe he was going to be drinking his newly arrived cup of tea with one.

"Well, what was I supposed to do? I actually started living with *two* men, Jordan and his friend. After I got free from Simon, I didn't have drugs and without them, I slept for most of seven days. But when Jordan wasn't with me, which was most of the time, I started getting bored. I thought about going back to my old neighborhood in the Tenderloin where I could easily score dope to get high again but I was afraid of running into Simon. Jordon bought me some fancy clothes and took me to meet one of his friends, a manager of a restaurant in the Fairmont. He told him that I was eighteen and had experience working as a waitress. His weird friend offered me a graveyard shift and I started working it. I didn't like following in the footsteps of my mother, who worked as a waitress, but I needed money and wanted to change my life." She fell silent and it looked to Dylan as if her fries were the sole object of her existence.

"So...what happened next?" asked Dylan, who showed obvious interest in her story.

"If we didn't have customers at three or four a.m., my boss, who had been asking me to go home with him so he could make me breakfast after work, told me that I could rest or sleep in his office. Well, one slow night at work when I was really tired, I took him up on his offer and went to sleep. I woke up to find his hands going inside my underpants and I busted him in the eye. I ran away after only ten days working my new job. But that was OK with me. I didn't like the stiff-collared uniform I had to wear. It was yellow and gold and it made me look like a rotting banana. But without any money, I started living in so much fear that I almost wanted to return to my parents' home in Indiana."

"Why didn't you? Wouldn't that life be easier?" Dylan inquired, not knowing whether to feel sorry for her or admire her.

"My mother's third husband was a scumbag. She married him when I was twelve. Over time, he and I went from hating each other to becoming super friendly. He let me know that he liked me to wrestle with him and I liked having a chance to punch him. But after a while, my mom started getting angry at our bouncing around. She told me to stop bothering him and if I didn't stop, she wouldn't talk to me. She'd only yell at me to go to my room." Jodi looked almost robotic as she spoke. "Then, one night while she was away working a late dinner shift, my stepdad and I were clowning around and getting really rough with each other. Before I could stop him, he pulled my blouse over my head and grabbed my boobs. I kicked him as hard as I could in the balls to end our brawl. I ran to my bedroom and locked my door. He was really pissed. He swore at me from outside my bedroom door and told me that he'd torch my mom if I told her what he'd just done. And I was sure he'd do it. He had such a bad temper, especially when he was drinking, which was most all the time."

Jodi's demeanor was so matter-of-fact that Dylan thought he could be talking with a manikin if he didn't know better.

"After a couple weeks, I couldn't take him being so lovey-dovey with my mom and glaring at me like he wanted me to die, so I ran away from him as fast as I could."

"Wouldn't it have been safer for you to tell your mother?" Dylan said, feeling a sadness begin to overshadow him.

"No! She was too busy making money to pay the bills to talk with me about almost anything, and besides, we didn't have that great of a relationship. She let me know that she couldn't wait for me to start making it in the world on my own. I felt like some kind of a burden breaking her back. She was tired of working so hard and not being able to pay our bills, and her body was hurting. Anyway..."

Jodi's voice became barely audible and Dylan guessed she was trying to hold back the painful emotion that was obviously rising to the surface.

"The last time I called home I found out that my mom had died. Since no one knew where I was living, I wasn't told about her death and I didn't get to go to her funeral. I have a feeling she's still mad at me, even on the other side." Jodi began to cry.

Dylan didn't know how to react. Uncomfortable at hearing her list of misfortunes and realizing that she had problems bigger than what he could solve, he felt a heaviness on his shoulders. Now coming down from his earlier high, his mind felt like burning coal. After listening to Jodi's narrative, he felt even more of a sense of responsibility to take her somewhere safe, in spite of his weariness. Feeling fatigued and having finished his tea, Dylan decided it was time to leave. Perhaps he could figure out how he might help her once he got some sleep. With a little more time and a clear mind, he was sure he could think of something.

"Do you want to go to San Francisco with me?" he asked as he got ready to pay the bill. He felt strangely transparent to everyone who looked at him, even though he had on two layers of clothes.

"Well, I don't know...I guess so." Jodi got up from the table. She offered Dylan her hand, which he refused to take, making it obvious that he didn't think it was a good thing to do. He imagined that she knew how to rely on herself to get through hard times.

While Dylan waited for her, she swaggered to two different dining tables before she was offered the cigarette she was asking to borrow. Dylan was annoyed and realized that the entire night was not going at all like he had anticipated. *Damn*, he thought, *her life has so many problems.* But he didn't want to inherit a new set of problems because of her. Even so, he knew there must be a better solution than returning Jodi to the crazy scene at Norman's.

"OK, let's get out of here. And don't light that cigarette in my car," Dylan said as she approached him, looking for matches in her bag. He teetered between compassion and frustration as he opened the café door to go outside. "If you can't think of any place to stay, I might know where you can stay tonight."

"You're not going to take me back to Normans?" Jodi asked as they walked to the car and she lit her cigarette.

"No, I need to go back to San Francisco and go home, where I can get a few hours of sleep before going to work tomorrow. And besides, I don't want to cross paths with that Seega again." He took the cigarette out of Jodi's hand and threw it on the ground before helping her into the car.

Since it was the middle of the night, Dylan didn't want to argue about her cigarette or taking her back to Norman's. Besides, she was still too stoned to know where he was going as he started to drive. No longer strangers, the misfit couple began to accept one another's company without complaint as they drove the back roads, watching the fog rhythmically appear and disappear like phantoms dancing in the dark.

Without warning, a deer jumped out in front of the car. Dylan immediately slammed on the brakes only to have his car skid across the slick highway. Within seconds he hit the deer with enough force to make a loud, smashing crash.

"Lucky there aren't any cars coming from the other direction or we'd be in big trouble," Dylan remarked to Jodi, who began to cry again as he steered back to the right side of the road.

"I hate hurting innocent creatures. Did you kill it?" she sobbed in a disapproving panic.

"I don't know," Dylan sighed with obvious stress, annoyed about the potential damage to his car and how Jodi didn't seem to care about that. "I need to pull off the road and look."

He pulled over, put the car in park, and grabbed a flashlight from the glove compartment. The cold slapped his face when he opened the door and jumped out. He walked over to the deer, which was lying on the road in a pool of blood. He shined his flashlight into its eyes and the deer stared back without blinking. *Oh no, this is a sign from the gods that something is very wrong,* he thought. But Dylan was someone who would always try to find something positive in any situation. With a short invocation, he whispered a prayer for the deer's peaceful passing, then took out his knife and cut off its tail. He had wanted a deer tail for his juju pouch and the universe had just provided it. He offered a note of thanks to the Great Mystery for the tail and the fact that his car was still intact, even if its left front fender was a bit smashed.

"What is that!" screamed Jodi when Dylan re-entered the car and started looking for some paper in which to wrap the tail, which was bleeding in his hand.

"It means the deer's life was not lost in vain," Dylan said to Jodi, who was crying again. "A deer's tail has the power to invoke the spirits of nature."

"What do you mean?" Jodi asked between sobs.

"I mean you should stop crying and just be happy we didn't get hit by another car when we swerved across the road," Dylan grunted, not feeling like sharing his hard-earned shamanic wisdom with a kid who wouldn't understand.

"I feel terrible," Jodi wailed.

"Get your head together. Life has bigger problems than a dead deer. More importantly, do you have any place you want to go in San Francisco?" asked Dylan, wanting to change the subject.

"No but you don't have to worry about it. You can just hold your deer's tail or your dick or whatever you want to do," she muttered.

"Listen, smarty pants, if you keep mouthing off to me you can walk in the cold back to Norman's house," Dylan replied, annoyed with her again as he pulled back out onto the highway.

"Aren't you a super-cool dude. You just want to leave me stranded on a highway to nowhere?"

His foot automatically started to press the accelerator with more force than was practical for the foggy, dark road, but he desperately needed to get home and return to his normal life. He was hoping to get a few hours of necessary sleep in his warm, welcoming bed, and he wasn't going to let her stop him. With a little luck and the bribe of a fragrant bud, he was sure he could drop Jodi at his old girlfriend's apartment in San Francisco for the night.

"I have an idea of where you can stay, just for tonight," Dylan said, hoping he could count on Destiny's kindhearted nature to offer her a place to sleep.

Leaving Marin behind them, the Golden Gate Bridge looked like a welcoming friend as they approached it. The lofty, illuminated towers looked like an enchanted entrance to a fairy castle partially hidden in the mist. Feeling a sense of relief, Dylan was sure he was doing the right thing for both himself and Jodi. *Everything will work out for the best,* he silently told himself.

Chapter Eight

Strength
The Loss of Innocence

"*D*ylan..." moaned Destiny as she answered the door of her apartment. "What are you doing waking me up at three o'clock in the morning?"

Destiny was Taylor's oldest daughter. She stared at her ex-boyfriend and his barefoot friend, whose red, swollen eyes looked as if she had been partying far too late into the night. Giving them both a half-awake look of disgust, she invited them inside, slammed the door shut, then turned and ran down the hallway to her room, where she jumped back into bed and pulled the blankets over her head. Perhaps Dylan and his disheveled friend would leave, she thought, hoping that the knock on her door had only been a dream.

Dylan followed Destiny to her room. He gently pulled away her covers so that she couldn't ignore him. With wide eyes and raised eyebrows, he spoke in a whisper. "Will you be a sweetie and help? Jodi needs someplace to stay and I can't take her home with me. Can she sleep in your living room?"

"You must be out of your mind," Destiny wailed.

She pointed to the door. "Get out! Leave me alone!" She tried once more to pull the covers over her head. Why did Dylan only knock on her door when he had a problem? Her anger began to awaken.

Dylan's voice took on a pleading tone. *"Please...* I can't take her home with me. She desperately needs a place to stay. I will leave you to go back to sleep as soon as you say yes," he implored while gently stroking her hair, which was sticking out from under the covers. Knowing Destiny's generous nature, he felt sure that she would give in to his request.

Former teenage sweethearts, Destiny and Dylan had remained good friends even after they had broken off their once stormy relationship, and in spite of their differences, they still had an endearing connection. After all, they had both lost their virginity to one another during a wild escalation of passion, and that special gift of love could never be repeated with anyone else.

"Who is she and what kind of problem is she running from?" Destiny asked, opening her eyes to scan the darkness in the room before she reached for her pillow and put it over her head. She knew enough about her longtime friend to understand that he wouldn't bring a stranger into her home in the middle of the night unless there was a problem.

"She doesn't have any place to go. Can you let her stay with you tonight? She's only sixteen," Dylan said, pulling back a corner of her pillow and giving her a gentle kiss on the forehead.

"Take her home yourself, you've got a bedroom," Destiny mumbled, then turned away from Dylan to show her annoyance. But her heart had a weak spot for him and that always gave him an advantage.

"My apartment is so small, I'd be walking on her if I tried to go to the bathroom. You've got a lot more space. And besides, you're a woman and you can talk woman-to-woman with her. I've got to go to work early in the morning but tomorrow I'm sure I can find someone else who will be willing to help her. Otherwise, she's going back to living on the streets and that is a serious problem for someone so young."

"Do you think I'm so asleep that I don't know the real reason you don't want to take her home? Stella isn't going to be too happy knowing you're hanging out with some other woman, let alone a teenager. But I also know that I won't ever get back to sleep tonight if I say no. Get a sleeping bag out of my closet for her. She can sleep on the futon in my living room. And then get out of here."

"You're the greatest. Honestly, I mean it. And 'may the kisses of the stars rain upon thy body.' I owe you a big one," Dylan said, not wanting to confront Destiny with the fact that she knew nothing about the character of his frustrating relations with his wife, bittersweet Stella.

"Let's see...you're quoting from Crowley's *Book of Thoth*, aren't you? Hmm, that's almost worth being woken up from my dream." Destiny sat up and looked at him with narrowed eyes. "But the big question is, what do I want you to do for me?" She was already thinking of what she wanted in return for taking in a stranger. "You will have to crawl in the dirt like the worm you are to repay this one."

Jodi, who had been listening to the two friends talk while she was standing in the hallway, walked into the dimly lit room. "Thanks," she said meekly, looking at the floor. "I won't be any bother."

"Jodi, this is one of my dearest friends," Dylan said, smiling. "She had a tough time growing up with her dad too. We used to call him Taylor De'Toro because he was so domineering but we made our own decisions in spite of his heavy-handedness. I'm sure she can understand your struggles and I promise that she'll take good care of you. Tomorrow, after I get some sleep, I can help you figure out where it's best for you to go." Dylan opened the closet door, quickly found the sleeping bag, and threw it to Jodi. "Your bedding, madam," he said, then turned toward Destiny. Without making eye contact, he gave her a kiss on the forehead. "Thanks for being a sweetie and letting Jodi stay the night. I'll get out of here now so you can go back to sleep. Come on, Jodi, let me show you the way to the futon," he said as he walked out the bedroom door. "I'll check in with you tomorrow, Destiny. Adios."

"You're such a nice guy," Destiny yelled sarcastically as the door shut behind him. She guessed that, as usual, he was oblivious to her feelings. She was really pissed at him for waking her in the middle of the night. Now her mind was awake—awake enough that she started to think about her recent absurd argument with her present boyfriend, and with those kinds of thoughts, she wasn't sure she would be able to get back to sleep for a long time.

He had left her alone in a bar earlier that evening after she couldn't find a way to forgive him for losing their vacation money after playing poker with his card buddies, and their planned trip to Brazil was canceled. She tried to distract herself from thinking about her handsome, curly haired Nick by spending the late evening studying ancient Greek rites of passage. After she had fallen asleep with her book as her pillow, she was awakened by dogs running and barking in the hallway outside her apartment, and people shouting loudly for them to shut up. Her night was starting to look more and more like she was watching a soap opera called *Untamed Emotions*.

It was especially upsetting that others took her kindness for granted. She was always expected to do things for others, even if she didn't want to. Early in life, she had been assigned the role of being a good girl since she was the oldest sibling and the "responsible one." Too many times she had done things for others not because she wanted to, but because other people demanded it and she had been conditioned to always say yes so that she would be liked.

She shouldn't live solely to please others, she told herself. She needed to learn to do things differently and the sooner the better. Maybe she would just start telling everyone who wanted something from her, no! Absolutely no way! No, I'm not going to take in your stray friend for the night, no, not me!

Thinking more clearly now, she realized that's what she should have said to Dylan. *One sheep, two, three sheep, four, oh damn!* Would she ever get to sleep again?

∽

A daring, bright teen, Jodi knew more about love and hate than most people her age. By the middle of the next day, she was tired of listening to Destiny advising her about what she should be doing with her life. Destiny sounded too much like her mother, who always told her what to do. By the time she had put her sleeping bag away and their late lunch was finished, she was rudely told to wash the dishes. It didn't take long before she could feel the cold truth behind Destiny's fake smile and sensed she was an unwelcome guest. Disappointed that Dylan hadn't called, she didn't want to waste any more time hanging around grumpy Destiny. She was ready to do something more exciting than sit in an apartment waiting for someone to *maybe* arrive.

She had lots of experience being out on her own. Because she hated the cold, windy city of her childhood, she had longed to travel, and San Francisco, the "free love" hot spot, had beckoned to her. To follow her freedom-loving dreams, she had stuffed her backpack with her favorite well-worn clothes, her first childhood teddy bear, a couple cans of tuna, potato chips, and cookies, and used her school bus pass to go downtown. She had saved just enough of her babysitting money to buy a one-way ticket to California. Without even saying good-bye to her mother, she jumped on a westbound Greyhound bus and rode solo across the country.

Mature for her age and naturally endowed with assets that many women pay highly to surgically obtain, she attracted men's attention and knew it. Hanging out and listening to music in Golden Gate Park created a world where romance was easy to find. When she first arrived in the city of love, she experimented with different relationships and sampled an endless, easily available supply of euphoric drugs. Her favorite pastime was dancing exotically, without a partner, to the beat of conga drums that rocked her core. But when she hooked up with Simon, he wouldn't let her do that anymore. She was heterosexual by nature but once he made her walk the streets to get fast, easy cash for his drug money, she was forced to explore what it meant to swing both ways. But thankfully, her life had been better lately. She had found new strength and she didn't like to dwell on that part of her past.

Jodi sneaked out the door when Destiny was busy talking on the phone to some dumb dude. She was happy to get away from Destiny and to be outside in the fresh air. She gingerly walked down Haight Street in the purple-blue twilight to catch a bus downtown. Even though the sidewalk was alive with colorful characters, she didn't feel like trying to connect with anyone and kept to herself. A young man with a guitar and a wide smile stopped to talk to her but she wasn't interested in having a conversation with someone who wanted her spare change—as if she had any to share. She was lost in her thoughts about her new friend, Dylan, and couldn't stop giggling about the weird, ridiculous night they'd had bouncing together on Norman's water bed. Knowing how crazy men were, including Norman, she wondered if anyone could ever make her believe in the prospect of having a true-love relationship.

The blow on her shoulder came suddenly, as if she had been hit by lightning. When she finally got a glimpse of her assailant's fiery eyes, horror overcame her. Her pain surged as his strong arms forced her to walk toward his car, which was parked in a back alley, one rough hand clutching her arm, the other covering her mouth so she couldn't scream. Caught in his vise-like grip, she could only stumble in the direction his forceful command moved her, and no one was close enough to notice. Jodi bit his hand and started to cry out but he quickly muffled her screams.

"Shut up, bitch!" the brut hissed as he forced her

into his car on the passenger's side. He held her painfully immobile with his massive weight, then got into the car by climbing over her and into the driver's seat. "Don't try to escape or I'll kill you. You're coming with me," he said, as he pulled her close to his side, one hand tightly holding her shoulder and the other starting the ignition. With masterful precision, he backed out of the alley and started down the street.

"Please," she pleaded, grasping to find courage in her voice. "Please stop holding me. You're hurting me!" With all of her strength, she struggled and freed herself from his grip. She lunged toward the door and frantically pulled on the handle to open it, willing to risk her life to leap from his moving car.

Acting to secure his captured prize, he swiftly grabbed her hair and held tight. Pulling her to his side once more, he grabbed her by the arm, almost breaking her wrist. His silence made Jodi aware of the frozen muscles in her body that were locked in fear, struggling yet unable to move. Her mind raced to find a way to escape but she couldn't break free from his threatening grasp. While the car moved along, currents of adrenaline pounded her entire body, making her feel like her heart was about to explode. There was no one to hear her scream and she couldn't run. Where was he taking her? And...would she live through this night?

The car slowed as they drove toward a freeway underpass. Without streetlights, the eerie darkness came into the sedan like a parade of angry panthers. He parked the car and turned off the ignition and lights. Jodi could see dim shadows frolicking menacingly in reflections from distant lights, and the waning moon appeared to frown in sympathetic understanding.

"I'm afraid..." were the words Jodi repeated silently in an unending refrain as her mind raced to find a reality other than the one she was facing. *Please God, let me wake up, please let this be a bad dream*, she prayed. Her stepfather, angered by her disobedience and her teenage rebellion, once told her she'd probably get killed if she left home. Was he about to be proven right?

Her driver, grinning in a grim, macabre way, tore off her shirt and pushed her to where he could slap her repeatedly, sucking away her ebbing will to escape.

"Please don't hurt me," she repeated while gasping for air, trying to move her face away from the sour, putrid smell of his alcoholic breath.

"I'm not going to hurt you," he said, grabbing her crotch. "Just take off your panties. Now!"

Even though her body was rigid with fear, her resolve was still intact. "No!" she cried.

"Well then, I guess I'll have to do it myself."

His fist slammed her shoulder like a sledgehammer hitting a nail. Again yanking her hair, he forced her to lie beneath him on the seat, engulfing her with his bulky, sweating torso. The desire to run enabled her to hit him with all of her strength, but in response, he forced grotesque kisses on her mouth. Jodi tried desperately to move away but the pain from another blow rendered her immobile. With all the anger she could muster, she spat in his face. But he seemed to take it in stride and showed his crooked teeth in a lopsided smile, as if enjoying her plight.

She could feel his hands moving toward his zipper. She started trembling as she realized that she, who would freely give herself to a sincere appeal of love, was about to be raped. His fingers racing to rub her soft private parts felt like multiple bullets piercing her soul.

"No, please, no!" she pleaded.

His answer came with his lips reaching for her mouth.

The lingering pain from his forceful blows invoked a feeling of terror she had never before imagined. Fearing the end of her life, her body quaked with a throbbing dread. Was death near? She wanted to vomit but she was frozen, motionless with fear.

Crushed by his brutality, and hoping her life wouldn't be taken, she couldn't summon the strength to refuse his words, "Do it or I'm going to kill you!" he yelled.

"I'll do anything you want," she blurted. "Just please don't kill me!"

Time lost all meaning as the present became an eternity of living in the hell of his enduring, loveless passion. Never before had Jodi felt such misery. Her pain was entwined with anger, as if a fire had gone wildly out of control. She tried to detach from the horrific sensations that she felt as he continued to penetrate her.

The thrust that signaled his climax came after what seemed an eternity. He removed his body's offensive embrace with a jerk and her body went from rigid to limp.

"That was so good," he remarked as he zipped his pants. "Where do you want to go now?"

Jodi could hardly believe his words. Weakly, she fumbled to get back into her torn clothes. "Can you take me home?" she spoke, feeling a faint flash of relief that she was going to live and her nightmare might soon be over.

"Sure. Where do you want to go?" he grunted as if he truly cared for his prey.

In shock, but so happy to hear his words, Jodi blurted out the names of the cross streets where she had once shared an apartment with her previous boyfriend, Jordon. Feeling like she was nearly released from the grip of approaching death, the prospect of being taken to a safe haven felt like an unexpected miracle.

Silently, the man drove through the city. Jodi's sense of hope returned as she saw her old familiar neighborhood and she realized that the man wasn't going to kill her. He was really going to let her go.

Even though time seemed to stand still, eventually he stopped at her designated street corners. Because of her pain, she could barely open the door, but she managed and swiftly jumped out of the car. She tried to read the license plate number as her predator drove away but in the dim light, the rapidly receding numbers blurred, making them impossible to read.

In the cool night air, the flame of her spirit reignited. She ran to the entrance of the apartment building, rang the bell, and waited for someone to unlock the lobby door. Soon she was excitedly standing in front of the former sanctuary that Jordan had once so kindly provided.

Even though the door to the apartment didn't open fast enough, the familiarity of her surroundings slowed the tremulous beating of her heart. Once inside the cozy living room, Mike, her previous roommate, and Jordon, her one-time knight in shining armor, turned down the stereo to listen to her tearful outrage.

Jordon's eyes became as large as saucers while he

listened to her story and his brow tightened with stress. "I'm out of here!" he said, acting like a cowardly lion. He turned away and got his jacket before he made his way to the door.

Jodi struggled to hold back her tears. Her heart sank as she watched him walk out the door without as much as one glance in her direction. Under her present circumstances, how could he not consider giving her a few seconds of emotional support? Stunned, sadness stabbed her heart as she saw him quickly disappear from view.

Mike, who had always liked Jodi, could not believe his friend's callous behavior. "The pig!" he exclaimed, shaking his head in disappointment and offering her a supportive hug. "Let's call the police to report your situation," he insisted. "Hopefully, they can catch the bastard who hurt you and that should help you feel better."

Jodi's body fell into a heap on the floor and her body began to shake. "Why me? I hate my life," she cried.

Mike tried to console her by trying to take her into his arms but Jodi instantly pushed him away.

"Don't touch me!" she screamed.

A short time later, two rookie cops were knocking on the door. They entered the room looking as if they were entering a crime scene where everything was suspect.

"Are you the woman who is reporting a rape?" one asked in a voice as cool as ice.

Embarrassment and tears accompanied her reply. *How do you talk with strangers about something this painful?* she wondered, feeling a red blush covering her cheeks. "Yes," she said through flowing tears. She couldn't think clearly about what she might say.

"Are those the clothes you were wearing during the rape? Please take off your underwear. We need to see them," one of the cops requested matter-of-factly, as though talking about the weather.

Shame became waves of oceanic torrents of anger as they held the crotch of her underwear up to the light. *Oh my God!* she thought. *This is just as horrible as being raped.*

"We're keeping these as evidence," one officer said, putting her torn panties in a plastic bag. "You need to come to the station with us to fill out a report. Our doctor will examine you for STDs and gather evidence for samples of DNA."

Can death be any worse? Jodi wondered while considering the attraction of suicide. An eruption of anger gave her the courage to walk out Mike's door with the officers, who were escorting her, wrapped in a blanket, to their police car.

"Get in the back seat," one officer said, opening the car door. "It won't take long for us to get to the station."

Quietly, she did what she was told. "I feel so dirty inside. I just want to die!" she murmured to herself as she got into the car. She felt her heart sink, closed her mind to the present moment, and started thinking about what she could do to end her torment.

Chapter Nine

The Hermit
Lighting The Lamp Of Wisdom

Dylan, still thinking about his recent experience at Norman's and trying unsuccessfully to focus on the work piled on his office desk, was obsessing about his own yearnings. He knew nothing about Jodi's situation but criticized himself for bringing her to San Francisco and making himself responsible for her welfare. He remembered telling her and Destiny that he'd call today but he was preoccupied. He was annoyed at Lisa, who hadn't returned his phone calls. Why was she playing this cat-and-mouse game with his emotions? He had bared his soul and confessed his love to her. How could she not know how much he cared? Were his insecurities being triggered by her lack of communication? It seemed that his uncertainty was definitely being triggered more and more, every passing minute his phone didn't ring, and now he didn't feel like calling anyone. Using work as a fitting excuse, he delayed calling Destiny. She could be depended on to take care of Jodi for just a little while longer, couldn't she? After he took some time to clear his mind, he'd return to the demands of his hectic world, then he would check on "Jailbait Jodi," as he'd come to call her.

In addition to his worries about Lisa and his headache from partying a bit too much the previous night, Dylan was also preoccupied with the uncommon sighting of the Seega and its spooky glow in the darkness. He was fascinated by the supernatural and wanted to scrutinize the ghostly presence in Norman's parking lot without the interference of Jodi's whimpering. And he needed to make sure Carmella was doing OK after Norman's strange antics.

At quitting time, he wasted no time leaving his consulting job in the city. Soon he found himself weaving in and out of the frustrating rush-hour traffic, watching day turn to dusk while crossing the Golden Gate Bridge on his way back to Stinson Beach.

Confused by his trial-and-error relations with women (lately, it seemed mostly error), Dylan realized how tired he was of worrying about his crazy love life. For a moment, he considered changing his plans and going home to bed but as he listened to himself analyzing his relationships, he knew that thinking about Lisa—or worse yet, his wife—would be more draining on his emotions than distracting himself by continuing his road trip to investigate the paranormal. He became increasingly excited as he thought about the invisible creature and wondered what he could do to change its grim fate. His mood brightened as he realized that this trip complemented his commitment to improving his magical skills and to more deeply awaken his inner sage.

After exiting the main highway, Dylan followed the same route to the coast that he had taken yesterday.

Lucky for me I don't need to talk to Stella anymore about where I'm going, he thought while rolling down his window for a breath of fresh air. "No, I didn't just think that," he said out loud, surprising himself as he heard his bitter attitude toward his wife in his defensive voice.

In the last phone message he'd gotten from Stella, she said she wondered why he hadn't called her and complained that he didn't love her anymore. He felt henpecked by her new form of nagging. Previously, he had responded to her demands concerning her new vision of love after she was so excited about dating someone new. But now, after spending so much time mending his upset emotions, he didn't feel like lending Stella his ear so she could complain about their relationship. Her changed viewpoint about the meaning of their wedding vows and the promises they had made to one another had broken his heart and changed his life forever.

The sight of a dead skunk on the side of the road and the smell of its putrid fragrance reminded him that he needed to pay more attention to his surroundings. As Dylan watched the oncoming dark shadows of dusk, he was happy to return his thoughts to the beauty of the countryside and to have another break from the crowded city and the endless labyrinth of his confused emotions. The narrow, curving Highway 1 began to feel familiar as he drove along looking for the turn to Norman's place. It didn't take long before it appeared and he was zooming up the gravel road toward his destination.

While parking his car, Dylan saw no sign of the Seega, who presently seemed less of a concern than the knots in his stomach that signaled he wasn't as confident returning to Norman's home as he thought. As he got out of his car, he realized that he didn't know what to expect after the strange drama he had experienced the previous night. Remembering that he had taken Jodi from Norman's home without saying a word about it to his friend gave him a slight sense of apprehension. Nevertheless, he was pleased to see the little house in the woods shining with lights that indicated Norman was home. As he walked away from his car, Dylan realized that he didn't know what to expect after the strange drama he had experienced the preceding night. Alert to the growing tension in his shoulders, he slowed his approach to the front porch.

"Anybody home?" Dylan called into the crisp air as he knocked. "Hello! I'm… I'm here! You told me that I'm always welcome back. Can I come in? Norman! Come on, open the friggin' door. It's cold as hell out here." Dylan stared behind him into the dark to see if the Seega had followed him, but nothing was there.

After waiting patiently, Dylan heard footsteps approaching the door.

Norman, with his hair in disarray, peeked his head outside. "Are you alone?" he asked, staring out into the yard to see if anyone was with him.

"Yeah, alone. Can I come in?" Dylan asked, offering a large smile in response to the strong aroma of pot that drifted through the door.

"Sure, Dylan, hurry up," Norman said while scanning the empty darkness behind him. "It's cold out there. Where's the brat?"

"Do you really think she's a brat? I took her to stay in the city with my ex-girlfriend. You two certainly went at each other in a weird way last night," Dylan said, trying to make his mind stay calm and his conversation lighthearted as they walked into the living room.

"Maybe. But I really like her, even if she is a bit crazy and stubbornly pig-headed. With her around, I always have a sassy friend who wants to get high with me," Norman answered without looking at Dylan.

"Sure...like you only want to get high with her," Dylan teased, insinuating that there was something more to their relationship.

"You can leave right now if you think you know more about me than I do," countered Norman, showing dislike at his friend's remark. His eyes were bloodshot from lack of sleep and Dylan suspected that he would quickly become irritated at any more innuendos concerning the tattooed teen he called "Hot Cross Buns."

"Oh, come on, it's no big deal," Dylan playfully exaggerated, hoping to lighten their conversation while taking a seat on the edge of a chair. "Like, I came all the way from the city just to offend you? You know, I think you tripping out with her is really cool."

Norman looked at Dylan in his kingpin manner, then stared coldly away, as if something important needed his attention. Speaking with his lips drawn tightly together, he muttered, "What's up? It's a little strange for you to be here two nights in a row, isn't it?"

Dylan knew it was time to tell Norman what was on his mind. "Something I saw here last night made me want to return."

"Oh, really? It wouldn't be that you want to take Carmella to stay with your ex-girlfriend in the city, would it?" Norman smiled but his voice sounded guarded, as if he were talking to a rival. He moved close to the fireplace and threw in a log. "Damn place is so damp. Living among the redwoods, I never seem to see enough sun." He turned around, ignoring Dylan, and focused his attention on the TV. He laughed as he caught a glimpse of a punk rocker provocatively riding an elephant on a video show.

Not wanting to take Norman's attention away from the bad-ass babe in the video, Dylan waited for the program to finish before he spoke again. "Ya know, the native Californians seemed to be a lot more clever about living in the redwoods. They said not to reside under the great green giants because bad spirits live among them. And to be honest, this is the main reason I had to return tonight. Do you know that you have a Seega living in your parking lot?"

"A what?" Norman replied, sounding curious at Dylan's strange remark.

"A Seega. It's an evil spirit who's condemned to live chained to the earth. It's not free to go to the other side," Dylan explained. "I saw him last night, right in the middle of your parking lot."

"What?" Norman asked, suddenly sounding more alert.

"Really," Dylan replied enthusiastically. "I learned about them the hard way when I was sixteen. I got stuck living with one in a house my dad rented that was built on an old Indian burial ground. The damn thing drove us out."

"Here we go again," said Carmella, who had silently joined them just long enough to hear Dylan talk about the phantom. "Are you seeing more ghosts? You must be hardwired to see ominous things that go bump in the night."

"I believe him," replied Norman. "Not too long ago, a friend of mine was sleeping in his van in the parking lot. In the middle of the night, he felt something pounding on his chest. It woke him from his sleep with a terrible fright. He jumped out of bed and came screaming up here at four o'clock in the morning, wanting to sleep in the house, yelling that there were spooks in the parking lot. The next day, he moved his van as fast as he could and I haven't seen him since."

"I want to go see this spook," Carmella said. "Seeing is believing."

"OK. We can all go but you'd better take a flashlight," Dylan suggested, realizing that her eyes told him she was high enough to see anything.

"Oh, you mean we need a hermit's lamp to illuminate our path?" questioned Carmella.

"Carmella, this isn't about the Tarot."

"I can't help it, Dylan. I was just reading Aleister Crowley's *Book of Thoth* and you remind me of the hermit—someone who hides under the disguise of being a computer geek but he's really a messenger from the gods who lights the path so that others can follow. Here you are, once again, taking me on a mysterious tour to see the underworld of invisible reality. You'd be a perfect match to the hermit if you just wore a hooded cloak and carried a serpent staff."

"Well, I don't know if I'm being flattered or not but what's important here is that we each find a flashlight so we can see the path in the dark," Dylan answered sounding aloof. He made a conscious effort to avoid sounding interested in her comments or forming a connection with her.

Norman joined the conversation with a cynical tone. "Dylan can't be a hermit 'cause he's married. And what about me? How come you never say any of that cool Tarot stuff about me?"

"Don't be jealous. It's because you're not into metaphysics," Carmella replied as she turned away from both men.

Norman grabbed Carmella. "You don't know what I'm into."

"OK. Are you into metaphysics?"

"Not really," Norman replied with a grin while pinching her thigh.

Carmella glared at him and walked away to find her jacket.

Soon they each had a flashlight and had walked outside to follow the meandering footpath. In the dark, the tall sequoias looked like Titans boldly defying the wind. Coyotes howled in the distance, affirming an untamed restlessness in the air. Moving in a surefooted manner, Dylan remained quiet except for his exhilarated breathing, which made his excitement evident.

"Where across the bridge did you see this thing?" asked Norman when they neared the ravine leading toward the parking lot. "I don't see anything."

Dylan's eyes scanned the distance. "Look to the left. There's a circle of light vibrating close to the earth that continues upward toward a faint, cone-shaped light that's higher than my head."

"I don't see anything. Where exactly is it?" chirped Carmella. "Maybe what you really saw is a space alien and it already transported itself home."

"Perhaps reality's too boring and you need to communicate with imaginary friends," Norman said sarcastically, walking in the direction where Dylan had pointed.

"It's not a fantasy. I see it. I can't believe that neither of you can," Dylan declared. "Can't you see it?"

"Maybe if we had more to smoke we'd see it too,"

Norman announced, giggling like a child.

"Oh, sweet!" replied Dylan in a serious tone. "Aren't you funny? If I were you, I wouldn't go over there. You don't want to provoke it. It looks like it's getting ready to—"

"Norman, let's not walk any farther," Carmella said, looking into the darkness. "Come on, let's go back to the house. I don't need to see any blinking lights to believe Dylan. I'm willing to take his word that there's something over there."

With his extrasensory vision, Dylan could see the Seega arching its ghostly back like a tiger getting ready to attack. Within a matter of seconds, Carmella was jerked up into the air like a puppet being pulled on a string. Faster than Dylan could blink his eyes, she fell back to the ground flat on her back. Norman moved quickly to help her stand up but she screamed when he tried to pull her upright. In an instant, the night became more ominous with her wailing cries of pain. Dylan felt an unwelcome stream of adrenaline shoot through his spine.

The gurgling sounds came next. "Give...stone... back..." reverberated in an echoing hum of vengeance.

Dylan strained to decipher the nearly inaudible words the ghoul muttered. *What is it trying to say?* he questioned in his mind.

"Come back over here! Hurry up!" Dylan said to Norman and Carmella. "You both need to get back across the bridge where he can't easily follow."

Norman seemed to be failing to help Carmella, so Dylan chanted a mantra for psychic protection and ran to help them. Carmella sobbed from both pain and fright.

"I can't put any weight on my leg," she groaned.

Her body began to shake.

"You'll be OK," Dylan said. "Just try to stand up and walk. We're holding you."

Dylan tried to lift Carmella with Norman's help but it soon became obvious that Norman was too stoned to be useful. Norman swung his arms in the air like a scarecrow blowing in the wind, trying to fight off the invisible presence. Dylan tried to lift Carmella on his own but he could hardly support her weight. He watched the Seega grow in height. The light emanating from its brow changed color from violet to blood red. As Dylan knelt next to Carmella, he watched the Seega pull something ominous out from behind his back. Dylan focused his eyes and realized that the object was sparkling light beams woven together in the shape of an ax.

Just as it was about to use his etheric weapon to strike against them, Dylan, in a fit of desperation, felt a rush of adrenaline give him a surge of unexpected strength. In an instant, he picked up Carmella and carried her back across the bridge where he knew they would be safe. Norman lagged behind, swearing defensively into the air. Once across the bridge, Norman fled in the direction of his house.

Although Dylan was left behind with Carmella, he didn't mind. He knew Norman was too stoned to be at all helpful on an emergency mission. Besides, he enjoyed holding Carmella, even though she was moaning in pain. With his support, she relaxed enough to stand on one leg and attempted to walk, or at least stumble, on her own, even if they had to stop every other step as they made their way back up the path.

"Thanks. Let me try to get up the stairs myself," Carmella said when they arrived at the house. She tried to take a step, then grimaced. "Well, maybe I could use some help," she said as she sank down onto the bottom step.

"OK, how can we best do this?" Dylan asked. "Can you put any weight on your leg?"

Norman looked down at them from higher on the path above them. "Shouldn't you try to hurry? That thing can't bother us here, can it?" he asked in near panic.

"I can't move. I hate pain. I want to just sit and let someone beam me up the stairs," Carmella said with a touch of anger.

"Teleportation isn't going to happen and getting chilled from the cold isn't going to help, either. Come on, let's get you into the house," Dylan said, summoning up his strength to carry her up the stairs as if she were a Barbie doll.

Norman, who had turned on all the lights in the house, began racing around in a panic. "OK, let's see what you've done to yourself," he said as Dylan set Carmella down on the living room couch. Norman squinted his eyes to look at her leg. "Oh, shit! Your ankle's twisted."

"Is it that bad?" Carmella asked. "I was just standing there when I felt something push me down. You were there. Did you see what happened, Dylan? Did you see it push me down? Did you? Whatever happened out there happened so fast. It's so weird...and the smell was as if someone had opened a coffin."

"I tried to warn you both but you didn't believe me," Dylan replied in a matter-of-fact way. "I thought I heard it say something about wanting a stone. Did either of you hear that?" He turned to Norman. "It looks like she needs to see a doctor, doesn't it?"

Norman nodded. "Yes but not this late. She'll have to wait until morning because I'm not leaving the house tonight."

"What do you mean?" Carmella asked.

"Just a minute," replied Norman as he went off to a different room.

Carmella rubbed her throbbing ankle. "It's swollen. I need to go to the emergency room. It's open all night. I can't handle waiting till morning. I'm in too much pain," she wailed. "Call 911!"

Norman quickly returned to Carmella's side. He had a gallon-sized glass pickle jar filled with a variety of different colored pills. "This is my very own pharmacy in a bottle," he boasted. "Come on, baby, let's get you stoned. You won't feel so bad after you take a couple of these." He handed her several brightly colored tablets from the jar.

"You're crazy. I'm in pain. I need a doctor, not pills. I can't even walk." Carmella started sobbing while Dylan gently touched her badly twisted ankle.

"Take these pills and you'll feel no pain," Norman told her. "I promise to take you to the doctor in the morning. I'm too wired to drive you to town now. Hurry and take these," he commanded, sounding like a cornered wild boar. "You need to get comfortable with the idea of staying home 'cause we're not going anywhere tonight."

"Dylan, you can take me to the hospital, can't you?" Carmella pleaded.

Norman looked at Dylan with disdain. Just then, the phone rang. "Don't answer it," he asserted.

They all stopped talking long enough to listen to the person leaving a message on the answering machine. Dylan's eyes widened as he heard Jodi's feeble voice.

"I'm at the police station in downtown San Francisco. Can you come and get me?" she pleaded before hanging up.

"Oh, crap," Norman said. "Sounds like more bad news. It's time to put Carmella to bed."

Dylan thought Norman sounded like the captain in charge of a sinking ship but he hesitantly agreed. He felt overwhelmed. Disagreeing with Norman could ruin their friendship, especially after his blunder of taking Jodi away the previous night. Perhaps he could persuade Norman to take Carmella to a hospital. In reality, Dylan was in mental agony about both his own and Norman's enormous role in Carmella's condition. And what about Jodi's phone message? Rescuing one friend was enough for him in one night but with the ring of the phone and Jodi's somber message, it sounded as though he needed to go back to the city.

"Carmella, you're one of my favorite friends but I just can't right now. You'll be OK staying with Norman. Jodi sounds like she's in a mess and may need my help more than you do," he said, trying to be stoic. Turning away from Carmella, he followed Norman out the door to have a private moment to discuss their situation.

"You know, man, I don't want to go anywhere past my front door for a while," Norman confided. "Even going to the parking lot is way too much of an ordeal for me. I'll reward you with some really good Cabo Wabo if you go pick up Jodi and give her a ride back here."

"Sure. I'm all for that. Or at least I'll try to find her," Dylan said, shaking his head in dismay while searching his pocket for his car keys. "I'm curious as to why Jodi's at the station and I'll do everything I can to get her out of there. So, I'm on my way."

The two men walked back into the living room, where Carmella was still moaning.

"I'm too stoned to drive anywhere," Norman said to her in a voice that proclaimed to Dylan that he was feeling sorry for himself.

"You self-centered jerk!" Carmella screamed from the couch. "I've called 911."

"I told you those pills will take away your pain. You're acting stupid!"

"I don't want your damn pills. I can't walk. While you were playing Mr. Cool with Dylan I called 911 for someone to come and get me."

"Carmella, you're a dumb shit!" Normal shrieked. "Dylan! Don't leave. You've got to help me get my pot plants out of the living room. And I need to hide my stash. Do you see anything that I could get busted for?" Norman started running around the room.

"Not if you get your powder out of site," said Dylan, not believing that he was witnessing another crisis happening for the second time within an hour. Feeling like he was becoming a rescue service for drug mishaps, Dylan anxiously questioned, "How 'bout if I leave now and go get Jodi? It's not the police who are coming; it will be the paramedics in an ambulance. They don't bust people. But it will be better if you open the windows so it doesn't smell so much like weed growing in here."

"Sure, man. Can you help?" Norman asked hysterically.

"Just for a quick minute. I've got to hurry 'cause I don't want to get stuck on your one-lane driveway facing an ambulance in the dark with no place to turn around." Dylan quickly opened windows and doors without saying another word. A grimacing cold filled the rooms. "It's time for me to go," said Dylan as he moved to walk out the door. "I'm sorry, Carmella," he said, already wrestling with the sadness that had descended upon him once he had heard Jodi's pleading phone message.

As Dylan was leaving, he heard Carmella scream to Norman in a tone as cold as a winter wind, "There wouldn't be a problem if you had listened to me, you crazy idiot!"

"Stop bitching! It's not too late for me to carry you back down to the parking area for you to wait for your ambulance. Maybe then you'll get a broken jaw to go along with your broken ankle," Norman retorted with hostility.

From outside on the front porch, Dylan watched Norman rush about carrying his stash of powder and his pill jar out of the room. "I was willing to take you to the hospital but I wanted to wait until morning, when I'd be sober enough to drive," Norman yelled.

"Sorry, but I need someone to help me now. If you were in pain and your ankle was twisted, you'd find a way to go to the hospital, too," Carmella said, bursting into tears.

"Enough crying! You win. Thanks to your phone call, I don't have a choice in the matter. You're going to the hospital. Dylan's going to get Jodi and I'm going to be alone. I don't like being alone, especially now when I know there's a spook nearby," Norman whined as he rushed to hide his oversized bong.

Dylan took a deep breath in the cool night air and was happy to get away from Norman, who sounded like a spoiled child. Before leaving, he took one last look at the house and raised his open hands to send Carmella some Reiki healing energy. Almost cartoonlike, Norman was rushing around the room precariously holding several pot plants in his arms. Dylan wanted to laugh but held it back. After all, this was a serious matter.

Chapter Ten

The Wheel of Fortune
Steering The Helm of Fate

Too bad Julie had to get pregnant. Mark shook his head in dismay, trying to relax his mood while he played with his hair to get it to set just right over his receding hairline. It was obvious he would have to do more than his fair share of grandparenting after Julie had her child. Seventeen years old, unmarried, and showing all the signs of having a hard time adapting to motherhood, his daughter's pregnancy remained an unhappy thought. Who would have imagined that it would be his youngest child to first make him a grandpa?

Perhaps he could more easily forgive her situation if she hadn't annoyed him by trumping his authority when she slammed shut the doors of communication, refusing to name her unborn child's father. Foolishly, Julie, whose flat chest was noticeably expanding in relation to her growing belly, had followed in her mother's footsteps by getting pregnant too early for her own good. Why couldn't Rowan have saved their daughter from this dire fate, Mark wondered, a smoldering resentment toward his ex building inside him. "What a pity she has to tarnish my good name," he grumbled, trying to calm his emotions.

He detested the burden this unexpected situation placed on him. Although he had been happy to be a dutiful father and share custody of his daughter after his divorce from Rowan many years ago, he would never willingly volunteer to have their daughter's infant move into the room next to his. But now he didn't have a choice. Mark gradually became aware of the knot in his stomach and wondered if Julie's announcement that she planned to live with him instead of Rowan was going to trigger his ulcers. His frequent visits to the doctor had shown him that it didn't do any good to hold on to anxieties and let them eat a hole in his stomach. He tried to relax and breathe away his tension. "Be here now..." he told himself while resolving to put Julie and her pregnancy out of his mind.

Taking his mental focus away from Julie, Mark began to think about his responsibilities. He needed to organize his mind and prioritize his imminent duties. At the present time, besides freeing himself from his worries about Julie, his most important mission was going to his lodge meeting, a long overdue gathering to support men's liberation. Quite different from most of his lodge assemblies behind locked doors, this one was being held at an outdoor campsite near Devil's Slide and it had sports competitions. Not that he was fit enough to win in any of those activities but he possessed other qualities. He'd had to crusade for popularity votes to claim the prestigious role of Master of the Hermetic Initiation Ceremony and had won. And tonight he looked forward to hearing two young men recite their secret oaths, a prerequisite for joining his fraternal order and getting permission to read the Golden Lotus secret transcripts for sharpening the sword of personal power and financial gain.

Mark hurried to pack his bag of ceremonial clothing. Before long, he had finished everything he needed to do, picked up his baggage, and left his home to walk to his car, which was parked in a nearby garage. He shivered in the brisk wind and hoped that the chilly weather wouldn't deter the men from venturing out or wearing only their briefs to battle their opponents in the games. Once in his driver's seat, he kicked over the engine, which grumbled to a start and made him smile with satisfaction as it growled like a tiger. He accelerated his way through the hills of Twin Peaks and made fast strides toward his destination, and by the time he reached the coast, all previous concerns had left his mind. He enjoyed his drive on the southbound serpentine highway. It wouldn't take long to find the hidden place where he could join his lodge brothers and play his part to jolt the party into high gear.

He felt so alive driving to the countryside, away from the confines of his apartment walls. Even though his home was comfortable, he yearned to be in nature, to feel its healing soul, but seldom took the time. He used the excuse that it was more important to watch environmental programs on his large-screen TV with a drink in his hand than to drive to the country without one. Lost in thought, Mark was amazed at how short the forty-minute drive seemed when he drove past the *No Trespassing* sign into the camp parking lot. *What a rich world,* he thought as he looked for a parking space among the many cars and trucks that had arrived earlier.

As he got out of his car, Mark felt an unwelcome chill and grabbed his heavy coat. He looked through the tall trees until he spied a glimmer of light from a bonfire, then followed a well-marked trail up the shadowy path to meet his group. Upon approaching the welcoming crowd of about twenty-five men, he shouted to everyone the call of the brotherhood, "Greetings, Serpents and Warriors!"

"One circle, joined destiny!" many answered amid tribal shouts.

"You're late, Markus," said an older man who was smoking a cigar. "We've been waiting for you to begin our ceremony. So get yourself a beer and let's get this show on the road. The natives are restless!"

"When you get to the top of this organization, late is being on time," Mark replied with a tone of superiority. Even though Mark knew he was in a group of extraordinary men, he wished they wouldn't be so anal. "While you get our initiates into the Westward quarters, I'll take a few minutes and get into my robes."

"You're the boss, Markus," one man replied. "Don't worry. We'll be having another drink while we wait."

Mark went by himself into the darkness of a circle of trees where he could change his clothes in private. He took his ceremonial headdress made of bear claws, bullets, and the skull of a tusked boar surrounded by golden pheasant feathers out of its bag, held it out in front of him, and admired it. He loved having the opportunity to strut his hard-earned authority by wearing this ornate crown of achievement. Besides, it made him look physically larger, and in his dark robes, he would be almost invisible in the flickering shadows of firelight if he didn't wear the headdress. If destiny agreed, he'd never miss an opportunity to parade the cosmic symbol of his office and show off its magnificence.

When Mark came out of the dark in his regalia, the other men made way for him in a titanic wave of movement. He proudly walked to the front of the group and stood on a bench to tower above everyone. "Put down your drinks, brothers, it's time to listen to the fresh voices of those who wish to join us," he orated. "Each of us needs to hear their oaths, which will join them as one with our brotherhood. Once they swear their allegiance to embody the values that we uphold, no one can destroy our unity. Listen closely to their voices to hear whether they are worthy of wearing our crest."

Mark looked stern as he waited for everyone to become quiet. His voice was tranquil yet commanding as he spoke to the two hopeful initiates. "Your fortunes may be *bueno*—good, or *mala*—bad. As you join our community, your goal is to go beyond this world of duality, the good and the bad, the wealthy and the bankrupt, and learn how to turn the wheel of fortune toward the destiny you wish to achieve. Initiates, what is the Wheel of Fortune?"

The first initiate, a tall, handsome young man named Richard Wiseman, answered in a way that made it apparent he'd had too much to drink. "A game show on television with a foxy lady who turns the wheel for prizes."

Oh no, thought Mark, *I don't think Mr. Wiseman, good-looking or not, belongs here. But we'll soon find out. Hopefully, our next man can do better.* "OK, Jason Green.

It's your turn to answer the question. Will you please explain the Wheel of Fortune?"

"Head Master, with all due respect to the wisdom of my fellow initiate, the wheel holds the essence of the principles of the brotherhood. It is the Sri Chakra of ancient times, the all-seeing eye of God, the karmic wheel, the evolving mandala of the zodiac, the sacred hexagram that bears truth beyond thought."

"Yes, very good," replied Mark, feeling a sense of relief. "Also, the wheel is related to the goddess of fate, Dame Fortune. As it spins, it is Lady Luck who turns destiny in your favor—or against you, if she disagrees with your ways. In days of old, gamblers prayed to her to win wealth and greater prosperity. Let us all call to her by her name!"

The men shouted loudly in unison, "Fortuna, mistress of our night!"

"Sustainer of our fortunes, for our silver, gold, and material bounty we give thanks," Mark bellowed. "All right, initiates, what do you need to start this journey?"

"Only faith," they answered in unison.

"What expectations do you have of our secret works?"

The first initiate, Richard, uneasily blurted in a broken slur, "I know that you will guide me to a better life."

Jason, the second young man, replied without hesitation, "Understanding and power over the universal vexations of success: anger, greed, bewilderment, delusion, envy, slander, and scorn."

Mark suspected that he had spent many hours studying the brotherhood's teachings. "Good answer. You'll do well in our brotherhood." Mark spoke his approval directly to Jason without looking at Richard. He stepped down from the podium and approached both initiates. Mark reached for a Grecian urn that was filled with cabernet, then poured a shot glass measure of wine for each man to drink. He commanded, "Drink this to empower your body, mind, and spirit to win over antagonistic forces." He then changed his tone. "Initiates, hear what I am saying. If you are inwardly drawn to take this path, you are requested to show your trust for your new family. To prove that you deserve to enter our inner sanctum, you must do one thing we request. Tonight, both of you must allow one of our worthy archers to shoot a beer can off your head with a bow and arrow."

"Oh, shit...I can't believe this!" Richard said to Jason, grimacing with apprehension.

"Yes, it's true," Mark continued. "You said you had faith in us and the foundation of our group connection is built on trust in one another. By submitting to this trial, you will prove your trust. And most importantly, once you have passed this test, you must each sign an oath with your own blood that you will consciously rise above mundane mediocrity and strive to elevate your standing in our brotherhood. Also, in your first year you must agree to do fundraising for the noble purpose chosen by our group."

"That sounds less difficult than having someone shoot a beer can off my head," Jason moaned, looking at several of the men who stood around him. "How are we going to raise funds if the arrows end up going through the middle of our foreheads?"

"Yeah," Richard agreed. "Do we really need to prove that we want to join your group? 'Cause if I must let some drunken lodge brother shoot a can off my head in the dark, I'm leaving now."

"OK, that's your choice. But the person who's shooting the arrow is an excellent marksman and is stone-cold sober," Mark maintained.

"I don't care. I'm not doing it. I'm out of here. You guys are a bit too weird for me anyway. And that hat you're wearing should be put in a coffin and buried," Richard sneered as he took a few long steps away from Mark.

Even though Mark wanted to tell him off, he held himself in check since he knew everyone was watching. In his position of leadership, he always had to prove he was worthy of being followed and he suppressed any strong reactions. Trying to sound totally detached, he declared, "We don't need your disrespect. You don't have a clue what's going on here. Lucky for us, you're the lesser of the two initiates and the stronger man is smart enough to know the value of our group. He's not a coward."

"Well, fuck off, Markass! I'm leaving this dumb ceremony! Jason's just more stupid, not more courageous…that's all."

"Enough nonsense. We bid you farewell, Mr. Not-So-Wise," Mark replied and turned his back to Richard. "Come, Jason. It's time to show your valor," Mark directed, dragging him by the arm.

❧

The city streets seemed endless as Dylan drove away from the police station. Feeling like a navigator through the outer boundaries of time and space, he was enveloped in a mental fog. Colors that his logical mind knew didn't exist darted in front of his headlights. *Spirits from another world,* he thought. Every few minutes, Dylan heard a muffled sob from Jodi, who sat in the seat next to him curled up in the fetal position. He reached over, put his arm around her shoulder, and gently stroked her head. Jodi didn't respond.

"So much for the tough girl living in the city," Dylan tried to joke. In his heart, he knew that her barely audible moans were natural to the misery she must be feeling. *If she only had more common sense,* he thought, *maybe she wouldn't be in this mess.* And neither would he. Luckily, the coke Dylan had snorted earlier in the evening hadn't totally worn off and he still felt awake enough to pilot through their middle-of-the-night odyssey. Driving through an inhospitable maze of avenues, he turned the car away from the flat grid of streets and started ascending the hills of Twin Peaks.

"This doesn't look like the road that will take us to Norman's," Jodi wailed.

"Don't worry, it'll be OK. I'll take you back across the bridge to Norman's after I get some sleep, which I desperately need to be able to go to work tomorrow morning. I'm barely awake, so I'm taking you to my father's house in the city for the night. It will be easier for us to think of what to do after we've both had a good night's sleep."

Dylan did not want to believe that those words had come from his own mouth. He knew he was getting more and more drawn into feeling responsible for Jodi and he wasn't happy with the thought. Any optimism he'd had about her not interfering with his life had waned an hour ago at the police station, when she announced that she had been raped. Seeing her misery triggered his willingness to do anything to help her, even though being with her went totally against his common sense. He tried to detach from thinking about the consequences of taking her from Norman's and bringing her to the city. What role had he played in the unfolding evolution of Jodi's karma and her present pain? Was he responsible for what had just happened?

The one thing he knew for sure was it was definitely time to find his own bed and end the current craziness of driving all over the Bay Area. While trying to push away an imploding cloud of guilt, he began to feel like a taxi driver, driving all over the city without getting paid for his time or his gas. "I'm not going to make that sixty-mile round trip again until after I've had a good night's sleep," he told Jodi, hoping that she could understand his quandary. His energy was waning and he started looking forward to his dream time, which would refresh his mind and perhaps bring answers to questions concerning Jodi's uncertain future.

"Toxins in my mind, toxins in my brain..." the man on the radio was singing.

While listening to the rhythm of the beat, Dylan could easily relate to the punk lyrics. He dreaded getting up early and going to work later that morning. He felt a sense of relief that his workweek was almost over but he became more aware of his frustration when he remembered that he hadn't seen or heard from Lisa. Fortunately, pushing her and their last erotic encounter out of his thoughts was a lot easier with Jodi sitting right next to him, whimpering like a baby.

"I want to go back to Norman's," Jodi persisted. "I have a place to go."

"I'm delighted that you have somewhere to go. I

would be glad to take you to Norman's but I've already had one exhausting trip across the bridge to his place earlier in the evening. When I left Norman's to come back to the city to pick you up, Carmella was waiting for an ambulance to take her to the hospital. It's not a good time to go there. And can you please understand that I've got to get up at six in the morning and get ready for work? I need to think clearly when I get to my job. So I'm going to go home before it's time for me to go to work in the morning, and get some sleep. I'll take you to Norman's tomorrow as soon as I can pick you up. And because we've just arrived at my dad's, you'll be able to get some sleep soon too. He's a really good guy. You can trust that he won't let anything happen to you. And most likely, my sister Julie is staying there too."

Dylan knew it would be better if he arrived at his father's home with a gift of pot but he had forgotten this protocol as he had been preoccupied with the Seega and the teenage runaway sitting in his car.

Things were far from perfect. His dad hadn't been answering his calls. But surely, he wouldn't mind giving a needy teen a place to stay since he had an empty bedroom in his place. If he or Julie weren't home, he'd use the key his dad had given him to "come in any time"—a privilege that he hadn't previously wanted to use.

Dylan knocked several times and was relieved when his father opened the door. "Hi, Dad. I was worried that you weren't home 'cause you weren't answering my calls."

"I wasn't. I just got home."

"I have a favor to ask of you. Can my friend stay here tonight until I can pick her up and take her to

Norman's tomorrow after I get off work?"

Mark looked at Jodi. *Lucky Norman!* he thought. *He always has young, pretty women hanging around.* "Sure, come on in. She's welcome here. A friend of yours is a friend of mine."

Once Mark looked at her, frozen in the light, he wondered what horrible kind of mess she'd gotten herself into. It was obvious that she'd been crying. He hoped Dylan hadn't been giving her a bad time. "Show her my spare bedroom in the back. I was just getting out of my clothes to go to bed myself," Mark said.

"Where have you been?" Dylan inquired.

"You won't believe it but I've been at a campout gone wrong."

"What do you mean?" Dylan asked, noticing an unusual furrow in his father's brow.

"First, show your lady friend to her room and then we'll have a chat before you go home to your Stella."

Dylan quickly showed Jodi to her room, which had papers and boxes spread all over the bed. "You can shower in there," he said, pointing to the bathroom. Without further conversation, he spent ten minutes clearing the covers while Jodi sat on the floor with a look of doom on her face.

When he finished, he said, "Everything will be all right. I promise to return as quickly as possible and give you a ride to Norman's. Tomorrow will be a better day." Dylan bent down and hugged the unresponsive Jodi good night. Then he gave her a little kiss on the top of her head, turned, and left the room. He tried not to notice the middle finger she pointed his way.

One minute later, Dylan was in his dad's kitchen. "So, what's up with the campout that went wrong?" he asked Mark, who was pouring himself a large glass of vodka.

"I was master of ceremonies for our club's gathering and we had chosen a new initiate. As part of the orientation, and to show faith in our fraternity, he was supposed to allow our longtime member and renowned expert archer to shoot a beer can off his head with a bow and arrow. The archer wasn't supposed to drink any alcohol but I found out after he missed his target and hit the poor guy in one eye that he'd had one drink too many." Shaking his head in dismay, he continued, "I can still hear him screaming. We called an ambulance and rushed him to the hospital. The doctors said that he may have permanently lost sight in his eye and he was lucky the accident didn't cost him his life. To make matters worse, his buddy, who witnessed this fiasco from afar, got into his truck to run for help. Because he was so stressed, he accidentally put his truck in reverse and drove backward into someone's new Mercedes. The Mercedes rolled forward and crashed into a tree and got smashed in both the front and the rear." Mark gulped for air, sounding totally exhausted. "I wish I would have had your friend Carmella's magic stone with me. Then maybe this mess wouldn't have happened."

"What magic stone?" Dylan inquired.

"She was here the other night with Norman after he crashed his car and was too stoned to get home. She showed me a magical stone that glows in the dark and said she found it in some abandoned house," Mark told him.

"Oh, really?" Dylan said, feeling a bit surprised. Instantly, his intuition told him that Carmella had found it in the haunted house they had recently visited together. *Oh no*, he thought, remembering the words he'd heard the Seega speak about returning a stone.

"Yes," Mark continued. "But now I just want to get on a plane and fly to Timbuktu because I don't want to be here tomorrow to answer the damn phone. I know it's going to be ringing off the hook. I'm usually happy to lead our prestigious pack but not now. I can't even imagine how much the legal fees are going to be to sort out this fiasco. It might even mean the end of our lodge," Mark lamented. "I just need another drink and then I'm going to bed."

"Dad, it's not your doing. It's the wheel of destiny turning to compose a new chapter. You can't control it. Best thing is that you relax, try not to worry, and get some sleep. I'm going home but I'll come over after work tomorrow, find out how things are going for you, and pick up Jodi. Please tell her to stay put until I can get back here to take her to Norman's. You can keep her busy by letting her watch TV." Dylan gave his dad a sympathetic pat on the back and hurried out the door.

What a crazy night, Dylan thought as he walked back to his car. He had wanted to tell his father about Jodi's situation but after hearing his father's problems and seeing him so shaken, he decided not to add further complications to his evening. And now, on top of everything else, he couldn't help but wonder about Carmella's stone. How had she gotten it? Why didn't she tell him about it?

Feeling a migraine starting to emerge, he turned his thoughts to finding his car and making his way home. All he wanted was to put everyone's problems out of his mind, fall into bed, and go to sleep.

Chapter Eleven

Justice

A Spirited Fling

"*I*t's very complicated and hard to talk about," Stella confided to Naomi. "I just want to cry when I think about it...and usually I do. My pain is so deep, I haven't talked with anyone about it. Even though I've been keeping my situation a secret, I feel like if I don't tell someone soon, I'm going to explode. That's why I'm here. It's taken me a while to get up the courage but I want to tell you what's going on, and then maybe you can help me. Dylan and I have been married for five years. He always talks about you and your family and says that you're an amazing card reader. I feel like I can trust you."

"Thanks for your vote of confidence. I hope I'm worthy of Dylan's good review. Please tell him thank you for me." The older woman sat back in her chair and looked deeply into Stella's eyes. She felt Stella's sorrow and decided it would be better to stay quiet and give the young woman an opportunity to unburden her soul. *Young people seem so plagued with torturous emotions and a lack of trust,* she thought. *These days they can talk*

to their computers but are afraid to talk with one another.
She was glad that her storefront office was inviting
and that people felt safe coming inside to share their
concerns with her.

Stella squeezed her hands in silence as if she were
wringing out laundry. "I was very attracted to
Thomas, a man I met at a spiritual retreat. I couldn't
stop thinking about him. I felt that we might be past-
life lovers and I wanted to pursue our connection but
Dylan, my adoring husband, would never allow such a
thing. When I first started telling him that I wanted
our marriage to become an open relationship, he
became angry and didn't want to hear about it. He was
opposed to letting me see someone else. He seemed so
insecure and immature, and we fought a lot about it. I
told him that having an open relationship would be an
exciting opportunity to grow. We could become wiser
by opening ourselves to new experiences than if we
stayed in our same, old-fashioned way of being
together."

Naomi nodded with understanding. She was glad
the sun had started coming through the star-shaped
crystals hanging in her window and that rainbows
were beginning to dance throughout the room. The
sparkling prisms of light helped her distance herself
from feeling sad for Dylan. She liked Dylan and
respected him as a gentle soul. She had watched him
grow into a young man in junior high school when he
began dating her daughter. She thought that he and
Destiny made a perfect couple, even if he was a bit
Mercurial. Secretly, she wished that they would have
stayed together but what vote did she have in teenage
affairs? Not many young men were as in touch with
the supernatural as Dylan, and that made him a perfect

match for her family.

Naomi watched Stella sit nervously in her chair. She wished she could say something to help her relax. She looked at the statue of Kuan Yin, the Asian goddess of compassion, standing in the corner, then looked around the room, searching for a sign of approval from the gods that they would help her give an impartial reading to the young woman sitting in front of her.

Without changing the expression on her sad face, Stella declared, "After arguing for several weeks about transforming our traditional marriage vows, and watching Dylan sulk around our apartment, I told him that he didn't have a choice. I didn't want him controlling me with his conventional ideas about our relationship. We didn't sign a contract to have an exclusive connection. I was so sure about what I was doing that I persisted in creating a major change in our lives. It's as if each detail is engraved in my memory. I kept telling him to be happy about new possibilities instead of being stuck in his narrow-minded view. Since I believe in being honest, I wanted him to know that I was going to start seeing Thomas whether he liked it or not. I longed to be free without needing to hide my actions or feel guilty. Dylan, my sensitive, supposedly freedom-loving husband, complained that he 'didn't see it coming.' I thought it would be great if we were both seeing someone new. I knew that if Dylan could be with someone else, he wouldn't be so angry with me and I wouldn't have to deal with his insecurities." Stella's tears ran down her cheeks.

Naomi interrupted her, trying to be supportive. "Before you go any further, please stop, take a deep breath, and take a tissue to dry your eyes."

"Yes, thank you. I haven't been feeling very balanced lately. It's like I'm obsessed with Thomas. He's been absorbing most of my waking thoughts. I was even willing to risk my relationship with Dylan for him. When I first met him, I couldn't wait to spend more time with him. I felt like a piece of ripe fruit and he was going to be the man to harvest me. We talked on the phone for hours. Thomas bought me a cell phone so that Dylan wouldn't know how often we were talking." Her cheeks flushed. "He made me so hot, even on the phone."

Naomi didn't reply. She smiled, waiting for Stella to go on.

"My relationship with Dylan became more difficult as he tried to adjust to having a new kind of relationship," Stella continued. "We stopped talking about open relationships so that we would actually keep talking to each other. Our communications became more and more stressful. We would argue and our quarreling became heartless. We soon stopped being intimate. I watched him mope about in a slump. Then he stopped coming home after work. Between his work schedule and mine, we hardly saw one another. And when he was home, he wouldn't tell me what was on his mind or what he had been doing. His retreat into cold silence seemed more aggravating than our previous arguments. After I became enraged at his strange behavior and at not hearing a word from him, he let me in on his little secret. He told me that my plan to change the terms of our relationship had succeeded. He also had a new lover. I acted delighted for him but inwardly I felt a cold chill go down my spine.

"I couldn't sleep that night. My mind spun as I

questioned my choices. What I had with Thomas was playful, affectionate, and I could talk to him about anything and everything. But then I slept with him and he totally changed. Everything that created a passionate connection for us stopped. Whenever I saw him, he continued to stimulate me like a lone wolf nearing a she den...but he was no longer available. I tried to be nonchalant when we spoke and embarrassed myself by shamelessly offering him an opportunity to make love. He told me that he had something more important he needed to do."

Naomi thought about the sword-yielding hand of justice and took a deep breath. Trying not to judge Stella's personal choices, she said, "Eros sometimes plays tricks on our hearts when we get too attached to the physical side of love."

"That's for sure." Stella sank down further into her chair. "A week later, the last time we talked, I joked with him about the craziness of our relationship and told him about my lusty passion for him. After all, he was responsible for provoking our initial sexual relationship. That's when he told me that he wasn't willing to be with me because his extended family didn't want him to be involved with any other women. I was livid. Extended family! How crazy is that? I hadn't been sleeping with Dylan because of the avalanche of feelings Thomas had triggered in me. I put my life on hold waiting to be with him, and now he 'wasn't willing'? I tried to hide the disappointment that ravaged the deepest core of my being. After all, I was a patient woman. I had waited a long time for Dylan to finally propose to me, and now I would need to wait for my new man to want to continue our relationship."

Stella stopped to wipe away her steady stream of

tears.

"I became agitated and anxious," she went on. "As Thomas felt me needing and wanting him more, he started withdrawing. He made it clear that we weren't going to have an intimate relationship. Why did it take him so long to let me know? I'll never know and I'll never understand him or any other man. I feel like such a vulnerable fool. What was he thinking when he bought me my own cell phone so that we could talk?"

It was half a minute before Naomi spoke. She adjusted her position in her chair, watched the moving rainbows the crystals cast upon the wall, then looked back at Stella. "So, you exchanged your harmonious relationship with Dylan for the dream of a more fulfilling but unborn love. How strange the twists and turns of romance." Naomi shook her head sadly.

Stella nodded. "After many hours of sobbing into my pillow, I began thinking that perhaps it was my wedding ring that made Thomas feel safe with me. When I took it off, my freedom to be with him prompted him to show me his phobia of commitment. The closer I tried to move toward him, the farther he moved away. When I became fully available to him, he froze like ice on a winter pond."

Naomi could see Stella holding back her anger at Thomas as she reached for another tissue.

"Now, although the opportunities are scarce, whenever I find the chance, I'm trying to improve emotional communications with Dylan. I feel so vulnerable and don't know where our relationship is going. Maybe I've killed any chance of getting back together with him. I know he's involved with someone else right now and I'm alone most all of the time. He says he still loves me and I know I have only myself to blame for setting him free to become involved with someone new. He keeps telling me to stop resisting the changes I've set into motion."

"Dylan's a good-looking young man. I wouldn't expect him to stay home waiting for you to finish your affair," Naomi said with a bit of sharpness in her tone.

Stella winced.

Naomi examined Stella's eyes to gauge her reaction. She had been consciously trying not to judge Stella's confession in a negative way but knew her last comment implied cynicism.

Stella tried to lighten the conversation. "He wants me to get into metaphysics. Dylan says that magical energy can be used for healing the body and mind, opening our heart, and transforming consciousness. He says, ultimately, that is what life is all about."

"That may work for Dylan but who are you? Do you want to study metaphysics? Because of your sexual openness, it might be more worth your while to study sexual alchemy or Tantra. What's really important is to focus on your personal needs and what you can do to mend the broken link in your connection."

"The truth is that right now, I'm clueless about what to do," Stella said. "Tantra sounds beyond me. I know it has something to do with yoga but that's about it."

"Don't worry, dear," Naomi replied. She picked up a wooden box that sat on a nearby table and took out a deck of cards. "Let's use my Tarot cards to get some clarity. Why don't you shuffle them and while you do, think about your relationship with Dylan."

Naomi handed Stella her cards.

Stella closed her eyes and slowly mixed them.

After a few moments, she looked at Naomi and asked, "Is that enough shuffling?"

"Yes, dear, now cut the cards wherever your intuition tells you to cut."

Stella closed her eyes again, took another deep breath, then cut the cards.

"Now, choose a card to answer a question about your relationship," commanded Naomi. "The card you select will tell you something about the best direction for you to go with your husband."

Stella hesitated, fingered one card, then pulled out another that was hiding just beneath it. "What card is this?"

Naomi smiled. "This card is a good sign. You have cut the cards on the eleventh major arcana card, Justice. It corresponds to the sign of Libra, which is the sign of equilibrium, harmony, and commitment in love. It represents the importance of staying centered and keeping your inner balance in order to find your way to happiness. Carefully weigh the pros and cons of your present choices in relation to your husband and your romantic path together. Check resources on sex, such as Tantric texts. Or, if you can't find any of those, read the latest issues of *Cosmo* to research how you might gather your strength to seduce him into making love with you again. The planet Venus linked with love rules this card, so you should be able to find a pleasurable solution." Looking into Stella's eyes, Naomi searched for visible signs of her immediate reaction. "You're still living together, right?"

"Yes but he's not home much except to sleep."

"Trust me. Sooner or later you'll find the right time to talk with Dylan and rekindle his passion for you. Don't obsess over your fear that your marriage is destroyed. You have time to fix it. Find the balancing point where you feel centered in your power as a beautiful woman."

"But what should I do?"

"Focus on healing your communications with your husband," Naomi directed. "And start being sexually playful again, even in little ways, like running your fingers through his hair. Remember the best times you had together and start acting toward him now as you acted toward him then."

Naomi saw that Stella's tears had stopped and felt her mood change.

"Negatives don't have to play out in life," she said. "Request a healing from your guardian angel, who is always with you. In your mind, visualize Dylan coming home and embracing you. Dark forces can more easily play themselves when there is fear. To help you clarify and improve your situation, literally change the lighting in your home. As a reminder to connect with your healing light, get some light bulbs that emanate a natural yellow glow. Yellow rays link you with your solar plexus, where you can feel your personal power and connect with your confidence. Stop worrying about your recent transgressions and open up, communicate your sense of loss without him. And don't forget to forgive yourself. You can't always be right about everything."

"Thank you for being so encouraging," Stella said. "But honestly, things feel so wrong that I have knots in my stomach. The more time I spend alone now, the more time I have to fantasize about having children with Dylan. I feel so sad that I can't tell him how much I want to become the mother of his children since he hardly ever talks to me."

"You sound so passive and weak," replied Naomi, annoyed. "I'm going to give you an affirmation that I want you to remember. Whenever you start to worry, mentally utter the command 'stop!' and then repeat to yourself: 'I am balancing my inner scales of justice with love, peace, and harmony.' When you're trying to fix things with Dylan, think loving thoughts and send affectionate feelings toward him."

Stella looked doubtful and hopeful at the same time. Naomi watched as she sat anxiously in her chair and realized that she needed something more. She took Stella's hand in her own. "I could even," she said in a matter-of-fact tone, "give you a love spell that my grandma taught me for fixing broken hearts. But for this spell to work, you have to be willing to pay dearly. Stains of sin and ignorance can only be removed if you're willing to go beyond what appears normal."

"How? What would I need to do?"

"First, I must ask my guides for their consent to give you this spell. If they give me permission, I can offer you their magical instructions about how to heal the discord in your marriage. Also, I will pray to Mother Mary for Dylan's seeds to be planted in your body. If God is in accord with the sincerity of your spoken words, you'll have a baby growing in your belly in a short time." Naomi's eyes looked upward and she sat in silence for a few minutes.

Stella continued, "I'm so tired of trying to change my emotions without seeing any change."

Acting as though she didn't hear Stella, Naomi said, "OK, I have finished talking with my guides. They told me that you won't need to wait long for what you want most. They also said that you presently despise Thomas, and to jump-start your healing, you need to tell him the consequences of his flirting with you. They have also prescribed the payment for the spell. I can't just give it to you if you wish to use it. Because you are considered to be part of our extended family, you need only pay half what a stranger would normally be charged. Finally, if you want me to help you conjure this magic, you will need to do some work on your own and it may take a couple of weeks or a month to see any results. For my time and effort in working with you, you will need to pay me two thousand dollars."

Stella caught her breath. "Two thousand dollars? Can I take time to sleep on this decision?"

Naomi let go of Stella's hand. "No, you need to act like an adult and make your decision right now. You and I both know that you're whimsical and you'll let your fears cloud your mind if you take too much time to deliberate. My time is too valuable to waste on holding your hand while you tipsy-toe on puffs of smoke while thinking about it. Just say yes or no to working with me before you leave." Naomi's voice had become like that of a captain commanding an ocean liner that was about to sink. She exhaled in exhaustion.

"Yes, I want you to help me." Stella's voice sounded pleading yet resigned. "I'll do anything to get Dylan's love again."

"All right. First, complete your obligation to pay me and then I'll ask you a couple of important questions. Besides that, you need to have complete faith in me. I need to warn you that once I start working invocations for you, if you do anything to counteract the energy I send, you will be in danger of psychic attack by astral entities and even my guides won't be able to protect you."

Stella visibly trembled, then said earnestly, "Dylan told me that you're a powerful healer. I won't do anything to block your energy. I promise. I need your help." She got out her purse and found her checkbook. "I can give you seven hundred now and the balance day after tomorrow when I get my paycheck. Does that work?"

"OK. We have an agreement," declared Naomi as she took Stella's check. "Can you bake an apple pie?"

"Yes."

"Great. I'll go to the kitchen for some items that you'll need to get started." Naomi got up and went through the back door into an adjoining room. She returned to her parlor with nine red apples in a wicker basket. "These apples will be an essential part of your love potion. Their red color inspires the blood of passion to flow and their sweetness will help you attract your husband's love back into your life. Nine is the number that signifies transition and moving through life's hurdles. To create a positive emotional environment ripe for love, you will weave together a spell using the Biblical serpent's choice for Eve's seduction of Adam—the apple—said to contain the seeds for the birth of the human race." She handed the younger woman the basket. "Now, take these and go. Don't let anyone touch them. I will call you and give you detailed instructions for their use once I know you and these apples have arrived safely home."

Stella looked bewildered. "I'm excited but a little afraid...I've never done a spell before."

"Don't worry. Everything will work out," Naomi said as she gave Stella a good-bye hug and walked her swiftly to the front door.

Chapter Twelve

The Hanged Man
The Sacrifice of Trust

*U*nfortunately for Dylan, the next day when he was supposed to pick up Jodi and take her to Norman's place in Stinson Beach, he couldn't get off work at his usual quitting time. On his desk sat a time-sensitive proposal marked "must be completed today" in neon-red ink. Because of unforeseen changes, he had major editing to do and was in a panic to finish before the 8 PM deadline. If he didn't have it done, he could count on his boss giving him a truckload of criticism that he didn't need. Worried about Jodi, he called his dad once again to check on her and to tell him that he'd arrive a little later than expected.

Julie answered the phone.

"Hi, brother, what's up?" she asked.

"I need to check in with my friend Jodi," Dylan replied. "Can I speak to her?"

"You could if she was here but she went out with Dad," Julie said with a humdrum lack of concern.

"What? Where did they go?"

"How do I know? Dad said something about taking

her to see dolphins. He didn't bother inviting me."

"That's crazy! Where are they going to see dolphins?" Dylan said in a voice that showed an unusual degree of concern.

"How am I supposed to know?"

"You could have asked where they were going. Do you know when they're going to return?" Dylan, who was normally calm, covered his feelings of anxiety with a veneer of irritation. "You're joking, right?"

"No, not really," Julie replied in a cavalier manner.

Dylan became more agitated as he sensed her unhelpful, defiant attitude. He changed the subject. "What are you doing at Dad's if he's not home?"

"Mom's got this new rich boyfriend who's taking her on some tree-saving eco vacation in Brazil and she doesn't want me to stay home alone. So I'm moving in with Dad. I was just unpacking when you called. I can't believe it. It's disgusting! Mom goes from this guy to that guy, yet tells me I can't have boyfriends at home past eleven at night. She must think I'm blind and can't see her parade of men coming and going late at night. And I can't handle her constant complaining that I don't do anything but mess up the house. She's always yelling at me to pick this up and pick that up, and to hurry up and clean the living room because her friend will be there any minute," Julie complained.

"I just visited Mom a few days ago and when I was leaving, I saw a dark-haired man coming to the door. Is that the guy who's flying her to Brazil?" asked Dylan.

"That must have been Moe. No, that one's out of the picture now that she's met her latest Mr. Wonderful with his hot little sports car. He's about six feet tall and fourteen years younger than she is. I think he's a dork but Mom is all excited about him and can't talk about anyone else."

Dylan didn't think he could handle more drama. "Thanks. I'll phone Mom and check to make sure she's not doing anything stupid. Hey, do me a favor. Tell Dad to give me a call when he and Jodi get home. Better yet, tell him not to go anywhere with Jodi because I'll be picking her up right after work to take her to Norman's."

"Why are you so hung up on Jodi? She's almost my age, ya know. She told me so. Isn't your Stella giving you enough love to keep you from hanging around jailbait?" Julie's voice dripped with sarcasm.

"Cut me some slack here, Julie. I told her I'd help her and I'm not interested in her except to keep my word that I'll give her a ride back to Norman's. Stella couldn't care less about what I do, anyway." Dylan tried to sound upbeat but beneath his emotional surface, Julie's question about Stella caused a heavy feeling in his chest.

"Really? Your wife doesn't care that you're hanging around with big-boobied young girls?" Julie teased. "Perhaps I should talk with her and get some lessons in not caring about the man I love."

Dylan's fingernails dug into his palms. "Don't horse around with me and please don't call and bother Stella. I'm at work and I've got a deadline to meet. I don't have time to talk to you right now."

"Well, I won't call Stella, not just yet. But I'm not an idiot and if you don't tell me what's really going on with you and Jodi, I might."

"I did tell you," Dylan replied, a note of panic in his voice. "Now please, be the sweetie that you are and don't hassle Stella. Maybe I'll see you later when I pick up Jodi. Bye."

Dylan hung up the phone, exhaled deeply, then looked at his computer screen. He could feel the knots of tension in the back of his neck. Where had his dad taken Jodi? Jodi was so young. Certainly, Mark wouldn't make the mistake of being interested in someone Dylan left in his care who was almost the same age as his teenage daughter. *No*, Dylan thought, *that would be crazy.* There had to be a good explanation. Dylan needed to focus on his work and he didn't have time to waste thinking about his father and Jodi if he was going to meet his looming deadline. He looked at the clock and told himself that soon enough he'd be driving Jodi north across the Golden Gate to Norman's. Besides, he certainly didn't want to play the role of her daddy who needed to worry about her. Or so he told himself as he tried to keep what had happened to her the previous night out of his mind.

As he worked furiously to meet the pending proposal deadline, he accidentally hit the wrong key on the keyboard and erased his last hour of work. Damn! He'd been working so fast that he hadn't hit the save key as often as he normally did. He went through a momentary downward spiral of panic, then pulled himself together with the realization that even his crazy feelings would have to wait until later. Maybe when he had a spare moment, he'd have some time for self-examination...or even make an appointment to see a shrink.

"I am happy and opening my heart to greater wisdom," he told himself. But despite the repetition of his positive affirmation, there were way too many things weighing on his mind, especially the where-abouts of Jodi and the unexpected, curious thoughts he was having toward Carmella. He was beginning to feel more and more like the Tarot Hanged Man, needing to take an inner journey to find truth. Looking around the empty room, he felt relieved that most everyone had left the office and no one was there to witness his aggravation.

His mind raced from one recent episode of his friend's world's falling apart to another. He thought his stress levels had peaked until normal, good-natured Carmella had sent him several distressed text messages to convey her hurt and anger. She told him she was thankful that after last night's grueling episode at Norman's, the doctors only needed to put her ankle in a temporary cast. Nevertheless, she was walking slowly, with pain, and she blamed him and Norman. Later, a phone conversation had gone from bad to worse when Dylan asked her if she had found any stones when they were exploring the haunted house together.

"It was only a stone," she had replied with what Dylan thought was an undertone of embarrassment. Then she asked, "What else did your father tell you?" after complaints about Dylan's father's assertive behavior with her. "And how was I supposed to know that you wanted me to report every detail of my experience walking behind you in that creepy house? You didn't even talk to me after we left."

"I'm sorry. After we were driving home I was in a state of shock and didn't have the energy to talk. Of course, I would want to know what you experienced. I'm so sorry I didn't communicate that to you," he replied. "When I do magic, I try to control what happens but I can't know for sure what's going to happen or how I'm going to be affected."

It was only now, in retrospect, that he realized how

cold he must have seemed on their drive home together. But understandably, today hadn't been the best time to talk about it and thinking about her now wasn't helping him meet his deadline.

To make matters worse, between her tearful calls, Norman, in a depression, had phoned and angrily accused him of being at fault for Carmella needing to go to the hospital. His string of swear words also let Dylan know how annoyed he was because Dylan hadn't delivered Jodi to his door as planned.

"Name calling isn't going to help," retorted Dylan after Norman had called him a "flaming asshole." He had bit his tongue to keep his cool at work and certainly was not going to tell Norman what was really on his mind. He felt guilty that he hadn't acted more assertively to stop Norman and Carmella from walking toward the phantom. After all, he was the only one who could see it.

Dylan shook his head and sighed. Right now he needed to push down his panic and focus on recovering the hour of work he had just lost.

At that moment, as if fate was playing pranks with his sense of responsibility, Dylan's work phone rang again. Thinking it might be his dad, he anxiously picked up the receiver. He was happily surprised to hear Lisa's voice on the other end of the line. He immediately perked up.

"Lisa, what's going on? I've been worried because I haven't heard from you in a while."

"Oh, sweetie, don't be mad. I've been missing you so much. It's just that I've been so busy at work, I haven't had a spare minute to call you."

"Yeah, I know work can get really busy. I've been busy too. But not too busy to miss you. I'm happy to hear from you. What's up?" Dylan felt his heart beat faster. Lisa sounded excited to be talking to him.

"I was wondering if we could get together tonight. My mother-in-law, who lives in Florida, fell down the stairs, hit her head on a metal railing, and landed with her legs in the splits. My father-in-law thought she was dead and called 911. Luckily, she survived the fall but is in the critical care unit in the hospital. So my dutiful husband bought a plane ticket to Miami and is already on his way to visit her in the hospital. For now, I'm a free woman."

Dylan groaned. Time with Lisa was what he had been desperately wanting and now everything else seemed to need his time. He searched his conscience. "I've promised someone I'd give them a ride to Marin County later." He fumbled for his words, trying not to lose Lisa's offer or to complicate the conversation by telling her that he felt responsible for helping another woman.

"Oh, darn. I need you to give me a ride too," Lisa giggled.

Dylan was pulled in two directions at once. He felt his craving for Lisa in his body but he remembered Jodi's anguish and the commitment he had made to take her to Norman's. If he was going to feel any peace within himself, his need to be with Lisa would have to wait.

"Lisa, I want to be with you but I can't just rush over right now. I'm working against a deadline. I've got to finish a proposal that has to be turned in tonight, and my time's already committed after work," Dylan said. He could hardly believe that his sense of responsibility was being a roadblock to fulfilling his urgent desire for Lisa. "But after that I'm available, and

I'd really love to see you. Once I have a better idea about things, I can call you and let you know what time we can get together later tonight."

"OK. Since my husband is out of town, you can come to my flat any time, really. This is such a great chance for us to be together. As long as I know you're coming, I'll stay up and wait for you."

"OK, my love. I'll be there as soon as I can." Feeling breathless, Dylan hung up the phone, then immediately tried phoning his dad, but Mark still didn't answer. Dylan felt the claws of frustration scraping against his mood. He sighed, rubbed the kinks out of his neck, and looked back at his computer screen.

∽

Mark had wasted no time trying to get to know Jodi but she seemed suspicious of his interest in her. Still, he knew how to sweet-talk his way into becoming her friend. Any pretty lady friend of Norman's would be welcome in his own list of friends and his dignity wasn't going to let their age difference interfere with having a good time, even though she seemed to barely notice what he said to her. He made it a challenge to get her to talk with him for longer than her usual five-second replies and to turn her frown into laughter. She was an ambiguity that he wanted to clarify, and a welcome distraction from the numerous calls he was receiving concerning the problems resulting from his recent lodge meeting.

After he had made Julie and Jodi dinner, then watched Jodi wait impatiently for Dylan, Mark used his finesse to get her to agree to go to the beach with him to watch the sunset and look for dolphins. He knew he wasn't misleading her by tempting her with the possibility of seeing dolphins jumping in the waves. In San Francisco, anything was possible. Even if he had spent his entire life going to the beach without seeing a dolphin there, they might see them today.

"I'm so sorry we haven't seen any dolphins," lamented Mark as he tried to console Jodi. "But even so, the sunset's lovely."

The fog began to move close to the beach, hugging the incessant crashing waves against the shore. The mixture of the fog and the last rays of the sun turned the sky into a pink-and-orange symphony of shifting light.

"I have a headache and I'm really upset," Jodi said, sounding a bit annoyed. "All I see are signs saying 'stay out of the water—sharks.' Can we go back to your place and see if Dylan's there yet?"

Mark had spent the day trying to make her feel comfortable in his home and wished she would show some gratitude. "Yes, of course. But I need to make a stop at my friend Taylor's house to pick up something. He has a daughter who's about your age. Maybe you two could chat for a few minutes while I talk with my buddy."

"OK," groaned Jodi with a heavy sigh. Disappointed that she hadn't seen any dolphins, she passively went along with Mark's request. If she hadn't felt so miserable, instead of waiting for Dylan she would have gladly left his place to hitchhike a ride to Norman's. But after what had happened last night, she didn't have the strength to venture into the unknown. It felt safer to wait for Dylan, even if that meant taking a drive around town with his father.

Darkness descended on them as they arrived at

Taylor's front door and said their hellos. Jodi preferred not to look at Taylor when they walked into his house and was annoyed that she was forced to listen to Mark complain like a baby about some recent accident that had happened the night before, his innocence, and how this could mean a potential lawsuit. She knew that if anyone had the right to object to the unfair, troubling events of the preceding evening, it was her. Yet she had no desire to tell these strangers about her problems.

The air in the large room seemed to disappear when Taylor reached out and put his long-fingered hand gently on Jodi's shoulder. "Would you like to join my friends and me tonight? We were just getting ready to do a ritual to create a path to spiritual love. Do you know that young women have magical powers equal to that of a dragon breathing fire?"

"I don't believe in dragons," she replied, jerking away from his touch. She knew the instant she heard his strangely melodious voice that it was time to leave.

"Maybe you should," he responded, smiling at her while putting his hand under her chin and lifting it so that she had to look up at him.

Jodi froze, looked in Taylor's eyes, and said nothing. *If this guy believes in dragons, he must be crazy*, she thought. Taking a deep breath, she summoned the courage to shuffle several steps away from him. Even though he seemed nice enough, there was something odd about him.

"I think fate brought Mark here to help us find the door to the labyrinth in the Matrix," Taylor continued. "My friends are waiting for me to lead them in a very important ritual. I'm going to summon the departed so we can speak to the spirits on the other side. Perhaps, among other things, they can give us some needed answers to Mark's predicament. You can join us in this rare opportunity to talk with the deceased. Do you know anyone on the other side you would like to speak with?"

Jodi couldn't believe it. All she wanted was to get back to the relative comfort of Norman's house in the woods. She looked at both men and wondered if there was any truth to Taylor's mumbo jumbo. Could this man with eyes like an eagle really talk to the dead? If so, it seemed like a chance she shouldn't pass up. Slowly, Jodi replied, "Well, my mom's on the other side and I'd really like to talk to her."

"And I'm sure she'd really like to talk to you too," Taylor responded, his voice carrying a note of certainty that made Jodi cringe. "Mothers always miss their children and long to be reconnected. I'm sure that, with your help, we can invoke her spirit to appear."

Although Jodi's first instinct was to leave, she missed her mom and longed for a chance to tell her she was sorry for running away and not being home to help her when she was sick and dying. Maybe her mom would forgive her and help her escape her unrelenting sense of guilt and grief.

"What do I have to do?" she asked.

"I'm sure Taylor will let you know," said Mark, who was intrigued by this shadowy yet interesting synchronistic occasion.

Without speaking, Taylor gestured for Mark and Jodi to follow him down a long, narrow hallway to a door. After Taylor opened the door, they quietly trailed behind him as he walked down a dozen short, narrow steps into a noisy room that looked like an old two-car garage converted into a meeting hall. Turkish rugs decorated the wall. Several ornate ceiling candelabras lit the space, which was crowded with about thirty people dressed in black, mingling about, talking, laughing, and drinking. Some were dancing wildly to a loud African drumbeat being broadcast from overhead speakers, and others were eating while standing next to a banquet table covered with chocolate, candy, and sugar-glazed desserts.

"Help yourself to anything you want," Taylor offered before leaving Mark and Jodi at the food table and disappearing into the crowd.

Somewhat hungry, Jodi was attracted to the decadent feast but her stomach was too knotted to eat. Although she wanted to look away, she couldn't resist staring at the mix of people in the spirited crowd. Soon the dim lights became even fainter and the music stopped. Jodi could hear her heart beating as the crowd fell silent and everyone turned and faced one corner of the room. There sat Taylor in a throne-like chair with large palm fronds behind him. He wore a kingly helmet made of what looked to be bones, a black robe decorated with unusual gold symbols, and a large, bejeweled cross hung from his neck. Attended by two semi-naked women kneeling before him, he looked like the King of the Apocalypse. Taken aback, Jodi felt a shiver run down her spine.

Using their fingers as paintbrushes and the flow of their emerging menstrual blood as an artistic palette, both women methodically drew a magical circle on the floor around Taylor and themselves. When the circle was completely drawn, they each sat on the floor on opposite sides of Taylor, looking toward him as if they were loyal dogs protecting their master.

"Tonight we are going to use the hermetically sealed Ritual of Archaic Magic to create the impossible," Taylor announced. He stood up and raised his staff, which was topped by a crystal skull. "I welcome you all. This ceremony will summon those spirits who are free to roam the ancient Matrix of the Netherworld. Also, on this special occasion, it is our honor to ordain Angel as a virgin priestess and sojourner to the sacred conjunction of alpha and omega, where only the pure of heart can find their way. She has agreed to ask the guides, gods, and goddesses of the four corners of the earth's magnetic field for our redemption and privileged rebirth. Following the traditions of our ancestral path, she has been instructed in how to travel the astral planes where she can follow Hecate's invisible path to the sphere of seven mysteries. With the blessing of the goddesses, she can bring light out of chaos, understanding to the misunderstood, and access the forbidden scrolls. These crucial documents map the route to the rainbow treasures guarded over by the shadows lurking in the subterranean planes."

Is this for real? Jodi silently questioned.

As if a green light had turned on, the crowd started to murmur.

Someone in the back of the room shouted, "What if she succeeds in getting there but doesn't find her way back?"

"Don't corrupt our vision of success with your lack of foresight, and cast the doom of doubt by asking such a question," Taylor said. "Her very DNA knows how to travel these webs of nether reality and her purity functions as her talisman. This work is meaningful for us all and Angel is first in line to achieve the reward of such an honor. If she doesn't feel right about accepting this prestigious invitation, she can withdraw at any time."

Suddenly, the lights flickered on and off and on again, and a brass bell chimed three times. The silent crowd parted to open a path down the middle of the room, and Angel, dressed in a long white wedding gown with a lace veil covering her face, walked rhythmically toward her father's throne. She pulled a large black pit bull on a chain behind her and together they walked proudly into the magical circle.

One of the two women inside the circle spoke sharply, "Before you can enter, you must say the magic words to open the invisible gate."

"I knock three times on your door," Angel whispered. "One knock for each of the Teutonic masters, the Three Witnesses, by which the invisible is made visible and light becomes tangible space."

"If you are not afraid to embrace the darkness, you may enter," the other woman inside the circle said, sounding a genuine echo of concern.

"I'm not afraid," Angel replied.

I would be if I were her, Jodi thought, feeling anxious for Angel.

Then Taylor's assistant took a dagger from her belt and cut an invisible door through which the young woman could enter their private, magic circle.

Angel walked to the foot of the ceremonial chair and her dog followed. Just as Taylor was getting up to give Angel his chair, the dog lifted its leg and peed on his black boot. "Damn dog," he complained loudly while shaking his foot. "Angel, by your own free will, you agree to be part of this ritual, is that right?" Taylor asked.

"Yes. I want to do it," Angel replied.

"And you have been instructed in how to vacate your conscious awareness and dive into astral space to explore the hidden inner planes?"

"Yes."

"And you have been instructed in maintaining your mastery over any chaotic spirits or grosser elements that you may encounter as adversities along your way?"

"Well...I hope so."

"You must answer yes or no."

"OK. Yes, I've been instructed," she stated matter-of-factly.

"Remember, at all times you must hold the cross that you are wearing around your neck with your right hand. Your left hand is free. If you encounter any difficulties, lift your left hand and we'll bring your conscious spirit back to the room as fast as we can. The elixir for the strength of your magic is in your faith to be triumphant. Visualize your success at all times. Now, sit in my chair," Taylor commanded, motioning for her to take a seat.

Angel moved quickly to the chair. Jodi thought she looked like a small child on a too-big Papa Bear chair. Taylor's two women attendants drew near, lifted her veil, and kissed her on the forehead.

Taylor called out, "Mistress of Cryptome, please recite the sacred code and come induce our Angel so that she can enter the inner planes."

Following Taylor's directions, the woman who had opened the unseen door in the magic circle chanted a song in a foreign tongue while she walked around Angel and her dog three times in a clockwise circle. She stopped chanting when she reached Angel's left side and pulled from her pocket a golden locket on a chain. "Angel, watch the golden ball. Watch it swing back and forth, back and forth. Relax your mind. You are falling asleep...you are falling deeper and deeper into sleep. You are relaxing. You are falling fast asleep. You are now asleep. Feel your spirit as it frees itself from your body. Let your unconscious spirit awaken and let yourself fly through space." The woman fell silent for a minute, smiled an all-knowing smile, and then said, "Tell me where you are at this moment."

"I'm surrounded by dark clouds and I can't see anything," Angel answered, sounding as though she was in a state of deep sleep.

"Angel, to help you go where you are needed, we won't talk with you for a while as you must be alone to take your journey," Taylor spoke softly. He then turned to the crowd, and as if he needed to supply a reason for everyone to assemble, he spoke loudly like a thunder-bolt, "Let us all remember those on the other side. Use your soul longing to invite the departed into our room." He fell silent for several minutes before continuing. "Ascend! Descend! Awaken all who sleep in dark shadows. Offer yourself as a host to the spirits. Spirits, we welcome you. Walk among us and anchor in our bodies to light up your lives this night. Eat through our mouths, dance with our bodies, experience and enjoy this soul feast of wine and food. Are there any spirits here with us tonight?" Taylor continued without skipping a breath. "I am calling the spirit of the mother of Jodi. Jodi, raise your hand so everyone can see you. Jodi, call your mother. We are humbly asking you to be one with us. Your daughter wants to hear from you and I will deliver any message you have for her."

Embarrassed, Jodi raised her hand and looked back at everyone staring at her. *If only I could hide,* she thought while Mark pushed her closer to the front of the circle.

Taylor was silent for a few minutes.

"Yes, she's here, Jodi," he finally said. "She wants you to know that she loves you very much. And she's trying to help you from the other side. She knows that you miss her and she misses you too."

I'm sure he's not channeling my mom, Jodi thought. *Anyone could come up with those lame comments.*

Taylor continued channeling. "You need to be reminded of your pure heart. Since you were a child, you have been vulnerable to those who want to use you. Your soul is pure but you have forgotten this truth, and your heart is being contaminated by the lust of the world. You have sacrificed your innocence and your honor. By playing into the temptations of the dark forces, you are losing your sensitivity to hear the murmur of your own soul and forgetting your higher purpose. Your mother says to tell you that she waits patiently to hold you and looks forward to the future time when you'll be together again. And just so that you know it's really her, she wants me to tell you that she forgives you for stealing her pearl necklace that you keep in your pocket. She's happy that you have something to remember her by."

Jodi felt her body jolt into shock. No one knew that she'd taken her mother's pearl necklace when she ran away from home. No one! Jodi felt her cheeks turn blazing red and tears streamed down her cheeks. "Mommy, I miss you. What should I do with my—"

At that moment, Jodi was interrupted. Everyone's attention shifted when Angel roared a deafening screech that sounded like an eagle shot in midair. Taylor turned toward his daughter, who ripped off her cross pendant, threw it in his face, and jumped up to stand on the seat of his royal chair. Angel looked at the crowd and laughed uproariously. She screamed, "You're all going to die hideous and vile deaths. You think that Father Time will allow you to be late to arrive at death's doorway but you'll be there sooner than you think." Then she pointed to one woman and said with loud certainty, "Your husband is screwing his mistress right now while you're at this stupid party. Maybe if you didn't stink, he'd be fucking you instead." To another woman, she shrieked, "Do you think that by wearing that black dress you can hide how ugly and fat you are?"

Angel's pit bull started barking viciously at the crowd. Jodi turned and ran for the door, along with everyone in the crowd, moving toward the stairway like a disturbed hive of hornets. Pushing and shoving, everyone hurried to get to the upstairs door, knocking Jodi out of the way in their frenzy. She was relieved when someone illuminated the room by turning up the lights but now it became easy to see that the room had turned into chaos. Jodi looked back to the altar and saw Taylor reach for his daughter's hand. In response, Angel kicked him in the groin. Things were going badly.

One of Taylor's female attendants, who had been holding the dog's chain, now urgently dropped it in his hand. Slowly, both attendants walked out of the magic circle. Once out of reach of the angry dog, they pushed their way through the crowd, ran up the stairs, and flew out the door, leaving Jodi and the others trailing behind.

Before Jodi made it to the top of the stairs, she looked back at Angel and her father. Taylor, acting with a false sense of command, held the dog's chain to stand guard against its growling, drooling, and baring of its teeth. Angel, her eyes staring wildly, spat furiously at her father, then sat back down on the chair and became silent as stone. Jodi felt someone grab her hand, then pull her out the door and down the hall toward the front entrance.

"I thought you gave her instructions on how to protect herself," said Mark nervously to Taylor.

"I did," responded Taylor, who looked as if he was going to cave in from the pain of seeing his daughter in such an obvious state of possession.

"Angel, my sweet daughter, do you remember the chants for protection I gave you?" he asked. "We can chant them together. Om...Parve..."

"Stop, jackass! Those chants might work for virgins but...guess what, you stupid old man? I've been sleeping with my boyfriend for the past two months after you go to bed. I'm hardwired for sex, drugs, and whatever comes my way." Angel cackled like an old witch. "And right now, I'm planning on doing a lap dance on horny old Mark. You and I both know that he wants me!"

Greatly alarmed, Mark — who, in spite of his urgent desire to run, had stayed behind hoping he could help — jumped back. "Angel! Come to your senses. You're the child of my dearest friend. Taylor, I'm going to leave and phone for help. I know you can communicate with Angel and bring her back to her normal self. Just keep encouraging her to reclaim her body."

Keeping his eyes on the makeshift stage, Mark

walked backward toward the stairs. As he turned to go up the steps, he looked back toward Taylor and his daughter. Once he made it up the stairs he ran outside, where he found Jodi, tearful and stunned, waiting for him on the front steps. "Let's go!" he commanded.

They hurried to Mark's car. Jodi happily climbed in and locked her door. In her mind, they couldn't drive away fast enough for her own sense of sanity.

Chapter Thirteen

Death

Dancing the Soul Tango

When Dylan finally got out of work and arrived at his dad's, he was surprised that no one was home. He used his key to enter the empty apartment and waited impatiently for Mark and Jodi to return.

Some days don't work out the way you plan, Dylan thought.

Hadn't he told his dad not to let Jodi go anywhere? He didn't expect his father to be out with Jodi. He'd told him he intended to take her to Norman's as soon as he got out of work. With neither Jodi nor his father present, it seemed that something wasn't right. Even though he wanted to forget his promise to Jodi, his sense of guilt cast the winning vote to wait for her return.

Trying to focus on something other than his impatience, he called his father's cell phone but Mark didn't answer. Carmella, who had annoyed him on the phone earlier that day, also didn't answer when he tried calling her. And even though he wanted to talk with Lisa, his intuition told him it was better to wait until later, when he could see her in person. Again he began to think about Jodi and a strange chill went up his spine. He didn't have to worry about his father's intentions...or did he?

As he tried to put any doubts about his father out of his mind, he picked up the remote and settled on watching a television show about murder and mayhem on the streets of San Francisco. *Too much like reality*, he fretted and turned it off. After looking at his watch and sitting anxiously for another twenty minutes, his frustration could no longer be ignored. He began to question why he was wasting his time waiting around for people when he could be with Lisa. What a strange twist of fate it was that Lisa was finally free to be with him but he wasn't available to be with her. He became more and more annoyed as he wondered where his father had taken Jodi. Why couldn't he have left a note telling him when they'd return? And where was his sister? He decided he'd give his father fifteen more minutes and if they weren't home by then, he was going to Lisa's.

At that moment, just as he decided not to wait any longer, he heard the front door open. The mismatched couple—a tired-looking older man and a teenage girl with downcast eyes—was uncomfortably silent as they walked into the living room.

"Where have you two been?" Dylan asked impatiently as if he were the parent and they were disobedient children. "Didn't we have an agreement that I'd pick up Jodi after I got off work today?"

His father gazed at him with a strange mix of confusion and fear. "Sorry, Dylan. We just got caught up in some unplanned events. Jodi's been in a rush to come home to meet you but my errands got in the way."

Dylan was instantly annoyed. "You could have at least called me. Couldn't you be a little more considerate?"

"You sound just like your mother. You don't ask me anything about what I need, you just start judging."

"Dad, you're way out of line tonight and I don't want to get into an argument with you. I've worked hard all day and I didn't expect you to be out so late or keep me waiting. I don't have a lot of free time, you know."

"I thought you said you didn't want to get into nagging tonight?"

"No," Dylan clarified, "I said I didn't want to get into an argument with you. I didn't say nagging." He turned to Jodi. "Come on, it's time to leave. Norman's been waiting for you. Earlier today I told him I'd get you back to his place by sunset and that was a couple of hours ago."

"Jodi, maybe you can fill Dylan in on what happened tonight so he gets off his high horse," Mark snapped, avoiding eye contact with his son.

"Thanks a lot, Dad," Dylan replied sarcastically, wishing that his father would have communicated differently. If only he had opened up and said a meaningful word or two, perhaps Dylan could have gotten a sense of what was going on in Jodi's mind. But it had never been easy for Dylan to talk with his dad.

After awkward good-byes, Dylan and Jodi left Mark's apartment. Even though they didn't talk to one another, the cool breeze coming from the ocean persuaded them to walk quickly. Jodi lit a cigarette. When they reached Dylan's old sedan, Jodi blew a smoke ring in his face. In spite of her obnoxious behavior, he opened her door, trying to be a gentleman despite her behavior.

"Jodi, are you doing OK?" he asked.

"I've been better," she mumbled with her head down as she got into his car.

Dylan went around to the driver's side of the car and got in. "Where did you go with my dad?"

"We went to some weird séance," she answered robotically.

Instantly, Dylan felt a knot in his stomach and got a sense that something bad had happened. He wanted to know for sure. "Who had a séance? Where was it? What happened?"

"It with some weird guy dressed all in black and his weird daughter who was dressed in a white wedding gown. I think it might have been your old girlfriend's sister. Anyway, if you want the weird details, talk with your weird father who knows where it was. And don't ask me any more questions."

Ignoring Jodi's wall of defensiveness, Dylan responded, "I'm sorry I couldn't take you back to Norman's any sooner. Last night, I was so stressed, I had to get some sleep so I could go to work today and not be a zombie. But I'm here now, so please don't be angry at me."

Jodi looked at Dylan for a quick moment before looking away. She began to cry. "I'm not angry," she said between sobs. "I just think you're a jerk and I'd rather not talk to you. So I won't."

Dylan imagined that she was still upset from the events of the previous night. Even though she didn't want to talk, he felt relieved to know that his father had simply taken her to a séance. In spite of the uncomfortable silence, a heavy weight lifted off his shoulders from the knowledge that, at this moment, he was taking her to Norman's to fulfill his agreement. As soon as his task was complete, he'd get back to the city and hopefully connect with Lisa before it got too late.

After leaving the bridge and its dimly illuminated towers far behind, he began navigating the twists and turns on Highway 1. Even though he wasn't sure that bringing Jodi to Norman's was in her best interests, he couldn't think of anywhere else to take her.

Throughout their drive, Jodi remained silent until they reached Norman's driveway. She let out a sorrowful moan.

Dylan reached across the seat and put his hand on her head. "Everything will be OK," he said sympathetically.

"Don't pet my head like I'm some kind of dog," Jodi growled.

Dylan couldn't believe her response and pulled his hand away. He thanked God that they had finally arrived. He scanned the driveway for any signs of a ghostly presence before he parked in front of the wooden-plank bridge leading to Norman's house. He looked at Jodi but she just stared out the car window. Dylan got out of the car. With his flashlight guiding his way in the dark, he walked to Jodi's door and opened it.

Jodi appeared to be sleeping.

"Come on, we're here," he said softly.

"What about that Seega thing?" Jodi asked, not moving from her seat.

Dylan shone the light on the ground next to her. "I've already looked around and I haven't seen it. But just in case it's somewhere close, we should hurry up and get going before we see it or it takes notice of us." He took Jodi's hand to help her out of the car but she pulled away.

"I'm scared."

"Don't worry. It's only a short distance to Norman's and I'm here with you," Dylan replied, offering her his hand.

Acting as if she didn't hear him, Jodi got out of the car and started moving toward the bridge.

Dylan closed her door and rushed to follow behind her as she sprinted fearlessly up the footpath. Luckily, a smattering of moonlight beamed through the tree branches, which made it easier to dodge the uneven ruts on the trail and helped them find their way to the little house in the redwoods.

After a few breathless minutes, Jodi began climbing the steps that led to Norman's brightly lit doorway. She turned to look back at Dylan. "Aren't you coming?" she asked.

Dylan was already headed back to his car. After Norman's insulting remarks on the phone earlier that day, he didn't feel like doing anything but delivering Jodi to his door. When he'd explained what had happened to Jodi in the city, Norman had heartlessly blamed him for the incident. Why couldn't Norman realize that he wasn't empowered to stop the unrelenting hand of destiny?

"No. Norman's angry at me and besides, I need to get back to the city." He was late for his next date.

Even though Jodi felt angry with Dylan for his role in placing her in situations that had led to her recent terrible ordeals, he was at least someone familiar, someone who had shown her kindness in the harsh and frightening world of heartless people. She hated to admit it but she even enjoyed his corny outbursts about life and magic. "But I want you to come with me..."

The sound of her voice evaporated into the darkness.

Beneath her veneer of apparent indifference, Jodi was desperate for someone to care about her. In the shifting scenery of her life, she had only apathy, exploitation, and enmity. She realized that Dylan's attempt to take care of her and his commitment to drive her back to Norman's showed a trace of the simple human caring she so greatly desired.

But Dylan, being in a big hurry to get back to the city, didn't see the lonely look in her eyes or hear her weakly spoken request. He had fulfilled his responsibility and only wanted to leave. He didn't care whether the Seega was in the parking lot or not. He had one concern and that was whether or not Lisa would be waiting to see him this late at night.

Lost in his thoughts about a new love in his life, he returned to his car, started the engine, and turned his wheels in the direction of San Francisco. He was mindful of not speeding in order to avoid getting a ticket. He had gotten too many of those in the last year and didn't want to add the fear of losing his driver's license to his list of increasing worries. As soon as his cell phone regained reception after being in the dead zone around Norman's, he dialed Lisa's number and waited for her to answer.

"Lisa. Hi..."

"Dylan, where are you? It feels like I've been waiting all night." She sounded like she was barely awake.

"Do you still want to see me?" Dylan asked, his

mind whirling with the fear of rejection.

"Yes, darling," she answered. "Get here as quick as you can, before I fall asleep."

"I'm almost there. Wait up for me," he said, blowing her a telephone kiss before hanging up. He could feel his body tingling with desire as he turned south on Highway 101.

Dylan was happy to cross the Golden Gate Bridge and didn't think twice about paying its steep toll to enter the city. Every road winding its way toward Lisa's place gave him the agonizing feeling that he was moving torturously slow, even though he couldn't help but speed. Finally, he arrived at her street, then had to endure a frustrating twenty minutes of lost time while he looked for a parking place. *Good thing my car can fit into a tight space*, he thought as he finally squeezed his car into a narrow spot between two driveways.

Breathing heavily from excitement, he rushed to find her home. He'd never been there before and felt a bit taken aback when he saw the size of the two tall, stone pillars marking the entrance to her building. He stopped, took a minute to slowly inhale the salty air, and told himself to relax as he walked through a sculpted archway and up a stone stairway. Finally, he was knocking on his love's door. Now everything else in his life could wait. In spite of all the obstacles, he would soon be in her arms.

"Hello, Dylan. Come on in," Lisa said as she opened the large, carved wooden door.

Dylan hurried inside and reached to give Lisa a hug. "I've been in a rush to get here all night. I'm sorry it's so late."

Lisa embraced him. "I've been missing you so very much," she said as her lips touched his. "I'm so happy you're here."

Dylan's body came alive with the warmth of her kiss, as if a river of fire had begun to flow through him. Lisa's touch was electric. Without hesitating, she took his hand. She led him down a dimly lit hall and into a room that looked like a Moroccan caravan filled with the glow of candlelight. In an adjoining room, not far from a pillow-laden king-sized bed, a heart-shaped Jacuzzi bubbled a warm invitation. Lisa stopped holding his hand, moved two steps in front of him, and turned to look at him.

"I want you to see something that I bought just thinking about you," Lisa said as she took off her night robe and let it slide to the floor.

She wore a black lace, strapless bodice that showed the delicious curves of her slight breasts. Below it, he could see her pierced belly button adorned with a sparkling diamond chain. Her black, sheer hose smoothly entwined with a purple-and-black lace garter belt to highlight the outline of her thighs. A tiny g-string decorated in the shape of a heart glittered when she moved.

Dylan's body began throbbing with excitement. He stepped forward, pulled Lisa toward him, and melted into her arms. He could smell the fragrance of sandalwood incense and smiled at his good fortune to be holding her. Their heated kisses turned their lips into magnets that couldn't separate. Dylan's hands slid down to her nearly bare buttocks.

At that moment, the phone in his pocket sent a ring of harsh reality to disturb their special occasion. "I'm not going to answer that," Dylan murmured, without stopping the flood of their luscious kissing.

"OK with me," said Lisa as she tightened her arms

around him, making their bond inseparable.

After a kiss that seemed to last infinitely, she giggled, put her hands on his shoulders, then jumped up and wrapped both of her legs around his waist. His hands caught her firm bottom to support her weight. He felt like a scorched desert coming alive with the first drops of gentle rain.

Swift as a fire stoked by the wind, their kisses became more excited. Dylan carried Lisa toward the bed. Then, as if fate was playing a bad trick on his good fortune, Dylan's phone rang again. Lisa playfully reached into his pocket and took out the phone. Her eyes squinted to see the caller ID name and number.

In a cold, unfriendly tone Lisa said, "It's someone named Carmella."

Unexpectedly, Lisa hit the answer button and placed the phone next to Dylan's ear. Dylan looked at Lisa with exasperation, freed one hand, and took the phone. Falling from his grasp, Lisa pulled away, jumped back from his embrace, and glared at him as if he were an intruder.

The loudness of Carmella's cries made it possible for her voice to be heard clearly in the room. "Dylan, answer the phone! It's an emergency. I need your help. Please answer the phone! I'm freaking out. Help, please!"

Dylan looked sadly toward Lisa and took a deep breath. Their interaction had spiraled into a downward tempo, like a tango moving rhythmically without missing a beat. He felt a sense of disappointment ripple through his body.

"Dylan, are you there?"

"I'm here," he said reluctantly.

"Guess what Jodi did tonight?" Carmella screeched.

"What?" Dylan replied without emotion while looking at Lisa and trying to fake a smile.

"She drank a quart of vodka then took Norman's gun and shot a hole in her head. Her blood splattered like red vomit all over the wall!"

Shocked, and looking at Lisa, who now stood wide-eyed with a look of disdain on her face, Dylan froze and slid to the floor. "No!" he wailed. "Oh, God. Is she dead?"

"She's in the ICU at Marin General Hospital. She's alive but she's in a coma and no one's sure if she'll pull through. After the ambulance left, the police came and took Norman to the station to ask him questions about her and what had happened. He's there now. And you, Dylan, are at the top of my shit list. Why did you have to bring some psycho like Jodi to Norman's?"

Avoiding Lisa's stare, Dylan replied defensively, "I brought her to Norman's because he asked me to bring her back and she wanted to go there. She didn't want to stay in the city and Norman likes having her around. I would have preferred not to have had to drive to Norman's tonight but he made me feel like I was betraying him because I had encouraged Jodi to leave his place."

"Well, now his house has yellow tape around it and no one can go in. I feel so terrible," Carmella replied.

Lisa was vanishing into the mists of Dylan's consciousness. Part of his mind was spinning with thoughts of Jodi committing suicide and another clung to the thread of conversation he was having with Carmella about Norman. "Do you know where the bullet went into her head?"

"I don't know for sure. All I know is that Norman's really freaked out. When he called me from the police station, he wanted me to find him a lawyer. He didn't say much about Jodi except that after she shot herself and the emergency people came to help, he didn't want to go with her in the ambulance. He went nuts. Just like when he refused to go to the hospital with me when I hurt my ankle. After she was taken to the hospital, he ran to clean his drugs from all around the house and flushed as much as he could find down the toilet. When the police got there, he was drunk and extremely high. He locked himself in his room but had to open the door because the police were going to break it down. They asked him a few questions, then handcuffed him and took him to the station."

Dylan became noticeably upset. "Did he say if she was on drugs?" he questioned. "Do you know if he had sex with her?"

"How do I know? Norman wasn't willing or able to talk much from jail. Besides, he knows that I don't like talking about his other girlfriends," Carmella admitted. "But I do know that it's not going to look good if they find his juices in her body. You would think with that much of an age difference, Jodi wouldn't have wanted to make love with Norman anyway."

Dylan felt his grief ascend like a vise tightening around his mind. "If she managed to commit suicide, it doesn't have anything to do with Norman or having sex with him. Jodi's a little crazy to begin with. She probably would have decided to blow her brains out sooner or later. I know Norman well enough to know that he would never give her a loaded gun to play with."

"True. But she's a minor," Carmella reminded Dylan.

"That's definitely going to be a problem."

"Can't you get off the phone already?" Lisa interrupted with a note of irritation.

Dylan stopped talking and looked at her. He felt his face flush with a wave of sad, imploding anger.

"Whatever happened in her mind that made her want to end her life, we don't really know," Carmella continued in his ear. "Once, I overheard her say that the fear of death was controlling her thoughts. One thing I know for sure is that she was the one to put the gun to her head and pull the trigger."

"Get off the phone already," Lisa commanded while shaking her hips in front of Dylan like a sultry belly dancer.

Dylan ignored her. "Were you at the house when this nightmare happened?"

"No," answered Carmella. "The truth is, I was a bit jealous of her connection with Norman and I didn't want to be there when she was there, let alone watch her hang out with him. I made a point of leaving right after she walked in the house. And I thought she was a bitch because as soon as she saw me, she gave me the finger. But right now, I'm just angry with her for creating such a mess. Norman's in jail because of her. And who's going to clean Jodi's bloodstains off his bedroom walls? She certainly wasn't concerned about any of us when she decided to pull the trigger."

"If someone's crazy, they're not going to be concerned about anybody else. But this is no time for judgment." Dylan's brow started to bead with sweat. "What I really need is to help Norman. I owe him for all the good energy he's given me over the years. I wonder if I can get into his place."

"Maybe we can blame Jodi's father for this mess," Carmella suggested. "She told me he committed suicide after leaving her mother and her when she was a child. Maybe that's where she got the idea."

Lisa handed Dylan a glass of wine that she had poured, then interrupted once again. "Dylan, get off the phone. We don't have a lot of time together and we have something we need to talk about."

Dylan ignored her, sampled his wine, and went on talking with Carmella. "I don't want Norman to take the blame for what Jodi did. And we'll never know what really happened in Jodi's mind unless she survives the gunshot."

Lisa jumped to grab the phone away from Dylan and yelled loud enough that Carmella could hear, "I'm not going to stand here and be quiet any longer! You need to get off the phone. Tell whoever's on the line to go cry in their beer and let you enjoy your evening."

He snatched his phone back just in time to hear Carmella say, "Oh...I'm sorry for disturbing you. I didn't realize you were in the middle of something. We can talk tomorrow. I'll try to find out what's happening to Norman and see if he can be released from the police station. Don't worry about anything. I'm sure everything will be OK."

Dylan heard Carmella's phone line disconnect.

Dylan looked at Lisa, who was making clown faces at him. "This isn't a time to be funny," he scowled as he turned off his phone. He couldn't believe that at this moment, Lisa was dramatically balancing on one foot trying to do a yoga pose while holding her hand next to her heart pretending to feel his pain.

"Yes, my dear, darling love. I'm sure that you're sad after listening to someone cry on your shoulder about her foolish friends. But don't let your woeful call from a damsel in distress stop our party. Right now, I have something to offer you that will help you forget that nasty call, whatever it was about. I promise to make you feel so much better." Lisa extended her hand to Dylan and pulled him toward her bed, giggling like a schoolgirl.

Chapter Fourteen

Temperance
An Overflowing Cup of Love

"I love you, honey pie," Lisa said affectionately to Dylan as they sat on her bed, which was draped in dark-blue satin sheets. Lisa had thought about asking Dylan to explain his recent phone call but it sounded so serious that she was afraid their time together might turn into a murky discussion about someone else's problems if she did.

Live for the moment, she thought, *and don't worry about problems until they come home.*

She knew as she looked at Dylan that right now there wasn't a problem. She'd been hoping for a time when they could explore their relationship without the customary short time limits and interference from other commitments. Tonight she wanted things to be perfect.

Dylan shifted nervously and looked blankly at the floor. Lisa could see the sadness on his face.

Turning to look at Lisa, Dylan said, "I've been wanting to be with you for so long. I was beginning to think that we wouldn't see each other again. If it wasn't for your smile, I'd be going crazy thinking about my friends' problems right now. I just need a few minutes to get my head out of their troubles and shift my attention back to the present moment." He managed a weak smile.

"I want you to be happy. Remember when you told me that I stir your soul?" Lisa said, determined not to let anyone steal their moment. *I would do anything to distract Dylan from his worries,* she thought. Smiling, she unbuttoned his shirt, then began lightly biting the tight muscles that rippled down the front of his chest.

Her long hair tickled Dylan's bare skin. He loved the sensation of her tresses sweeping across his midriff and his mind gradually began to move away from the call he had just received concerning Jodi.

Lisa unbuckled Dylan's belt, untucked his shirt, and began to cover his belly with wet kisses. "I love that our evening has finally opened up for us to have some time together. We fit perfectly together," she murmured, putting her arms around him, gently pushing his upper body down onto the bed and moving her body on top of his.

Dylan moaned as she buried her head between his shoulder and neck and started to playfully nibble his ear. Finally, he relaxed and was able to let his body melt without reflecting on the coldness of Lisa's behavior while he was on the phone. The moment was becoming more agreeable with every kiss and their electric charge was turning passion's voltage on high.

"Yes, we're a great fit. What a wonderful surprise it was, getting your phone call asking me to come here tonight," Dylan said, pulling her bodice down to unveil her bare breasts.

"What a minute...you haven't said that you love

me," Lisa said, removing her bodice and strategically rolling her hips back and forth in an exciting rhythm over his body. She noticed Dylan beginning to smile.

"If I'm a little slow saying I love you, it's because I'm waiting to see how much you love me before I commit to telling you how much I love you. But I want you and find you so deliciously attractive," Dylan said. He grew silent and began to cover Lisa's soft, fragrant skin with an abundance of warm, moist kisses.

Dylan's stroking of her body became more intense and her body tingled with excitement. Her king-sized bed was just the right size for expressing the passion of their raging desire. Each movement turned the flame between them higher and higher until Dylan couldn't wait any longer to taste the sweet wetness between her legs. He slid his body toward Lisa so that his hands could gently open and caress her inner thighs.

But Lisa sat up abruptly and pulled away. "Wait a minute. I need to hear you say that you love me," she growled.

Dylan moved his hands to further caress her. "Let my actions speak for themselves," he said, kissing inch by inch up her inner thighs.

Even though Lisa had initially worried about inviting another man into her bed, any guilt she may have felt for doing so was crumbling with the warmth of Dylan's sensitive touch. She leaned back on the soft pillows to surrender to his tender expression of love's intimacy. Like an overflowing fountain of affection, she couldn't contain her happiness and began to coo like a lovebird.

Suddenly, Lisa bolted upright. "Oh my God! Stop, Dylan!" she hissed. "It sounds like someone's opening the front door. I've got to go look." Lisa jumped up and ran to the bedroom door, which was partially open. "Jesus, Dylan, grab your clothes and get out of here. David's home! He's home!" Lisa whispered in a fast, barely audible tone of distress as she watched her husband, suitcase in hand, walk through the front door and close it behind him.

"And where am I supposed to go?" Dylan asked as he jumped out of bed and started grabbing his clothes, which were scattered all around the room.

"Oh my God, quick! Get into my closet!" Lisa said, throwing his shirt at him and frantically straightening out the bed covers. As quick as lightning, she grabbed his hand and dragged him into her large closet, turned on the light, and closed the door. Lisa then ripped off her garter and slinky black hose, threw her sexy bodice behind some jackets, and grabbed a plush pink teddy bear nightgown, which she tugged over her head as fast as she could. Staring wildly at Dylan, who looked like a deer frozen in a car's headlights, she grimaced and made a sad expression to communicate her disappointment. Then she put her finger to her lips to signal no more talking, pointed to a corner where Dylan could sit and hide, then quickly turned off the light and scrambled out.

Dylan's anxiety skyrocketed as he watched her leave him alone in her closet. She left in a flurry without noticing that the door was slightly ajar. *Oh no... what if her husband looks in the closet?* he thought while trying to shrink into the shadows.

Ever so quietly, Lisa ran on her tiptoes, grabbed the two wine glasses, shoved them behind the bubbling jacuzzi wall shelf, and jumped into bed. She smoothed the covers so that the bed looked nearly undisturbed, pulled the sheets over her head, and pretended to be sound asleep.

Lisa was relieved to hear nothing but silence coming from her closet but she couldn't stop her heart from pounding like a drum being played in a ritualistic frenzy. She tried to calm her breaths and told herself that everything would be all right. Within seconds, she heard the bedroom door open and David's soft footsteps thumping toward the bathroom. Lisa heard water gurgling in the sink and the toilet flush. She worried about Dylan hiding in the closet as she listened to her husband's steps coming into the bedroom. *God help me!* Lisa thought, once again trying to calm her pounding heart.

With barely a sound, David made his way to their bed. He turned back the neatly folded covers and climbed in. He moved close to Lisa and embraced her. "Honey, are you awake?" he asked. "Lisa, I need to talk to you," he said, gently tapping her on the shoulder. "Sweetie, sweetie….I'm home. Please, I need to talk to you. I need you to wake up..."

Lisa rolled toward her husband and sat up. "David," she said pretending to be startled and sleepy. "What are you doing home?"

"Honey, I needed to be home with you. I talked for a long time on the phone with my dad and my mom's going to be OK. My dad told me that he didn't think I needed to visit her in the hospital since I wouldn't be able to do anything to help. She's on so many meds that she wouldn't know I was there. He knows how busy I am at work, so it wasn't hard for him to convince me to turn around and come back home. I changed my ticket when I was sitting in the Chicago airport and got the first available plane back."

"David, that's great," Lisa yawned. "I'm happy to hear that your mom's going to be OK. Welcome home, sweetie."

"While I was waiting at the airport I saw this necklace in a store window. It was so beautiful that it made me think of you and how beautiful you are. I *had* to buy it. Can I turn on the light so I can show it to you?"

"Um…sure, but not the overhead light. I'm still groggy. Can you just turn on the light on the night table?" Lisa answered, her neck muscles beginning to stiffen.

With knots tightening his stomach, Dylan watched David through the slightly open closet door. Like a shadow in the dark, he could see David get out of bed and walk to Lisa's nightstand to turn on the light. David leaned toward Lisa and gave her a kiss on the forehead.

"Are you awake enough to see what I've brought you?" David asked, sitting next to her on the bed with a big smile on his face.

Lisa sat up and made an attempt to act like she was just waking up. She rubbed her eyes and yawned out, "I guess so."

"While I was on the plane and waiting at the airport, I had time to think about our lives together. I thought about my dad and mom and how grief-stricken my dad was at the thought of losing her. While listening to his fear of her loss I realized that I have a fear of losing you too. I know that I'm not always available to you and I don't give you as much attention as you deserve." He squeezed her hand. "I'm sorry, baby. I want you to know how much you mean to me and how much I love you. This diamond is a symbol of how I feel." David opened a small box and handed it to Lisa.

Lisa's eyes opened wide. "Oh my God! David! What did you buy? I can't believe it," she exclaimed excitedly.

"It's a two-carat stone and it's surrounded by six small blue sapphire gems. The jeweler told me that blue sapphire has a magical property that acts as a talisman to guard the purity of love. I couldn't resist it, just like I can't resist you, and I want to protect our love. This gift comes from my heart, baby, and it's just a small expression of my appreciation of you."

"I don't know what to say," Lisa mumbled, wishing she could change the script of the recent events in their bedroom. "I'm in shock."

"Good. I want to make you happy. This gift comes with a promise to you, Lisa. I'm going to start putting our relationship before my other commitments. Yes, I'm dedicated to my work but I can start setting more boundaries there and make our relationship my priority. I make the company enough money for them to know my value. I don't want to be married to my career—I want to be married to you. I love you so much."

"I'm stunned," Lisa replied, resisting the urge to look toward the closet. Her face flushed as red as a beet.

"Good. I wanted to surprise you. That's why I didn't let you know that my plans had changed and I was returning home earlier than planned. Here, let me help you put on your necklace." David took his present out of the box and fumbled a bit while putting it around Lisa's neck. "It looks so beautiful on you...but I bet it will look even better if you weren't wearing your nightie. How about if you let me help you take that off so I can see your beautiful curves?" David reached to pull off Lisa's gown. "Yes, it's so much more beautiful against your bare skin."

He started passionately kissing his wife and began to tenderly stroke her body. Soon, he turned off the light. Climbing back into bed, he held Lisa's warm body close against his own. "I don't care if you're sleepy, I just want to make love to you."

At that moment, Lisa caught a glimpse of the open closet door. "Wait!" she shouted, jumping up and turning on the light. "First I want to look at your gift in the mirror."

Naked, she walked to the full-length mirror on the closet door, looked at her reflection, and closed the door tight. Dylan heaved a sigh of relief.

"Wow! This stone is amazing," she remarked, looking toward her husband. She walked slowly back to her bed, trying to keep her composure intact, and climbed back in.

"Remember the night we first met and the first time we made love?" David asked Lisa, who became unusually quiet.

"Yes," she answered while inwardly trembling with the fear of David discovering Dylan.

"I'm sorry I've been too busy to express gratitude for our time together. I want you like crazy and I'm going to make love to you with more passion than you've ever felt," David said as he started to feverishly kiss Lisa and gently stroke her between her legs. "Oh my, you're so juicy..."

Lisa was thankful that their foreplay didn't last too long. But she was surprised that David immediately started keeping his promise to be more present for her and made love to her with greater enthusiasm than she had experienced in a long time. He explored every private nook of her body and did everything he could to drive her crazy with excitement. The resounding moans of her pleasure reverberated loudly throughout the bedroom, letting David know he hadn't lost his touch.

As the intimate enjoyment of the loving couple became more and more apparent through the closed closet door, Dylan, sitting on the floor behind heaps of expensive shoes, felt his heart becoming heavier and heavier. As he heard Lisa groaning with pleasure, he wanted to scream out in agony from the pain he felt pounding his heart. Every time he heard Lisa moan, it felt like she was throwing a grenade into the core of his very being. He didn't know how to contain his emotions. His eyes filled with tears.

Damn her, he thought, feeling trapped in an intolerable situation. He sat there quietly, not wanting to listen or be a voyeur, not wanting to make a noise and blow Lisa's cover, and not wanting to be stuck in a closet surrounded by the sweet smell of the woman to whom he had given a piece of his heart. Soon, his emotions turned to anger. He was angry with himself for being caught in this horrible situation and he was angry with Lisa for placing him in a trap from which he didn't know how to escape.

To distract his mind from the sounds of the erotic melody being played on the body of the woman he had falsely imagined was his soul mate, he began to think about Carmella and how sweet she was. Why couldn't he find someone as nice as her to be with? And then he thought about Jodi and how much pain she must have been experiencing before she shot herself. Why couldn't he have had more compassion for her? Why couldn't he have sensed her pain and prevented her from committing a hideous crime against herself? Why didn't he, who was known in psychic circles as "the best intuitive in the city," see the tumult of her pain and her impending doom? Dylan wanted to vomit. *Even Norman, sitting in jail, must be having an easier time than I am,* he thought.

Instead of giving in to more jabbing pains of jealousy and anger, Dylan took hold of his emotions and shifted his focus. Holding himself as still as a stone, he recalled a lecture on morals that his mother had given him when he was a teenager and she had found him sneaking out the window late at night with the hopes of seeing his sweetheart, Destiny. "You're only hurting yourself when you lie. Dishonesty holds you prisoner in the misery of self-created illusion. To hear the song in your heart, you have to be honest."

As much as he had hated his mother for blocking his attempt to go out that night and for disciplining him by grounding him for a month, her words now helped him listen to his present inner truth. Kicking himself for ignoring his own integrity and not seeing what should have been clear as the light of day, he knew he was living a lie. He missed Stella. Stella was a good woman. When she wanted to be with another lover, she didn't lie or hide her truth; she had told him what was going on in her mind. As Dylan sat there, alone in the dark, he realized that he actually respected Stella for being honest, even if her truth had stung deeply and had changed his idyllic perception of love. And now he was treating her like dirt. He was making sure that she would pay for hurting him by ignoring her and her attempts to make amends, even though they were living together. By refusing to talk to her, he felt his power over her and could repay the pain she had inflicted on him. But right now, all he wanted was to hold Stella and be with her again.

Stuck in the closet, he decided to distract his mind from the revolting moans and shrieks of love coming from the bedroom. He wanted to listen to the truth of his soul. He quietly moved into a cross-legged, yogic sitting position and searched for the reason he was in this mess. Was he placing too much importance on chasing an impossible reality? Listening inwardly, he followed the somber trail of voices in his mind that reminded him that joy and sorrow, love and hate, forgiveness and blame, and anger were all part of life. His libido completely flatlined.

Being stranded in the claustrophobic room reminded him how strange this world could be. People weaved entangled webs that caught unsuspecting souls as if one was but a meager fly.

Once I get out of here, I never want to see Lisa or hear her falsely sweet voice again, he proclaimed silently. *This nasty predicament certainly gives new meaning to the phrase "coming out of the closet,"* he laughed quietly to himself.

He focused his attention on his breath and began to meditate and calm his emotions. He listened to the voice of his sorrow and tried to detach from its intensity by visualizing unconditional love erupting from his heart like molten lava streaming from a volcano. Then he made a commitment to himself that he would buy a plane ticket and leave behind all this craziness, and fly to some destination where he could feel free. He imagined himself watching the lava flow into the sea around the big island of Hawaii and for a moment, almost forgot that he was sitting in a dark closet.

He played with thoughts of alchemy and subtle vibrations. He called upon the Angel of Temperance to guide him to quiet the exploding fire of anger that continued to erupt each time he heard sounds of intimacy from the adjoining room. He imagined angel wings fluttering a cool breeze to help him find his equilibrium, and that a celestial being was pouring him a cup filled with soothing waters of eternal love. He heard his inner voice spark a dialogue with the angel and began to commune about moderation being a godly virtue.

His thoughts were interrupted by a sound he hadn't previously heard coming from the other side of the closet door. Someone—he assumed David—was snoring so loud, it sounded like a lumberjack cutting down a tree with a chainsaw. Dylan's mind jumped to the possibility of escape. Crawling slowly on all fours, quiet as a mouse, he moved to the closet door and opened it just a crack. As the snoring continued, Dylan pushed it open wide enough to look out into the room. He could barely see but immediately spied a way out. Lisa silently waved to him but he ignored making any eye contact with her. His escape route toward the bedroom door became instantly clear.

Thinking of himself as a courageous lion and following the rhythm of David's snoring, Dylan began to move swiftly out of the closet toward his freedom. Moving like a beast on his hands and knees, he was soon outside the bedroom and scrambling down the dark hallway at record-breaking speed. With every ounce of his strength, he stood up, and while trying not to make a sound, started slowly walking toward the front of the house. When he got to the large wooden door, the double bolts made his hopes drop like a boulder. It was not going to be easy to leave without waking up the entire household.

He turned and crept toward the kitchen. Earlier in the evening, he had seen a small porch with a fire escape at the back end of the building. He imagined that, being farther from the bedroom, the back door would make less noise when opened. He was right.

He felt in the darkness for a doorknob. His heart jumped when he found it. He unlocked the double bolt and let himself outside. The cool mist that touched his face made his heart soar with renewal and he felt that luck was finally on his side. He sneaked down the fire escape. Once on the ground, Dylan found himself trapped in a backyard jungle cluttered with nearly invisible yard furniture and creeping vines. It was hard to see in the darkness of the cloud-covered night but fortunately, his night vision helped him see a fence, which his fingers followed toward the front of the building. When it came to an abrupt end, Dylan heard a car going by and knew he was near the street. He quietly moved a large, potted plant so that he could use it as a stepladder to hoist himself up and over the wall.

Once on the other side of the fence, he looked around and was relieved to see that no one had witnessed his escape. Dylan had avoided being seen by David and was free at last. He rushed to his car, a tremendous sense of relief driving his steps. He fumbled for his car key, and even though he couldn't seem to move fast enough, he soon opened the door. Shouting out his happiness like a man freed from chains of disgrace, he jumped into the driver's seat and started the ignition with a burst of renewed energy. He let his shaking hands rest on the smoothness of the steering wheel to calm his nerves before he moved out of the parking place and began to drive. The fog was so thick it was like steering through a tunnel but whatever was happening outside didn't bother Dylan. He was glad to finally be going home.

Chapter Fifteen

The Devil
Chains of Desire

Norman sat in his jail cell on the one-inch-thick mattress that was a poor excuse for a bed. His mind, body, and spirit were in the utter horrors of withdrawals. He would have been willing to do almost anything to get a fix. His aching muscles twitched violently, forcing him into a fetal position of consuming despair. Cramping and hardly able to move, he groped his way across the mattress toward the rimless steel toilet to vomit the contents of his already nearly empty stomach. *What the hell did I do?* he asked himself over and over again as he tried to rub an ever-present, phantom itch that couldn't be soothed no matter how much he scratched. He fell to the floor just in time to see a metal-barred window slide open and an eye peeking into his cell.

"Obviously, whatever he's on didn't kill him," Norman heard a voice say. "I wonder how much he's enjoying getting high now?" The window slid closed with a clang that echoed endlessly in Norman's delirious mind.

Feeling as if he was about to be disemboweled, Norman could hardly string words together coherently enough to complete a thought. A tremendous pain was rising within him, increasing with every breath, but there wasn't a remedy anywhere in sight. Surely, death would be better than this horrific suffering.

Out of the jumbled confusion of his mind, his thoughts staggered together without much meaning. He realized that he hadn't known how high he was until this moment, when he was falling into a hopeless abyss. The upset circuitry of his nerves sent his body into intermittent spasms as if he had lost control over his physical senses. His mind raced to find answers but his thoughts were like ants crawling through soft glue. Through his mental haze, he searched for answers as to what had happened that brought him to this cell. He barely recalled the police banging on his door and Jodi bleeding on his bed. Surely, the small dose of crystal meth he had given her wasn't enough to cause an overdose. What had happened to her?

His gut-piercing, dry heaving finally subsided. With intense effort, he turned away from the contents of the toilet in disgust, dragged his body to the metal door, and attempted to pull himself up on its horizontal crossbar. He screamed into the dimly lit space, "Hey man, I'm sick. I'm not high. I want a lawyer. I have rights."

Minutes seemed like hours. No one answered. Norman could not bear the pure hell of his pain and started yelling with as much force as he could muster. Finally, a gruff voice answered from somewhere in the distance, "Shut the fuck up. I'm trying to sleep!"

Startled, Norman fell silent. His mind was on fire

and while going in and out of his mental haze, he thought that perhaps he had died and was experiencing the flames of hell. Even so, he could feel drops of cool water falling from his closed eyes, and for a moment he imagined that he was standing beneath a pounding waterfall. But as he opened his eyes and saw the metal bars, he had to work hard to push away his fear. He started grinding his teeth together inside his tightly locked jaws as his mood turned into violent, self-condemning anger. Moaning like a wounded dog, he told himself that he was a powerful man and men don't cry. If only he could call Dylan, his mind-over-matter buddy. Without a doubt, Dylan could wake him from this unearthly dream, chase away the devil, and wave a magic wand to pull him from the depths of hell and make everything all right. And where was Carmella, his hot friend who was always pulling Tarot cards? She and Dylan would come at any moment and help him get back home. He was sure of it.

Fat chance.

At that moment, in a prison of his own making, Dylan was busy licking his own wounds caused by the unpredictable fallout with Lisa. He was lost somewhere beyond Pluto in the solar system of his mind. Even though he was not the kind of person who normally felt sorry for himself, Dylan was sure he could hear a violin playing a soulful tune of lost love as he turned the key to open the door to his apartment.

Quietly, he walked into the front room, turned on the light, and started to tiptoe toward his private room. To his surprise, Stella walked out of what was once their bedroom and met him in the hall.

"Where have you been? You look like you've been in a catfight," she said, looking at his disheveled clothes, then directly into his eyes.

Dylan gazed unresponsively at Stella, whose dark hair fell in picture-perfect waves over her bare shoulders. Then he noticed what she was wearing and went into shock. She was dressed in a black lace teddy nearly identical to the one that Lisa had worn earlier that evening. Even though Stella looked deliciously invitingly, Dylan's libido went limp. He blinked hard.

"What are you doing up? I figured you'd be asleep," he managed to blurt as he tried not to think about how he had removed Lisa's lingerie just seconds before the mind-numbing experience of jumping from her bed to hide in her stuffy closet.

"Well, truthfully, I've been waiting for you. I've been hoping for a little time to talk to you."

"At this time of night? What about?" Dylan couldn't believe his terrible luck—that tonight of all nights, Stella wanted to talk.

"I'm about to go crazy because of what's happening to our relationship. I can't stand it that you won't talk to me. I want to tell you how horrible I feel about what's happened between us."

"It's been awful for me too but please...can we talk about this some other time? I'm exhausted," Dylan said, avoiding eye contact.

"Please, if I can just explain..." Stella said.

"Stella, are you hearing me? I'm beat. I'll be glad to talk with you about what's happening in our relationship but another time. Right now, I need to crash. Please..."

"OK, I can wait a little longer. By the way, I made you an apple pie. It's in the kitchen. Can I bring you a piece?" Stella felt her heart beating with the faint beginnings of renewed hope because, for the first time in what seemed an eternity, Dylan wasn't avoiding her. Yet, even so, he didn't comment on her lingerie, which she had recently bought with the hope of attracting his attention. She wasn't sure how to read his shocked expression but she did feel herself breathe a little easier that he wasn't turning away from her as he had done on previous occasions.

For the first time that night, Dylan's eyes met hers. "Apple pie? What happened, Stella? I must be dreaming. You've never been the baking type. You must be going through some pretty major changes to start making pies. After I get some sleep I'll be happy to try your pie. Right now, it's too late at night and I'm not feeling that well." Dylan started moving down the hall.

"Dylan," she called after him. "Maybe I can give you a back rub to help you feel better."

"What is going on with you? No, don't tell me. Let's wait until tomorrow to talk. Right now I'm struggling to stay awake. I'm so tired that I'll fall asleep standing up if I don't get to bed. So really, it's not worth your bother." Dylan couldn't bear the thought of talking with anyone right now, and especially didn't want Stella to get a sense of his painful emotional predicament. Turning away, he stumbled down the hall toward his room without giving much thought to their brief interaction.

Stella followed him down the hall. "Sweetie, can we sleep together tonight?" she asked. "I've been missing you so much."

"What's up with you?" Dylan said, feeling a murky mixture of surprise and annoyance. Once again, it was obvious she was not listening to him but he was too tired to confront her about her weird behavior. Not waiting for her answer, he went into his study, closed the door, and turned on the light.

In the privacy of his room, he tried to relax but the inner voice of his overwhelmed emotions seemed louder than ever. Sleep would be the best remedy to block out the pain of his aching heart. As he started to undress, he realized that he was too tired to look for pajamas so he climbed naked under the covers draped over his futon.

Eager to enter the world of his dreams, Dylan closed his eyes. Just as he was about to fall asleep, he heard the door gently open and footsteps slowly walking toward his bed.

I must be imagining things, he thought right before he heard Stella whisper, "You didn't tell me that I couldn't give you a rub."

Dylan, too tired to resist, didn't make even the smallest attempt to reply. Instinctively, he felt that he and his wife would soon be having an emotionally charged conversation if he pushed her away. Right now, he couldn't deal with any more chatting and decided it would be easier to pretend to have already fallen asleep.

Stella's hands slid under the covers, found his bare shoulders, and began to knead the knots that connected them to his neck. Her soothing touch made Dylan realize just how stressed he was. He could feel her warm breath on his skin and smelled the sweet lavender scent of her perfume. His wall of defense melted as her hands lovingly caressed his back, helping him to relax. Soon, Dylan felt Stella crawl into his bed and lay her naked body next to his. He held his body in check so that he didn't make the slightest movement. He didn't want Stella to feel the nervous tension he had in response to her body touching his. He struggled to ignore her explicit signals that invited him to make love. After the erratic events earlier in the evening, Dylan didn't want to think about the possibility of having sex, above all with his wife, who had created an oceanic wave of distance between them with her demand that he let her be free to date someone new. Perhaps he was already dreaming and his subconscious imagination was playing tricks on him, he told himself. Maybe in his present state of mind, he was hallucinating and Stella wasn't really in his bed wrapping her legs around him. Whatever the truth of the present moment, he was too stressed to be emotionally or physically accessible for reopening his heart to her and making love. Stella and the rest of the world would have to wait for him to get some sleep before he would be available for anything.

At the same time Dylan was finally getting to sleep, across town, Carmella was once again awakening from her fretful dreams. She was nervous and emotional in a way that made her feel like crying. Turning on her light, with one eye open and one eye half closed, she looked at her clock and saw that it was four thirty.

Norman's nothing but a douche bag! Why did I have to get involved with an idiot? she thought, feeling her anger soar. Making a mental list of why she didn't need Norman in her life any longer made her feel less like crying. Stoically, step by mental step, she tried to detach from her emotions. Torn between compassion and annoyance, her inner voice was too loud to ignore and she sadly realized that Norman had proven himself to be an unlikely candidate for her love. If Norman hadn't been such a party animal, she wouldn't have left his house, and maybe Jodi wouldn't have had an opportunity to shoot herself in the head.

Reaching toward her nightstand, she switched off the light and rolled over in her bed to go back to sleep. Rambo, her beloved Maltese dog, was asleep at her feet. Her throbbing ankle, wrapped in its medical support, jerked painfully from getting tangled in the sheets. *Maybe Norman needs to be in jail to get his head in order*, she thought.

To compound her confusion, at the same time she was feeling angry toward Norman, she felt equally bad that she didn't know what she could do to rescue him. Perhaps the peculiar events at his house were caused by the invisible Seega. She'd have to ask Dylan if it was possible for that force of evil to come into the house and lure Jodi into trying to commit suicide. Just the thought of the Seega made her reach for her sweet Rambo and hold him close to her chest for comfort.

"Oh, Rambo, I love you so much," she said, giving her pet a squeeze.

Still unable to fall asleep, she got out of bed, turned on the light again, and found her black-velvet drawstring Tarot pouch. As she opened her bag, the stone she had found in the haunted house seemed to jump into her hand by its own volition. If she hadn't previously believed in magic, after feeling the stone grow hot to her touch, she now knew that it had to exist. A tremor of fear went through her. It was obvious from the intensity of the heat in her hand that this stone had some kind of power. Nervously, she put it back into the pouch and out of sight.

Carmella sat down on the edge of her bed. She took out her cards, closed her eyes, shuffled, and thought of a question to ask her oracle. In her mind, she asked, *What can I do to help Norman?* After cutting her cards, she turned the Devil face-up.

"Well, this card certainly seems to fit the occasion," she said out loud. *More gloom on Norman's horizon*, she thought.

She felt a vibration on her thigh and looked down. The stone, which she distinctly remembered putting inside her card pouch, was now sitting in her lap. Again, she held it in her hand and felt its pulsing warmth. *What kind of stone are you?* she wondered. As if giving her an answer, it started to glow and became increasingly hotter. *Maybe Dylan will know what to do with this stone*, she thought before fearfully throwing it back into her Tarot pouch once more, pulling the bag's string tightly closed, and shoving it to the back of a nearby drawer.

There were so many other things to occupy her mind that she didn't want to take the time to worry about the unusual stone or the Devil card. Besides, she would rather not think about scary things. Earlier in the day at the unemployment office, she had accidentally run into Mary, Dylan's father's friend, who she had briefly met in his apartment. Mary had told her in a shaky voice about her impending eviction. She was putting her meager savings into fixing her car and she was fairly resigned to the fact that it would soon become her mobile home. Feeling empathetic toward the discouraged woman and her sad situation, Carmella had offered to let her take showers in her apartment until she could find a job and afford to pay rent again. *Hopefully, this will work out*, Carmella thought, wondering who would come to *her* rescue if she couldn't pay her rent.

Carmella got back into bed but still could not sleep. She started thinking about what she needed to do in the morning. Because of her injured ankle, she couldn't do yoga, her usual morning routine. As soon as it was business hours, she would call the prison and talk to Norman to find out what she could do for him, then go to the ICU at Marin General Hospital to visit Jodi. Tossing and turning, she tried to put everyone and all of their problems out of her mind but to no avail.

Surrendering to her insomnia, Carmella continued making her mental to-do list and put the events of the coming day in order. She was excited as she thought about her afternoon interview with Mr. Stalsburg, the movie producer. Her mind started going over the most pertinent questions she could ask to create a gripping news story as she slowly fell back to sleep.

Her alarm startled her and woke her from a dream. Looking around to find her clock, Carmella sat up quickly in bed, knocking sleeping Rambo to the floor just in time to realize that the alarm was actually her phone ringing. Half asleep, she reached for the receiver. "Hello," she said with sleepy hesitation.

"Will you accept a collect call from Norman?" an operator asked in a robotic tone.

"Yes, of course," Carmella answered excitedly. "Norman! Hello! Are you OK?"

"No, baby, I'm not OK. Can you get me out of here?" Norman sounded like a five-year-old pleading for a favor from his mother.

"I'll try. What can I do?"

"Come down here and talk to these assholes. Maybe

you can find out why I'm here. I don't even know but I do know I want to get out right now."

"OK. Will they let me see you?"

"I've been told I can see one person for fifteen minutes today. Can you get over here quick? Maybe they'll tell you more than they're telling me and I can find out what's going on and when I can get out. All I keep hearing is that I've endangered the life of a young woman."

Carmella could hear Norman moaning with pain and there was a disheartening desperation in his voice. Suddenly, the phone went dead.

Alarmed, she looked at her clock. It was seven in the morning. Jolting into wakefulness, she realized that she didn't even know exactly where Norman was. She imagined that most likely her friend was in the Marin County jail.

After fixing herself a cup of coffee, Carmella started making phone calls to inquire about Norman's whereabouts. It didn't take long to find out where he had been taken after his arrest and with a few calls, she was talking to the receptionist at the county jail, an infamous holding tank for wrongdoers, addicts, and drunks. Norman wasn't a criminal, she told a police officer on the phone before asking what she could do to help him get out.

"I'm not allowed to disclose information," he replied gruffly. "It's better if you come during visiting hours and talk to him yourself. That will be this afternoon."

"I'm working this afternoon," Carmella replied. "Can't I come earlier?"

"Your friend isn't well enough to see anyone this morning. Perhaps you should come tomorrow," the indifferent voice answered, then abruptly hung up.

Carmella felt helplessly tied in invisible chains. Perhaps later in the morning she would call Dylan and ask him to help. Presently, the only thing she could do was dial Marin General Hospital.

The phone rang ten times. Impatiently, she waited for the robotic messages to finish before a real person answered and she could ask for Jodi in the ICU. Carmella sighed with relief when the receptionist told her that Jodi was still alive. When asked if she could visit Jodi, the woman replied that Carmella could only go into her room if she was a relative. Carmella quickly responded that she was her sister and that she would be there as soon as possible.

Carmella jumped out of bed, mindful of her in-jured ankle, got dressed, and decided against her better judgment to take Rambo with her for moral support. Soon she and her dog were in her car and Carmella was driving down the highway at lightning speed to check on Jodi. She needed to know what to tell Norman about Jodi's condition. If Jodi was going to be OK, maybe Norman could be released. Since her morning was packed full of important errands, she didn't waste any time getting to the hospital.

Carmella parked under the shade of a tree. She gave Rambo a quick good-bye kiss on the nose, left him in the car with the window cracked, and was soon riding the elevator to the third floor of the hospital. The nurse at the reception desk asked Carmella a long list of questions about herself and her relation to Jodi. Seeming satisfied with her earnest answers that Jodi needed Medi-Cal because her family didn't have health insurance, the nurse said, "She's in a coma. The bullet missed going into her brain by about a sixteenth of an inch. She's very lucky that she had such bad aim. Since she missed her target, she might recover to live a normal life."

Carmella's heart throbbed with a current of hope. "Jodi's not going to die?" she asked.

"Hopefully, she'll be OK." The nurse pointed down the hall to Jodi's room and said, "Go to room 303 and pay her a visit. She's still at risk but if her will to live is strong, she has a good chance of coming back to join us for afternoon tea. Hopefully, she'll be OK. By the way, do you know someone named Dylan?"

"Yes, he's a good friend of the family," Carmella lied.

"She had a letter in her pocket addressed to him," the nurse replied, pulling it out of Jodi's file.

Carmella reached for the letter. "I'll be happy to take it to him." She smiled once it was in her hand, then turned and walked quickly down the hall toward Jodi's room.

The door to room 303 looked like all the other doors in the white-walled, sterile-looking hall. Carmella took a deep breath, turned the knob, and walked into the room.

When she saw Jodi's pale appearance, she was afraid that she might be dead. The young woman reminded her of a ceramic doll lying still as stone under white covers with an IV line going into her arm. Carmella looked at the heart monitor with its blinking lights and her stomach tightened with worry.

She moved closer to Jodi and reached to take her tiny, limp hand. "Jodi, I'm sorry we didn't get along. I'll be nicer to you in the future. Please come back to us. We'll have fun hanging out with each other."

Carmella bent down and gave Jodi a kiss on her

white-bandaged head. After standing there quietly and saying a prayer to call on healing angels, she whispered, "I have my dog in the car with me, so I can't stay long. It's not so easy seeing you like this. And later I have to go see Norman. He's in a mess, too," she said. Releasing Jodi's hand, she wiped the tears from her eyes and turned to walk away. "I'll be back to see you soon," she said, looking over her shoulder while she moved quietly out the door, trying to dodge a sense of mounting sadness.

Once outside the hospital, Carmella moved slowly toward her car as if she were sleepwalking. She wished that she could wake up to a different reality. She closed her eyes and stood still to feel the morning breeze. If she didn't worry about her friends, she could improve her attitude and unwind from her state of panic. Without question, she needed to get out of her negative mood.

Looking at her watch, she realized that she had enough time to pull a Tarot card before starting her drive to the jailhouse to visit Norman. Before she did anything else, Carmella was sure that life would feel better if she took a moment to consult her oracle.

She reached for the cards in her purse, unwrapped them from their silk cloth, and began to shuffle. *What is my card for today?* she questioned. Within seconds, she pulled the Devil card. *Again? Oh, great, there's no escape from the fires of ignorance.* Reflecting on the unlikely chances of pulling this card twice in one day, she thought, *Norman's been catting around too much and has gotten caught in a web of negative forces. And Jodi has taken a nasty fall in the karmic Chutes and Ladders game of life. If only we could protect ourselves from trouble, our lives would be so much easier.* Carmella sighed deeply.

Just as quickly as she had taken her cards from her purse, she put them back and hurried to her car. After visiting with Norman, she wouldn't have much time before she needed to be at her afternoon interview. *This is a busy day*, she thought while getting into her car and turning the ignition.

After a short drive zooming down Marin County roadways, she pulled into the jail parking lot. Carmella felt a little guilty because, once again, she needed to leave Rambo alone in the car. Actually, she felt a little bad that she had brought him on this hapless journey in the first place but her dog offered her the cheerful company she so desperately needed to take her mind off of her problems.

Her personal challenge was remaining optimistic about her plan to make a living by selling her writing. Even though she had a verbal contract for the sale of her magazine article on the modern practices of witchcraft, she hadn't gotten written confirmation about its acceptance. As a freelance writer, the payment for the sale of her story would certainly take care of a few of the bills that sat on her desk waiting to be paid. *Be absolutely positive and remain confident*, she told herself, trying to pry her concerns from her mind.

After getting out of her car, she hurried to the jailhouse so she could speak with the prison officials and find out about Norman's release. If only her Tarot cards could tell her what was going to happen, she would be better prepared for this sudden mission of mercy. Trying not to stress, she hurried to the visitor reception room and walked inside. The large room was filled with wooden benches and crowded with pregnant women, crying mothers, and nervous friends. Carmella felt intimidated by its sterile unfriendliness.

"No, you can't see the prisoner and no, we can't tell you anything," said the impassive man in the dark-blue uniform, who looked like he was hiding behind his oversized desk. "When he's feeling better, he can talk to you and tell you whatever he wants to tell you."

"But doesn't he get to have visitors?" Carmella asked anxiously.

"Yeah but he's too sick right now to see anyone. Maybe he'll be OK enough tomorrow to see friends," the man replied indifferently, fixing his badge to make sure it was straight.

"What is wrong with him? Does he need a doctor? I'm really concerned because he called me today and asked me to come see him," Carmella responded. *"Today,"* she emphasized. She felt the urge to run past the guard to look for her friend behind the locked doors.

"We're taking good care of him. Don't worry. He needs a little time to sober up before he can visit with you." A phone rang and the man picked up the receiver. "Hello. Just a minute." He looked up at Carmella, offered a tight-lipped, phony smile, and said once more, "Come back tomorrow to see him. Sorry, but there's nothing you can do here. You'll have to excuse me now. I need to take this call." He looked away and started talking as if no one was standing in front of his desk.

Dejected, Carmella turned and walked out of the dismal room. She couldn't wait to be outside in the fresh air again. When she passed through security into the warmth of the sunlight, she realized what having freedom really meant. She rushed to her car and opened the door to find Rambo waiting for her. He licked her face and excitedly jumped out the door. She let him take a pee and walked him around the parking area before he eagerly hopped back into her car. Once again, she slid into the driver's seat.

"This is a beautiful, sunny day," she said, trying to convince herself that there was a reason to be happy. Soon she had joined the speeding traffic weaving in and out of the lanes on Highway 101. As she gripped the steering wheel, she took a deep breath to reduce her accumulating stress and rushed to get to her interview on time.

Chapter Sixteen

The Tower
Crumbling Truth

*C*armella rushed through the morning with help from her two cups of coffee. Although she felt sad when she saw Jodi lying there in a coma, her visit to the hospital and encouraging talk with the nurses had inspired hope that most likely Jodi would recover. But her trip to see Norman had been much more frustrating. It was heartrending but she figured denial of his visitation rights because of a debilitating sickness could only mean one thing—most likely, Norman was coming down from his addictions cold turkey. She shook her head. *Poor Norman!* she thought as she drove down Highway 101.

She had to be alert to the cars speeding around her and didn't want to dwell on her suspicions about what might be happening to Norman. Weaving in and out of all the traffic with her beloved Rambo sitting like an honored guest in the front seat beside her, Carmella was relieved when she finally exited the freeway and took the frontage road to her destination. She could hardly believe her good timing when she pulled into the large asphalt parking lot at the movie studio five minutes early.

After parking in the shade and turning off her ignition, she gave Rambo a good-bye kiss on the nose, jumped out of the car, and walked to building number five—a fire-house-red barn-like structure nestled among an oasis of buildings surrounded by lush gardens in full bloom, rock waterfalls, and fountains. In front of the building was a large white tent created a makeshift reception office for what appeared to be a hectic day at the studio. Out of breath, she tried to relax her jittery nerves before she went inside and approached the receptionist.

"My name's Carmella Ashera and I'm here to interview Mr. Stalsburg," she said politely.

The heavyset woman looked Carmella up and down with critical, narrowed eyes. "Yes, you're on the appointment calendar. Unfortunately, he needs to finish an important project before he'll be free to speak with you. He'll be busy for at least another hour, perhaps longer. Do you want to wait?"

Carmella didn't have to think twice. It was important for her professional credibility to get this interview and she was willing to stay as long as needed.

"Yes, I can wait," she said, "but is it OK if I walk around with my dog? He's in my car. Normally, I don't mind letting him sit for an hour but if I'm to be gone longer than I expected, he's going to need to stretch his legs."

"No problem," the woman said with a smile. "I like dogs. Just don't let him pee in here."

"Don't worry about that. Rambo's well trained," Carmella replied as she turned to head back outside.

The bright afternoon sun and a garden of yellow-gold three-lobed fleur-de-lis greeted her as she exited the tent. Smiling with the anticipation of what was to come, she moved down the pathway to get her dog. Within minutes, Carmella was back inside the large tent, sitting in the makeshift waiting room with a happy Rambo wiggling in her lap.

Her scheduled interview had the potential to turn into a large paycheck. It was also a sign from the gods letting her know that she could be successfully self-employed. With focused determination, she had made more than seven phone calls to set the date for this important meeting. Writing made her happy and since she'd spent so many hours seeking out her present opportunity, she didn't mind spending a little time waiting. Besides, life was always good when her little dog was with her.

After a while, restless Rambo jumped from her lap and started checking out the environment. A steady stream of people passed by and stopped to say a word or two about her "white fluffball." Rambo was becoming the center of attention.

Among Rambo's admirers were two young women, who approached them with enthusiasm.

"What a totally cool little dog! He looks like a Maltese. Is he yours?" the taller of the two girls asked.

"Yes. His name is Rambo," Carmella said with a smile.

"He's so cute. Can we take him to show our friend? She's right outside the tent," the other girl asked.

The girl's friendly manner made it apparent to Carmella that Rambo would be in safe hands. Rambo obviously enjoyed the affection he was getting and willingly jumped into the girl's arms. *A dog sitter couldn't come at a better moment,* thought Carmella. She agreed with a smile and handed the girl his leash. She could use a little undistracted time to go over her interview questions. A little break from Rambo would come in handy right now.

The girls waved as they left the tent, fussing over Rambo. Carmella smiled and pulled out her notes. After about twenty minutes, she looked up from her writing and surveyed the room. Even though earlier she had been able to see Rambo with the girls near the front door, she felt a shiver of alarm when she realized that her dog had not yet been returned and was nowhere in sight. She put down her pen and went outside to look for the girls. She walked in the direction she had seen them go and made her way along the path outside the tent.

"Rambo! Rambo!" she called.

Neither her dog nor the young women were anywhere in sight. Carmella began to feel an ache in her heart. As her sense of dread began to increase, she ran to the parking lot. Not seeing her dog, she dashed back toward the buildings to search the outdoor tent area surrounding the blocked-off façade of the movie set. Frantic, she asked a few people walking by if they had seen the girls and her dog but no one remembered seeing them.

Carmella ran back to the reception room.

"Did those girls bring my dog back yet?" she asked the receptionist.

"No, I haven't seen the girls or your dog," the woman replied, her fingers hovering over her keyboard. "You just missed Mr. Stalsburg. You weren't here when he left his busy schedule to speak with you. You should know that someone like him doesn't have time to wait. He won't be able to see you at any other time today."

Carmella held her emotions in check. Not only was her dog missing, but now she had just lost her chance for an interview that could have easily landed her a paycheck. Panic began to surge through her veins. Her logical mind went into battle to control her emotions, which were ready to fly out of control.

"What can I do to reconnect with Mr. Stalsburg? And I'm concerned about my dog. He isn't anywhere to be found. Do you know those girls who took him?" She was trying to give the impression that she was in control of her emotions but wasn't sure she was being successful.

The woman furrowed her brow and looked slightly irritated. "I wasn't paying attention to who took your dog but I'm sure they'll bring him back. I'll send a text message to alert the security folks working on the lot to keep an eye out for him. Most likely, someone has him sitting on their lap and they don't realize you're looking for him. Young people can be so unpredictable," she said, rolling her eyes in disbelief as she picked up her phone to text security.

"OK, thank you," Carmella said. Deflated, she returned to a seat to wait. She could hardly believe how horrible the afternoon was turning out to be. She was reminded of her powerlessness to control her own life and felt an overwhelming sense of helplessness. She wanted to scream. Her precious Rambo—her loyal, true love and longtime companion—was missing! Anxiety from her building sense of loss began to swirl with thoughts of losing her interview, Norman being in jail, and Jodi lying near death in the ICU. The dramas of the day were too much for Carmella. She started to cry.

"Here's some tissue," the receptionist said as she walked over to Carmella and handed her a box. "Maybe you should go back outside and continue to look for your dog." Now appearing to be concerned for Carmella, who was in an obvious state of panic, she added, "I can talk with Mr. Stalsburg about rescheduling his appointment with you but he may not be available. I'll let you know and will call you."

"Yes…that's nice of you. I'll go outside and look for those two girls again. If they come back with my dog, will you please ask them to wait for me?"

"I'll be leaving soon but if I see them before I go, I will tell them to wait for you," the woman answered, returning to her desk and moving a large stack of papers across it. Avoiding Carmella's eyes, she turned away and looked intently at her computer screen.

Trying to hide her tears, Carmella walked outside the tent to continue her search for Rambo. The sun disappeared behind a mass of clouds that hid its cheerful glow. Angry at her own naïve trust in strangers, Carmella's self-imposed criticism resounded like a dirge from hell.

After a fruitless search, Carmella returned to the office. The receptionist had left. Clutching her purse and her notebook in her lap, she sat in the nearly empty waiting room, hoping that the girls would bring Rambo back. Two hours dragged by as she watched people come and go, all too busy to pay any attention to her. No one she stopped to ask about Rambo had any helpful information. Carmella imagined that something terrible must have happened. She decided to call the Humane Society but no one had called in a report about finding a missing dog. She called her friend Dylan but he had just awakened, was eating apple pie, and was in an important conversation with his wife.

"I'll call you later when we can talk," he told her.

After a long day and an unsuccessful search for Rambo, Carmella was exhausted. To make her situation worse, she had to sneak around to avoid the security guards, who had asked her to leave the gated lot. She felt as though she had dropped like a leaden weight from her inner tower of strength. Finally, she decided to go home and unwind from the craziness of the day. It would soon be dark and there was nothing more she could do to find her pet. No one seemed to notice that there was a young woman whose heart was dying from the pain of losing Rambo. She would certainly never give up her search and she'd be returning to this horrible place early tomorrow.

While Carmella was suffering through her plight, Dylan's luck seemed to be coming out from hiding. Although it was late afternoon, he had just climbed out of his futon and given thanks that it was the weekend instead of a workday. Recounting his recent dream of being lost in a labyrinth, he wasn't sure about the strange twists of fate that had been occurring and had to take a few minutes to untangle what was real from his imagination. As he got dressed, he mused that the strange events of the previous night seemed entwined with the fiery forces of Mars, the planet symbolizing war and power, because his obstacles were so acute. It was as if he'd gone to battle and lost control. He grabbed his phone and listened to his messages, and afterward decided that it might be better to return to bed. His world of friends seemed to be in a state of mass hysteria, as if they had fallen from the Tower.

But perhaps things aren't as bad as people are making them out to be, he thought as he stumbled into the hallway.

In the sunlit kitchen, Venus, the goddess of love and seduction, seemed to be smiling at him as he looked across the room and saw Stella cutting him a piece of her delicious-looking apple pie.

"Hi, sweetie. I've been waiting for you to wake up," she said. "I've saved you a cup of coffee to go with my homemade pie."

Just then Dylan's phone rang. It was Carmella. "Hi, what's up?" he asked.

"My dog is gone. Something dreadful has happened. I think someone stole him."

"Oh, no. I'm so sorry..." He glanced over at Stella. "Can I call you back? I can't talk right now..."

Dylan seated himself at the table, happy for the first time in long while that he was home with Stella. Despite the disturbing phone messages from his friends, it was a new day and he could take a few minutes to enjoy it. He was ready to start fresh and leave his, and everyone else's, problems far behind.

"Hi..." he said to Stella with a smile as he eagerly reached for the pie and took a bite. With the taste of warm cinnamon on his lips, it was hard to remember why he had spent these last few months ignoring his wife. Today she seemed lovelier than ever in her sheer black lace blouse, which tantalizingly revealed her beautiful curves.

"Do you like my pie?" Stella asked, looking at him as if she had won a lottery ticket.

"It's amazing! I didn't know you knew how to make apple pie."

"While we've been too busy for each other, I've been taking cooking lessons. Someone told me that making you a pie might show you how much I care for you."

"And who told you that?" Dylan questioned.

"A lady friend," Stella replied coyly.

"Do I know her?"

"I don't think so." Stella crossed her fingers behind her back and smiled. She couldn't tell him the truth about her visit with Naomi. Certainly, he would be angry with her for paying a bruja to cast a love spell.

"Well, you should thank her for me. This pie is the best thing I've had to eat all week. Will you cut me another piece?" he asked.

"Are you sure? I don't want you to get sick from eating too much," Stella said with a false concern that hid her sense of delight.

"You don't need to worry about that. I love your pie. And I didn't have any dinner last night."

Stella looked at Dylan, her smile fading. "What were you doing last night that you came home so late?"

"I was out with friends. Why do you care, anyway? Isn't your new boyfriend keeping you distracted enough that you don't have time to worry about where I've been going?"

"Dylan, let's not talk about any of that," Stella said, looking down while mumbling something inaudible.

"Why? How are things going with him, anyway?" Dylan looked at her intently. He noticed that her cheeks had grown red.

Stella looked deep into Dylan's eyes. "He isn't my lover anymore," she blurted out. "It's finished." She hoped that Dylan wouldn't say something to make her feel worse than she already did. The warm glow of just minutes before had faded, and in its place, a sudden gust of cool wind was blowing through their conversation.

Dylan dropped his fork loudly. "Stella, is this what you wanted to talk to me about last night? I might have known there was an underlying reason why you'd be making me a pie. Do you think a pie is going to make me forget how much you hurt me when you told me that you wanted to be with someone else?"

"But Dylan…" Stella started to say.

Dylan interrupted her. "I trusted the love that you gave me. You promised to be my loving wife, then told me I wasn't enough for you. Am I just supposed to forget that you threw me out of your heart because you'd met your new 'true' soul mate? You can't make enough pies to take away the pain that you caused me."

Suddenly, the pieces of the puzzle fell into place and Stella's unusual behavior made sense. Dylan had felt it was a strange turnabout last night when she unexpectedly started playing the seductive she-wolf. If her recent affair had gone up in smoke, as seemed to be the case, then it made sense that she would become interested in him again. Even if his own love life was going poorly, his body contracted as he found himself feeling like Stella's second choice. His emotional nature wasn't fluid enough to immediately mirror the twists and turns of her feelings for him. He felt as if his next words were floating up from a deep well of sadness.

"Stella, I'm sorry things aren't going well in your romantic world. I wish it could be like a happily-ever-after soap opera and I could eagerly jump into bed with you again. But you made me feel like I was damaged goods. Just because your new boyfriend left you or you're changing your mind once again about what you want doesn't mean that I can easily forgive and forget."

As Dylan heard his own words, he was surprised that he could be so clear about his thoughts. Ever since their falling out, he had felt so confused about his emotions that he couldn't communicate much of anything to her. But now things felt different.

"What is it that you want this time?" he asked.

Stella held back the tears. She sighed deeply as she looked up from the floor to meet his glare. "Oh, Dylan," she said softly. "I want us to get back together. You're my husband. I'm sure I can make you happy. We can start a family and make a fresh start together. I'm so sorry for the pain I've caused you."

Her eyes fell to the floor again in a gesture of helplessness. This was not working. One apple pie was not strong enough magic to make up for what she had put Dylan through.

"You're moving a little too fast for me. I haven't had time to adjust to your change of heart. I'm still stuck in your demand for us to have other lovers. And now you want to start a family?"

Stella felt confused and ashamed at the same time. They were both young and it hadn't seemed so wrong to have a little extra adventure at this point in life. But now, as she heard Dylan's words and the layers of feelings that were beneath them, she realized how much anguish she had caused him. How sensitive he was beneath his confident, all-knowing veneer. Realistically, that sensitivity was part of what had attracted her to him from the very start. It was an endearing quality that had made her fall in love with him.

At that moment, Dylan's voice came back into her consciousness. She realized that he was looking straight into her eyes—something he hadn't done for some time.

"I don't know what to think or say. Especially right now. I need to breathe some fresh ocean air and wake up from my nightmare of the last few days. My dad is freaked out about something he can't talk about on the phone and needs me to hurry over. I've got a friend who just attempted suicide and is in a coma in the ICU in the hospital, and Norman's in jail. Destiny called and left me a message telling me that her sister Angel is in grave danger and wants me to do something. And another friend just called, crying about her dog being stolen. I'm starting to panic just thinking about all the calls I need to make to find out what's happening with everyone. My head is in too many places right now to make decisions about our relationship. For the past three months, my mind has been rehashing your harsh remarks that shut me out of your life. I can't just dismiss all that and pretend that nothing happened. Please, Stella, I need some time to figure out my feelings."

Dylan's laundry list of problems, as grave as they sounded, was the wrong thing to say to Stella at that moment. She felt invisible. Hadn't he heard anything she'd said? Her inner window on her own sorrow for the wounded feelings she'd caused Dylan slammed shut and her own feelings of being unheard moved into the foreground. "Can't you just get out of your head for once and listen to my feelings?"

"That's not fair. I have listened to your feelings. How rude of you to say that!" He wished he could tell her that he felt like an emotional train wreck but he couldn't. The soul-destroying truth was that the anger he felt toward Lisa was now merging with the memory of Stella's betrayal. "Stella," he said, "do you want me to suddenly respond to your needs when you didn't respect mine? You couldn't wait to stop sleeping with me because of another guy, and now you can't wait to sleep with me again. Like I said, I need to go out for some fresh air, think about all this, and go see my dad."

"OK," Stella said. An edge had crept into her voice. "Don't worry about our relationship. Go rush to help your friends. I can wait to talk to you when you're ready. I can keep waiting and waiting for you, just like I've been doing for the past couple of months."

"Haven't you heard anything I've said? This conversation is getting too crazy for me. I've got to go."

Stella's voice rose. "Damn it, Dylan, I love you! Will you at least hear that?" Then her voice fell into a whisper. "Can we please kiss and make up? Other couples have conflicts. It doesn't have to be the end of our relationship. We can make our life together better than what we had before."

Dylan felt numb. No matter what Stella said, her words were like messages painted on panes of glass that went sliding past him without making contact. "Stella, I'm serious. I just woke up, the day is almost gone, and I've got to find out what's happening with my friends who are all suddenly calling for help. Please, give me just a little time." He got up and put on his jacket.

"Well, OK. I get it. You're leaving. But if you truly need to go, you might as well take the rest of the pie with you, just in case you get hungry. I did make it especially for you."

"Thanks but no thanks. Save some for yourself." Dylan turned to look at his wife before walking out the door. The sight of her made him soften. "Stella, don't worry. We'll figure all this out," he said as he started to walk away.

"Wait..." Stella moved toward him. "Can I at least have a hug?"

"Yes," Dylan replied. He gave her a loving embrace but he didn't feel it in his soul. All he wanted was to find his car keys and get out the front door.

Chapter Seventeen

The Star
Hope's Dark Reflection

*T*he rhythmic *click-clack* of a cable car hurrying down the hill soothed Dylan's frazzled nerves as he walked to his parked car. Once inside, he squirmed in his seat to get comfortable, then hurried to call Destiny, who had left a frantic message on his voicemail.

"Hi, Destiny. What's the matter?" Dylan asked when she answered her phone.

Destiny was obviously distraught. "My dad just told me that Angel is acting so crazy that she needs to be under heavy sedation or put in a mental hospital."

"What? He actually said that? That doesn't sound like the Taylor I know. Listen, calm down. I'm guessing that he's willing to give my dad more information about your sister than he'll give to either of us. He and my dad are always talking together in their secret brotherhood code language. And my dad must know what's happening because earlier today I received a message from him telling me that something's going on with your sister. Is there any chance you can meet me at my dad's house so we can ask him what he knows about Angel? I'm on my way to see him now."

"Yes, you're right. Mark and my dad are always sharing secrets. I'll go right now," Destiny said and hung up without a good-bye.

Dylan began making his way to his father's home in Twin Peaks. He was relieved it was the weekend and he didn't have to worry about work. There seemed to be enough to do in his life without worrying about deadlines. Lost in thought, the trip to his father's place seemed effortless until it took the customary fifteen minutes to find a parking space. Dylan felt a momentary sense of freedom from his concerns as he got out of his car. He was happy to feel the refreshing chill of the cool air and didn't mind walking up the steep hill to his dad's place. He couldn't help but smile as he saw Destiny sitting on the steps waiting for him out front. Dylan helped her stand and gave her a welcoming embrace.

"I can't believe that my little sister's losing her mind because some demonic spirit has taken over her body. That can't be true...can it?" Destiny asked with a panicked look on her face. "Just hearing things like that coming out of my dad's mouth makes me want to scream."

"Well, it does sound pretty crazy. Jodi told me that she saw your sister involved in a séance and you know how weird those can get. But at this point, try not to worry. Let's see what my dad knows about it," Dylan said, trying to invoke his faith in divine providence as he knocked on his father's door.

Mark opened the door and ushered them inside. "Destiny, I haven't seen you in a while. Nice to see you again. You're certainly becoming a beautiful woman," he commented.

"Dad," Dylan started. "Earlier today both you and Destiny called me about Angel. I invited Destiny here because she's hoping you can help solve whatever problem Angel's facing."

"I've never heard my dad sound so hopeless," Destiny said, breathing a heavy sigh. "He told me that Angel's possessed and he doesn't know what to do. He says I can't help her and doesn't want me to come over."

"You should be talking with your father about this, not me," Mark answered with a somber look.

"Dad," Dylan said, "Taylor isn't answering his phone and yesterday, when he did talk to Destiny, he refused to talk about Angel except to say that she's out of her mind. He didn't want to scare Destiny with 'gloomy' details. Unfortunately, now she's more worried than if he'd told her what was really going on."

Mark walked to the bar at the other end of the living room and poured himself a double shot of scotch. Then he sat in the chair across from Dylan and Destiny and downed his drink in one gulp. "Look," he said. "I don't know how much you know, Destiny, but when I saw Angel the other day, she looked like a spawn of Satan caught in the grip of hell's fury. It felt dangerous to be near her. That's why your dad doesn't want you to visit. He's afraid for your safety."

"But maybe I can help her," Destiny replied in a wavering voice.

"Or maybe you'll attract the same dark energy to you. I'm sure your dad's trying to protect you from hostile forces. Taylor's going crazy watching Angel and not being able to help her."

"Dad," Dylan interrupted, "I think I can help. At least, I'm willing to try."

"And how are you going to do that?" Mark asked.

"I need to talk to Taylor and Angel and ask some questions. I've helped with other similar situations," Dylan said calmly.

"Dylan," his dad continued, "Angel is obviously stuck in some subterranean force field. She had been practicing astral traveling. Taylor said that he taught her to disengage her spirit from her physical body and fly to faraway places in her ethereal, light body. The day of the séance, he instructed her to astral travel on a mission to visit a sacred etheric temple but when she was out of her physical body, a phantom entered it. We saw her struggle to reclaim her body but whatever entered her is stronger than Angel and it's blocking her return. It became obvious that her body is possessed by a ghoul who enjoys violence and has a lack of restraint."

"If it's truly an evil force that has taken possession of her, I can get rid of it," Dylan said confidently as he reached for Destiny's hand to give her emotional support.

"My poor sister," Destiny said. "She needs me."

"No, you need to listen to your father and keep a safe distance from your sister," Dylan replied. "It's better for me to try to help her."

"Well, both of you should talk to Taylor before you try to do anything. And you know, she's not the only person in trouble," said Mark. "Earlier today, I got a call from that friend of yours, Carmella. She asked me if I could bail Norman out of jail. Do you know what's going on?"

Dylan nodded. "Norman's having criminal charges filed against him. He's been charged with endangering the life of a teenage girl as well as with possession of hard drugs for sale. He might even be charged with statutory rape but that hasn't been determined yet."

Mark's face contracted into a frown. "Damn! I feel sorry for him. It's always something with Norman. I've tried to tell him that he needs to slow down, to be more careful, but Norman always laughs it off. And that Jodi," he added, "the silent one—it was easy to see that she's trouble. But it's his own bad karma that got him busted."

"He wouldn't be in this mess if Jodi hadn't tried to commit suicide at his house," Dylan explained. "After the paramedics responded to 911 calls two times from his home in one week, and found his place smelling like a marijuana farm, it wasn't long before the police arrived with a search warrant."

Mark shook his head. "Two times?"

"Yes, Carmella got hurt in his driveway earlier in the week and called 911."

Destiny shook her head in disbelief, got up, and moved toward the door. She turned to look at the two men. "It sounds like Norman's got big problems but I'm focusing on my sister. I've got to go. Mark, thanks for telling me what you know about Angel. At least now I have a better sense of what I'm going to be dealing with at my dad's. Bye, guys."

"Destiny, you shouldn't go," Dylan responded, growing concerned. He hadn't seen Destiny this upset in a long time.

"I'll talk to you later, Dylan," Destiny said as she rushed to open the door.

Dylan was torn. Should he go with her or not? He

consulted his intuition and understood with an inner awareness that it would be better not to go with her. Since his romance with Destiny had ended, Taylor took delight in refusing to acknowledge him at social gatherings even though he and Destiny had remained good friends. He had a better chance of not stressing her father if she warned him of his arrival instead of coming in the door unexpectedly.

"OK. Call me later and tell me what happens," he said. "Tell your dad that I'm willing to help and I'll be coming to visit Angel soon."

"Thanks, Dylan. Will do. I'll call you." Destiny hurried out the door and quietly closed it behind her.

Dylan turned to Mark. "What about Angel's mother, Naomi? Was she involved in the ritual too?"

"No," Mark answered. "A few years ago she vowed never to attend Taylor's rituals because she wasn't willing to watch his 'ego on steroids.' And right now she's so mad at Taylor that she's moved out of the house and told him she's never coming back. I think she's staying with her sister. They're probably lighting candles for Angel and sticking pins in a voodoo doll that looks like Taylor."

"That would almost be funny if Angel wasn't in serious trouble," Dylan responded.

"Everyone's got big problems, it seems," ranted Mark. "I'm getting phone calls from collection agencies all the time telling me that I owe them money. I'm afraid to answer the phone and they're leaving threatening messages on my answering machine. You can't talk with those idiots. And to make things worse, now I've got my lodge brothers calling me and blaming me for setting a disaster in motion the other night at the initiate's rite of passage and I'm facing the threat of a lawsuit. Where's your mother when I need her? Even though we're divorced, she's the one person in the world who's always been strong enough to help me when I need it."

Dylan had never seen his father so shaken. "Mom's camped out in some redwood grove working to help save an ancient forest. Her cell phone doesn't have reception in the woods so you can't reach her."

Dylan was like a pot full of boiling water that needed to be moved from the burner. It seemed lately that his father was always having financial challenges and Dylan didn't want to listen to his long list of problems. He'd heard weird stories too many times before but the potential lawsuit story seemed to top the list. The only thing Dylan knew for sure at this point was that Mark's analysis of what might happen to him was based on fear instead of fact.

Dylan's cell phone rang just then. Happy for the distraction, he answered it. "Hello?"

Instantly, Dylan heard the panic in Carmella's voice. Upon hearing her crying about Rambo's disappearance, he turned and walked away from his father to continue his conversation in private.

"Oh, Carmella," he said sympathetically. "I'm sorry about Rambo. Do you really think it was a dognapper? Could he have just wandered off? Please stop crying. We'll find your dog."

Dylan was quiet as he listened to Carmella's unfolding story about how Rambo had mysteriously vanished. He wished he knew how to calm things down. Then he heard something that made his mood lift like the fog in the morning sun. "What? You have a letter for me from Jodi? I can't believe it. I'll come over as soon as I leave my dad's."

When Dylan hung up, he turned and walked toward his father. "Dad, you'll be OK. Pull yourself together. I've got to go. A friend has something for me and I need to get it before she goes to bed."

Mark sneered at him. "I hope it's something between her legs."

Dylan wouldn't listen to crude remarks from his dad. He had spent too much of his life listening to his father's traumas and most of what he received in return consisted of insensitive, abrasive comments. He felt lucky to have had his mother's warmhearted empathy to offset his father's surreal, twisted take on life and love.

"I'm outta here," Dylan responded.

"Don't you blow me off. I'm your father."

"Dad, I've got too much to do," Dylan said, edging toward the door. Sometimes it seemed like his father was more of a child than an adult. At times like these, Dylan didn't want to be around to play the role of the concerned parent. "We'll talk again later. Don't worry so much. This stuff will all go away sooner or later. Right now, I'm sorting through my own problems but I'll be back before too long to check on how things are going for you."

Concerned about how weary Mark looked, Dylan walked back to his dad and gave him a hug, then quickly left. The day was almost over and he needed to visit one more friend. He was saving the best for last. He hoped his next meeting would be better than what had transpired so far that day.

∽

By the time Dylan got to Carmella's apartment on Green Street, it had started to rain and he realized that not only did he not have an umbrella, but he was also emotionally spent. The day had been one long series of highs and lows with nothing in between. He knocked gingerly on the door, looking forward to being with Carmella more than he wanted to admit.

"Dylan, I'm so happy to see you," Carmella said as she opened her door and invited him inside. "Do you want some coffee or tea?"

"You forgot to say 'or me.' Do you want coffee, tea, or me?' That's how the saying goes." Dylan smiled as he saw her blush. He wondered if he had been too forward. "Sure, I'll have some tea," he said, looking around her brightly illuminated room.

"OK. Follow me to the kitchen and I'll heat some water." Carmella gestured him inside and Dylan followed, feeling himself relax in her presence. The more time he spent getting to know Carmella, the more drawn to her he felt.

"Have a seat," Carmella said as she poured water into her teapot and put it on the stove. "I'm sorry about the frantic phone calls. I hate to dump on you but I'm going nuts. Besides feeling devastated about Jodi trying to commit suicide, and that Norman's locked up in jail, now I'm going crazy worrying about Rambo."

"You're not dumping on me. I'm happy to listen," Dylan replied. "You've got a lot to deal with. And how's your leg?"

"It's getting better but I'm really upset about Rambo. He's like my child. I've had him since he was a puppy. I can't stop thinking about him. I'm going back to the movie set tomorrow to continue my search."

Before he knew what he was doing, Dylan stood

and took her in his arms to offer support. "I'm sure Rambo will find his way home," he said huskily. "My intuition tells me that you'll find him."

Carmella easily melted into Dylan's arms. She felt the warmth of his embrace and smelled the musk of his wavy hair. For the first time all day, she relaxed for a brief moment. She wished that the teapot hadn't begun to whistle, but it had, and she needed to turn off the stove. She slowly pulled herself out of his arms.

Dylan noticed that even though she was slightly limping, her body moved gracefully as she moved about the kitchen and reached into the cupboard to get the teabags. Dylan's heart pounded in his chest. He wasn't supposed to be feeling good right now but there was something about being near Carmella that made him happy. He didn't want to resist his happy feelings, especially since they seemed to occur so infrequently these days. He smiled despite all that was going on in his chaotic life. He couldn't be sure but he thought that he saw Carmella smile for just a moment as she filled his empty cup on the table, then sat in a chair close to his.

"I know you feel devastated but you've got to stop thinking about Rambo so you can get some sleep tonight," Dylan said in a soothing tone. "Tomorrow you can begin your search for him all over again." He moved his body so that his shoulders touched hers. They were both silent for a while.

"Thank you," Carmella said, breaking the silence. "I so badly needed to talk to someone who understands. I really appreciate that you took the time to come here and listen to me."

Dylan put his arm around Carmella and gently said, "You've got to be strong so that you can find

Rambo. And we've got to trust that our friends will make their way out of their crazy predicaments and will be OK."

"Thanks for your encouragement," Carmella said, turning to look at him. "Before I forget, here's the letter I told you about that the nurse found in Jodi's pocket." She took a crumpled envelope out of her purse that hung on a nearby chair and gave it to Dylan.

"I don't know if I can handle any more surprises today," Dylan said. "I think I'm going to open it after I get some sleep. I might start to lose my sanity otherwise. Please forgive me for drinking your tea and running out the door but I've got to go home and sort out some stuff with Stella. It's a difficult time and I feel like I'm at a test point to find out if I'm the master of my fate or if I'm just a puppet playing a part in a drama that can't be changed. You understand, don't you?"

"I think so. I'm still trying to understand my fate in relation to Rambo but I feel better after talking with you. Can we talk again tomorrow? Hopefully, I'll have more news regarding Norman and Jodi."

"Of course. And if I hear anything, I'll call you too." Dylan leaned over and gave Carmella a lingering kiss on her cheek, then stood and made his way to the door. "Good dreams, sweet Carmella. If you start to worry again, just remember that my intuition sees you finding your dog," Dylan repeated as he left.

Although Dylan was glad to have spent a little time with Carmella, he was happy to be going home again and happy that the rain had stopped. He needed some time with Stella to help him get more clarity about the choices he now faced. When he unlocked the door to his apartment and walked inside, it was quiet as a church. Stella was nowhere to be seen. He heaved a sigh of relief, happy to be alone. He felt exhausted from listening to the myriad complications of life that were weighing on the shoulders of his wife, friends, and family. Even his own mind seemed to be whirling. Should he reconcile with Stella? Could he find a way to heal the craziness that was going on between them? And what about Lisa? He felt his blood boil when he remembered what had happened the previous night, and it got hotter when he realized that the day was almost over and he hadn't heard a peep of an apology out of her.

After going to the kitchen and getting a soda from the refrigerator, he walked back to his private room, congratulating himself for having the willpower to resist eating another piece of Stella's tempting apple pie. He sat at his desk, turned on his reading light, and though he knew he should wait, pulled out the letter from Jodi. Even though the paper was crinkled, the words were clear. *Dylan*, Jodi had written. *You are my one true friend. I've written you a poem to thank you.*

Nighttime Stars

A glowing sun
Sets over a hill,
Caught in reflections of light,
As the earth stands still.
Now begins the glory of night
And the sky begins to fill
As a million stars
Sparkle and shine bright.
A deepening calm sweeps over the land
When the moon dominates the sky.

The dark horizon is moved
By the hand of night.
Stars shine bright.

Dylan reread her poem several times. He thought about her feisty nature, how real she was, and how much he really liked her. For someone so young, she was so bright. *Like a star herself,* he thought while sliding her poem into a book on his desk. Her inspiring words made him feel better. If he could only have cured her problems, he would truly be happy. He envisioned himself sending Jodi healing rays of Reiki energy just as he was falling asleep.

❧

Early the next day, Carmella returned to the makeshift reception office on the movie lot. Less friendly than yesterday, the receptionist appeared to be growing weary of Carmella's repeated requests for information about her lost dog. But Carmella had a knack for reading people and sensed that she would help find him. She knew she should listen to her instincts.

Carmella was happily surprised when Mr. Stalsburg walked into the office. Hoping that her timing had improved and she could somehow salvage her interview, she jumped up and stood in front of him.

"Sorry to bother you, Mr. Stalsburg. I'm the woman who was going to interview you yesterday. My dog disappeared while I was here waiting for my appointment with you and I went to find him. That's why I missed you yesterday."

"Well, I hope you found him. It's upsetting to lose a pet." Then, appearing to be in too much of a hurry to wait for a response, he made a dash for the exit.

Carmella was dumbfounded by his coldness. She felt the need for some fresh air to relieve her sense of panic so she walked outside. As she breathed in and out to calm her nerves, off in the distance she heard a dog barking. She listened, trying to locate the source of the sound, and moved toward it. It was coming from inside a nearby building that was marked with a sign that read "Off-limits to the general public."

Ignoring the sign, Carmella stepped into the building and walked unnoticed past several rooms where numerous people were working. She trotted down the hallway, following the familiar sound. With caution, she peeked inside the room where the barking was coming from. Her mind couldn't believe what she was seeing, so she pressed her face against the wood of the door to open it wider.

A young woman had secured the dog, which was wearing a muzzle, and another was using henna to tattoo an upside-down pentacle on its butt. The little dog looked nearly identical to Rambo except that it was shaved to its shiny pink skin. The only fur that remained was a tuff between the ears trailing down its shoulders fashioned in a rainbow-colored Mohawk.

"Is this my dog?" Carmella yelled incredulously as she burst into the room.

"What?" said the woman holding the tattoo pen. Both she and the other woman instantly busied themselves trying to relax the yelping mutt, who was becoming agitated in response to Carmella's voice.

At that moment, another girl walked into the room holding what looked like a cake made of ground meat molded into the shape of a cat. Carmella could smell ground liver as the girl walked through the door. The young girl obviously knew how to distract the dog from noticing that its butt was being used as an art canvas. Pulling free from the woman who was holding him, the little dog forgot about being the center of attention and lunged for the plate. Obviously hungry, it didn't care about anything in the room except for the appearance of its tasty treat.

"This isn't your dog," the girl said. "It's Roland's dog and he's paying us to get him ready for a role in a movie."

"But it looks just like my dog without its hair!"

The door opened and Mr. Stalsburg, the producer, walked in. He didn't act at all surprised to see her there and looked directly at her. "Do you know that you're trespassing?"

Carmella tried to choke back her frustration. "I couldn't help but come here when I heard this dog barking. I'm looking for my lost dog."

As if lost in thought, Mr. Stalsburg said, "Isn't he an interesting looking mutt? Too bad he can't eat through that muzzle."

"This dog looks just like my Rambo without its hair!" Carmella repeated. "You stole my dog and you've shaved off his fur," she screamed, no longer able to hold back her emotions. "You're heartless monsters!"

"Not only are you wrong but you're also insulting," Mr. Stalsburg hissed. "Girls, didn't you get this dog from the trainer who's under contract with our studio?"

The young women whispered to each other before one said, "Yes, we picked up the dog from its trainer."

Carmella couldn't believe what she'd just heard.

She lunged toward the table and reached for the dog's jewel-studded collar. The younger of the two women assertively pushed her away.

"I've spent half a day getting this mutt ready to play a role in a movie. You can't come here and just grab it."

"I want to have a closer look at him." Carmella was outraged.

One of the other two women quickly pulled out her cell phone to make a call to security. The henna artist grabbed the dog and started to leave the room.

"Just let me look at him for a couple of minutes," Carmella begged once again.

"Do you know what Terra Linda means?" asked Mr. Stalsburg calmly.

"Yes, it means beautiful earth," Carmella responded, trying to get a closer look at the dog, which was quickly being carried toward the door.

As if on cue, several security guards appeared. The young woman holding the dog ducked behind one of them and bolted out the door. Two of the broad-shouldered, towering men stopped Carmella, grabbed her, and assertively started to escort her toward the exit.

Just when Carmella thought that this day was becoming her worst nightmare, she heard the producer say, "Just a minute! Let her go. Your look is perfect for the part, Carmella. That's your name, isn't it?"

"Yes," she answered in a bewildered tone.

The guards released her.

"I could have the girls write up a report that details how you broke into our off-limits building. And I could charge you with trespassing. But you're such a beautiful woman and I feel bad that you've lost your dog. I understand how sad you must feel. To show my integrity, I'll have one of my assistants find the contracts that were signed by the owner to temporarily release this dog to us, and if it will make you feel any better, you can see them. But more importantly, I'm excited. I can't stop thinking that you have the perfect look, your slight limp and all, to play the role of a witch that gets burned at the stake in the production of my documentary. Your image makes such a strong statement. Seriously, would you be interested in being an extra in my movie? The woman we initially hired for this role is out of commission with a broken leg and I'm desperate for a replacement."

Carmella was in shock. She was sure that the dog she had just seen was Rambo but couldn't prove it. The offer of a part in a movie sounded great and the thought of getting a paycheck would ease her concerns over having enough money to pay her bills. She looked at the producer, who had a large smile on his face. She pinched herself to make sure she wasn't dreaming before saying, "Are you serious? I would love to be in your film."

"Great. I never suggest that someone play a role unless I feel it is absolutely right. There's too much at risk if I make a mistake," Mr. Stalsburg replied while dismissing the security guards with a wave of his hand.

"I'm flattered and it sounds like fun to play a part in a movie," Carmella spoke with calm reserve. "But I'm still hoping that you will let me do an interview with you."

"Sure. We can find time to do that next week when my schedule isn't so tight. We can talk about your interview later. Right now, you need to go back to the office where I first met you, and talk with the receptionist about filling out the paperwork. Tell her I want you to play the role of Sybil. She also needs to give you directions to the costume department and the dates and times for when we need you for filming."

"I can't believe this is happening, Mr. Stalsburg," Carmella said feeling like she wanted to give him a hug. Except for not finding Rambo, this day was turning out to be much better than she had imagined.

Chapter Eighteen

The Moon
Emotional Waves of Fire

As Carmella drove back to San Francisco, she decided to stop at the Marin County jail. She was still in time for visiting hours and she knew it would help her sleep better if she could see Norman and hear from his own mouth that he was all right.

Once in the reception room, she warily strolled toward the attendant, who sat behind a large glass partition, and asked to visit Norman. Without changing his sour expression, he gave her a form to fill out that would allow her a fifteen-minute meeting. She scribbled her information in the blank spaces and handed it back to the attendant, who said, "Have a seat. Someone will call you when it's time to visit your friend."

Although his monotone voice didn't sound very welcoming, Carmella was excited that she would soon get to see Norman. Even though he'd only been locked up for a few days, it felt like an enormous luxury to be allowed to see him. With her heart beating like a drum, she walked to an empty spot on a wooden bench, sat down, and tried to think of what she should say to Norman.

Twenty minutes crept by before she heard the metallic clang of keys, looked up, and saw an officer open a locked door that led to the interior of the building. Reading from a list, he called her name along with several others. Anxious, Camilla got up and walked over to where the officer stood. With a brutally official air, he motioned for her and the others who had gathered to show their identification and walk through a metal detector before he led them through another locked door.

In an unemotional tone, he voiced instructions to them. "Go down the corridor and turn left into the waiting room."

Carmella went down the windowless hall and into the waiting room, where she instantly smelled dry, stale air. She felt like she couldn't breathe and she tried in vain to calm the sense of anxiety that was flooding over her. Tears started to fall on her cheeks when she saw two men in orange jumpsuits and shackles walk past the entrance accompanied by an armed guard. Carmella sat on a wooden seat and scrunched her shoulders up toward her ears in an attempt to get rid of the stress triggering the onset of what she knew would become a migraine.

Another ten minutes passed before she heard her name called again. This time she was led to a private room that contained only a single chair placed in front of a thick pane of glass. A few minutes later, Norman walked through a door and into the room on the other side of the partition. He sat on a chair positioned directly across from her own.

"Norman, I miss you," Carmella confessed, blowing

him a kiss. "Do you have any news about your situation?"

"No, sweetie. It's so nasty in here." His voice seemed to shake with uncertainty. "All anyone talks about, if they talk to you at all, is getting a court date, felonies, and their attorney. I'm bored out of my mind and I want out of here. It's like time is at a standstill and I'm going crazy. This ain't no vacation, that's for sure."

Norman felt as if a swarm of snakes was wiggling through his body. His thoughts drifted momentarily to images of past drug experiences. There was the opium parlor in Chinatown where he was led through a maze of alleyways until he had no idea where he was. After stepping through a low, ancient wooden door, he found himself in a room with low-lying beds lining the walls. The walls were covered with ancient newspapers that bore headlines of major events, such as World War I— newspapers that had yellowed from the smoke of countless years and long thin pipes. Almost all the beds were filled with old Chinese men lying quietly amid their smoky dreams.

The small man who was in charge led Norman to an empty cot and motioned for him to lie down. Then he brought a filled pipe and offered it to Norman, who inhaled the bittersweet smoke with several deep breaths, then several more after the pipe-bearer indicated that he should stop. Obviously, he had been too greedy, for instead of disappearing into dreams like the others present, within half an hour he was violently sick and fell into a wretched state that bore more than a little resemblance to what he was experiencing now.

"Norman, can you hear me? What are they saying

about when you can get out?" Carmella asked, concerned about her friend's temporary silence.

Norman was jolted out of his reverie. "The reality of my situation is very confusing," he said. "My bond's set at a hundred grand, and who's got that much money sitting around? If I'm lucky, my dad might pay for a bail bondsman to put it up but in the meantime, I'm playing the waiting game and wondering whether that's going to happen or not."

Norman stopped talking and put his head down between his knees for a couple of minutes. Then he sat back up and shook his head sadly before continuing.

"Talking with the old man is like the Inquisition, and he keeps threatening me by telling me that I have to go into residential rehab or he won't help me. He's bullying me, like always, but I haven't got anyone else who's willing to front the money and get me out of here."

"Do you have a lawyer?"

"Yes, my dad hired a lawyer but he hasn't been here and I don't know anything about what he's doing to help me. Like I'm going to get justice when I can't even talk with a lawyer. I want out of this shithole. My head feels all groggy and I don't even know why I'm here except that it has something to do with Jodi. The one thing I know is I was just trying to help her."

"You know she tried to commit suicide, don't you?"

"She did? She isn't dead, is she?" Norman asked, putting his hand flat on the glass as if he could touch Carmella.

Carmella could see the tracks of scar tissue that covered Norman's veins running up and down his arm. His hand shook uncontrollably. She put her hand on the glass directly across from his, trying to comfort him.

"No, but she's in a coma. I told the nurses at the hospital that I was her big sister and they let me see her. She looked so lifeless but the doctors are supposedly hopeful."

"How bizarre. Try to find out more if you can. I feel really, really bad for her but I'm too sick to think much about anything. I can't sleep. I need some meds but I can't get them here. I'm about ready to go crazy. I just want to get out of here. Hey, you'll remember to water my cactus plants, won't you?"

"Yes, I'm happy to do that for you. I'll go there later and water them." Carmella stopped talking when she heard a loud buzzer signaling that visitation time was growing short. "Is there anything else I can do for you?"

"Just help me get out of here." Norman started to sob like a baby.

"I don't know how to do that," Carmella sadly replied, trying not to become too emotional herself. "But if you can tell me what to do—"

She stopped talking when the buzzer rang again, signaling that visitation time was over. Carmella gazed silently through the glass at Norman, who appeared older than she had ever seen him look. A guard came in to escort him out of the room. Feeling frustrated, sad, and lonely all at the same time, she got up to leave.

As she walked out the door, she realized it wasn't fate that was to blame for Norman's current situation and his rotten mood, it was his addiction to drugs. As much as she wanted him to believe that she could have a relationship with him, and maybe even love him, she knew in her heart that she didn't really love him. She was angry with him. He was totally out of touch with her reality. Perhaps if he had asked her even one little question about her life or had shown some interest in her, she wouldn't feel so upset. But he hadn't. Not even once. He was only concerned about himself and his problems.

Later that evening across the Golden Gate, Carmella's fortunes appeared to take a turn for the better. As she gingerly walked up the steps toward Luna's apartment door, her energy was surging. She made a commitment not to let the recent events get her down, and even if she didn't have her dog, she had her new rock in her pocket that in some strange way gave her strength. She had tried to call Dylan to tell him about her recent visit with Norman but he hadn't answered her calls. Because he had talked to her about his challenges with his wife, she knew from their conversations that he was beginning to spend time with her again. She wondered if perhaps they were trying to repair their damaged relationship. She imagined that if Dylan were her man, she'd be a happy woman.

Knocking on Luna's door made Carmella feel hopeful—hopeful that she would find her dog, hopeful that she would stop being mad at Norman, and confident that taking this novel opportunity to speak with the authentic high priestess of a coven would polish off her nearly completed article called "The Revolving Wheel of a Sacred Circle."

To overcome her nervousness, she applauded herself for taking the initiative and calling Luna to ask her about the practical uses of magic and ritual in everyday modern society. As she waited outside the door, which was decorated with a garland made from woven oat straw, she mentally recounted meeting Luna on the bluff with Dylan, and the benefits of why she'd accepted an invitation to Luna's woman's empowerment ritual. But now, more than anything, she was happy for a distraction from her present turmoil.

When Luna met her at the door, she gave Carmella a big hug and invited her inside to her cozy living room. After offering her some mead, she began briefing her on what to expect while more women arrived. Luna wondered whether Carmella had any idea that she had received a special invitation to her normally closed-to-newcomers ritual to celebrate the goddess in all women. Sensing her lack of knowledge of the craft, she felt that she needed to give Carmella a basic introduction to witchcraft, and decided to proclaim to all the women who were gathering, "We'll be performing our ritual tonight to give thanks to Gaia for fertilizing the gardens of our lives. We'll also be invoking Artemis, the great goddess who is the protector of the feminine and the mystic arts. We'll call on her to bless us with her healing guidance as we do our work to benefit Mother Earth."

Luna looked at Carmella, and although directing her conversation toward her, spoke loudly enough for the assembled group of women to hear.

"My prayers to the Great Spirit of Light involve meditation, breathwork, and invocations. Often, before starting the ceremony, we chant together. Chanting is a way to synchronize everyone's energy with our magical intention. But before we begin, I don't want to overlook the real immediate needs of any person in this moment. Do any of you have a problem or situation that you would like to work on in our healing circle?"

Intrigued by the offer, Carmella spoke softly but directly, "I'm fighting going in and out of a fabulous pity party that I keep throwing for myself. Within the last week, I've lost my dog and my boyfriend."

Luna looked at Carmella's striking face and figure and thought that of all the problems the young woman standing in front of her would announce, losing a man would not be one she would have imagined. She shook her head and smiled at Carmella. "All I can say is look inward. How you handle the situation becomes the situation."

"What do you mean?" Carmella asked.

Luna became aware that she needed to divide her attention between all the women and not focus solely on Carmella. "I don't have the time to explain right now but if you think about it long enough, you'll figure it out," she replied before being interrupted by a woman who had just finished placing flowers on an altar that sat against the back wall of the long, rectangular room.

While putting on her sparkling crescent moon crown, the woman told Carmella, "Situations always change. You might want to use our circle to pray to the goddess that things change in your favor. Really though, most of us here feel sorry for you losing your dog. But as far as we're concerned, you can celebrate losing your man. Men want to use women and take control of their manna, their innate power. Seriously, you'll feel better once you realize that you can do just fine without that man in your life. In the past, we invited men to join in our rituals but time and time again, they get into their egos and forget the true work we're doing. We don't need men to tell us what lies hidden beyond the veil."

Her words were almost drowned out by the sound of the women applauding in agreement. Another woman giggled before she began to tell her story.

"You all know that we choose to be skyclad and take off our clothes for our rituals," she said. "More than once I've seen some man's penis rise as he walked near a pretty naked woman, even when we weren't doing sex magic. Strangely, I always find myself becoming embarrassed even though I'm one of the women in the circle who doesn't cause a rise in the passing lord of the circle. Men, without even trying, can be so crude and insensitive."

"It's not just men who are insensitive," Luna broke into the conversation. "My parents are the worst. I can give them a big share of the credit for why I don't have men at my rituals."

"Why?" several women asked.

"Earlier in my life," she continued, "my dad and mom had a key to my apartment. Once they let themselves into my place while I wasn't home, and a friend of mine who'd needed a place to stay was sleeping in my bed. He didn't let them know he was there and he overheard them talking about me. While they were going through all my stuff, checking to see if I had any drugs in the apartment, they had a conversation about whether I was a lesbian or not. They even said that if I wasn't gay, I was probably suppressing my latent tendencies and it would be better for me if I was queer because then they wouldn't have to worry about me getting pregnant. How's that for being sensitive?" Luna asked sarcastically. "When they finally strolled into my bedroom and found a man in my bed, my friend acted as though he had been sleeping the entire time and didn't hear what they said about me. But I decided to interpret their tactless conversation as a sign from the gods that it would be OK to let the world know that I prefer the smell of a woman to the stink of a man. Women are so much more attractive to me than men."

Carmella's eyes opened wide at Luna's comment.

"Are all the women who come to your rituals gay?" Carmella asked, starting to feel a little intimidated.

"Women are women. Gay or straight, they're always welcome at my rituals. Large or slim, young or old, we are all daughters of the goddess. What's important is that we come together as sisters and share our desire to honor the goddess. But what about you, Carmella? Have you ever made love to a woman?"

"Well, honestly, I'm a man's woman."

"That sounds limiting. Be honest, haven't you ever thought about making love to a woman?"

"Sure," said Carmella. "You've heard the song lyrics, 'I kissed a girl and I liked it,' haven't you? It's a hot song that makes me think about kissing girls but I've always had a boyfriend."

"Where is he? You said you 'lost' him," one of the other women asked.

Another woman also broke into the conversation. "Where's any man when you need him?"

Carmella was quick to reply, "Honestly, he's in jail and he's being so weird. I really don't know what's going on between us at this point. He's too stoned too much of the time and I feel betrayed by his connection with another girl. That's why I feel like I'm not really with him anymore."

"Sounds like he's a loser," said the woman who had been clearing the room to create space to make a circle.

"I've got a really good spell that will help you find your dog. Are you interested?" she asked.

Carmella was relieved at the change of subject. "Yes, of course," she replied.

"What's your dog's name?" the woman asked.

"Rambo."

"If you choose to do this spell, you must do it in the moonlight for it to work. First, you must focus your emotions and attune your energy with Rambo's. Let yourself express your feelings toward him, as if he were standing in front of you. Then, take Rambo's leash and tie it into a noose and wrap it around a hand-held mirror. Stick the mirror with the attached noose into the earth near the place where you last saw Rambo. That will help you locate your dog."

"I can add to that spell," another woman chimed in. "It's similar to making a voodoo doll in order to affect someone's energy. While chanting Rambo's name, visualize him having all the furiousness he needs to bite free from his situation. It might help to cut out a picture of a pit bull and place it where he sleeps. The cut-out image will cause Rambo, who is psychically connected to you and his bed, to feel the energy of what you are thinking and summon his inner pit bull for courage."

Luna added, "It won't take too long for you to get some sense of a response from the energy you put into these spells. If the goddess knows your intention is pure, the power of magic will bring fast results."

"Thank you so much," Carmella spoke from her heart, wondering if she could handle doing spells, yet happy to have some guidance on what she might do to find Rambo.

"We're glad to help you," Luna replied. "Everything will work out if you stay even-minded. And our ritual will work better if we take some time to think about what we're trying to accomplish with our energy. Doing a ritual with people who share a singular purpose is very powerful. Let's have a minute of silence to harness our healing forces and meditate on our group intention. Does someone have the Moon Tarot card to place on our altar?"

A chubby woman stepped forward. "I was planning on doing that before I got distracted by all the talk about magic spells to find a missing pet," she said. She walked to an ornate table covered with crystals of various sizes and shapes, and placed a large Rider-Waite Moon card in the center of the altar near a large silver pentacle sitting inside a crescent moon.

Another woman called out, "The Moon is our Mother. Magic, come alive!"

A few more women filtered in through the door and Carmella could feel the room filling with silent anticipation. She was becoming familiar with the expectation that she should remove her clothes for the ceremony, and knew when she saw the other women starting to disrobe that it was nearing the time for the ritual to begin.

"Who will take the lead to invoke the elements so we can amplify our power and shut out the negativity of the world?" Luna bellowed above the chatter while raising a dragon claw crystal wand above her head.

The woman with the crescent moon crown shouted loudly in a rhythmic cord, "Yod, He, Va, He, earth, air, fire, and water."

From the deepest part of her inner self, Carmella surrendered to the alluring voice of what she imagined could actually be the goddess herself. The circle of women felt so familiar that she wondered whether, in some past life, her spirit had participated in this ceremony many moons—or for that matter, many centuries—ago.

But even though she found this all very amazing, and good material for the article she was writing, she couldn't help but wonder whether it would really help her find Rambo.

Luna raised a jeweled goblet above her head, looked upward, and smiled as she affirmed to the group, "We are one, we are all! Look to your right, look to your left, and see the goddess! She is one, she is all. Isis, Demeter, Diana, Artemis, Persephone, Sophia, Athena, Freya, Yemana, Quan Yin, Tara, Brigit, Oshun, Lakshmi, Shakti, Bhavani, Devi, Durga, Kali..."

❦

That same night, while a tormented Norman was tossing and turning on a thin facsimile of a mattress shouting for a fix, and Carmella was chanting to the goddess, Dylan was softly awakened by Stella stroking his thighs.

"Dylan, love of my life, wake up," she whispered. "I have a present for you."

Dylan, who had just recently fallen into a deep sleep, stirred from the dream he was having of walking on the beach with Carmella when he heard Stella's soft voice and felt her warm, naked body. The lavender smell of her hair and the touch of fiery energy from her hands on his thighs jolted his body into unexpected wakefulness. "Stella! You've climbed in my bed for two days in a row. What's happening with you?"

"I want us to get back to how we were when we slept together in our bed and told each other before going to sleep every night that we loved one another," Stella murmured in his ear. "I can't stand being without you anymore, Dylan. I love you so very much." She started to gently nibble on his ear. Her hands slid to his legs and the way she rubbed him felt like matches lighting tinder for a fire.

Dylan's body couldn't ignore Stella's gentle touch. His body didn't care that he hadn't resolved the issue of what to do about their problematic marriage. Their bodies were talking to each other and his mental defenses drifted off with the fleeting clouds of the night sky. His passions were hungry and she was offering him a delicious feast.

Stella opened her lips so that her tongue could deliver a moist kiss on his neck. She started biting his skin ever so softly and continued tenderly kissing his bare chest. She knew what turned Dylan on in bed and she wasn't going to wait for him to tell her whether he was ready for her or not.

Chapter Nineteen

The Sun
The Unexpected

*A*fter the previous night with Dylan, Stella wasn't about to let him sleep late. She wasn't going to hold back her feelings. Maybe she could entice him into wanting to make love again. She knew that if she waited much longer, he would wake up and make some lame excuse about needing to go somewhere or do some alchemical thing to save the world. Even after several years of marriage, she wasn't sure about his self-proclaimed visits to other dimensions and wasn't even sure that she liked the part of Dylan that she called the "spirit walker." It seemed sane enough when he was talking about visiting other worlds but when she thought about it, it didn't quite fit in with her perception of reality.

For now, the best thing she could do was use her own form of magic and decide how to successfully continue yesterday's conversation. Summoning her courage, she walked down the hallway, pushed open the door to his room, and peeked inside.

"Dylan? Are you awake? It's time to wake up."

"Do I have to?" replied a sleep-deprived Dylan, who hid his head under the pillow.

Stella walked into his room and sat down on his bed. "No, of course not," she said, gently rubbing his back. "You can choose to sleep the day away but I can think of nicer things to do. Did you enjoy last night?"

Dylan rolled over and looked at his wife. "Yes, that was delicious," he answered, his body feeling a tingling contentment. He smiled as he realized that his dilemma of what direction to go with Stella had been happily resolved when their bodies had become one in heated ecstasy the previous night.

"Dylan, I want to talk with you about something important. I'm at a crossroads and I need you to hear me out. You agreed to marry me for better or worse, right?" Her voice sounded soft, shaky, and childlike.

Dylan jolted into concerned wakefulness when he heard her question. Even though the sweetness of her lavender scent made him want to move closer to her, he steadied himself. He could feel something intense coming. He wished he was still asleep and the present conversation was part of a dream from which he could awaken.

"Stella, I married you because we loved one another. For the past three months we've hardly spoken so we've already been weathering 'the worse.'"

"I need you to not judge me or think me to be a bad person when I tell you what I'm about to say."

Dylan sensed a tightening in his chest and his emotions immediately became heavy, but seeing the look of panic on Stella's face, he gently asked, "How can I be judgmental about you when you're deep in my heart?"

"Dylan, it's because you are the love of my life that

I want us to be together," Stella said.

Dylan could hear the angst in her voice. "Well, I'm happy to hear that since we're married. Before I fell asleep last night I was thinking about my love for you. Even when I felt like I wanted to die after you said you wanted to date someone new, I knew I wouldn't be hurting so damn much if I didn't love you. I didn't give up on us. I'm here with you now."

During the preceding months, Stella had closed the door on him emotionally so she could have her adventures, and in return, he had done the same. Now he was remembering those waves of discordant feelings and trying to put them out of his mind. He told himself to relax, breathe, and to be grateful for the present moment and the beautiful woman sitting on his bed.

Stella took his hand and placed it on her belly. "Dylan," she said, "I'm pregnant."

"This is a joke," Dylan said, yanking his hand away from her stomach.

Stella appeared to be afraid. "No, I'm serious," she whispered.

"How many months pregnant are you, for God's sake? Until last night, we hadn't slept together for three months," Dylan replied in a fiery burst of emotion.

"I'm not sure how pregnant I am, honestly," she answered.

Dylan sat up in bed and moved to create distance from her. "What do you mean, you're not sure? Who's the father of this baby, Stella?"

In her sweetest voice, she said, "Sweetie, I want you to be the father." Stella began to plead her case. "As much as you are my husband, and the ground beneath my feet, I'm counting on you to do what's right for us. It's only reasonable to have a child together."

Dylan's mind jumped to an unsettling conclusion as he questioned, "What do you mean, 'you want me to be the father'? Who is the father? How many months pregnant are you?"

Stella lowered her eyes. This conversation wasn't going as she had hoped. She wasn't sure whether she should just run out of the room or keep trying to talk to Dylan, who had a wild, crazed look on his face.

"Did you know you were pregnant when you made me apple pie? Why didn't you tell me yesterday when you crawled into bed with me?" Dylan asked.

Stella found herself aghast from the terror of her self-disclosure.

"I just found out that I was pregnant this morning. Dylan, please, I need you to hear me out. I want our relationship to work and I want us to have a family. You said you wouldn't judge me."

"OK, well...I'm not judging you. I'm happy for you," he quickly replied with a bitter tone of disdain. "It only makes sense that when we were talking yesterday you must have also been questioning whether you might be pregnant. And if you just found out today, that means you can't be very far along, and that also means I can't be the child's father. Didn't you think that I might want to be involved in the decision of having a child? Do you think I will happily go along with anything you ask of me just because you're pregnant?"

"Dylan, please don't go there. You just said that you love me. If you truly do, and you just said that you do, you can be my child's—*our* child's—father."

"Are you crazy? I can't be your child's father if we

haven't been sleeping together for the last three months," Dylan said, jumping out of bed and starting to get dressed.

"But, Dylan, please listen to me! We can look at this child as a gift from God and our love can continue to grow. Our relationship can become stronger than before."

Dylan felt sick to his stomach as he looked away. He didn't know what to think anymore. Stella was making his life very difficult and he felt his anger surge.

"Thanks for trusting me enough to share your thoughts with me. And for letting me know what you're planning for *our* future," he said sarcastically. "Maybe I'll think differently after I have some time to think about this but right now, I don't see myself jumping into the role of being the father to another man's child. How can you so easily forget that you recently kicked me out of your life to run off with someone else? And now you expect me to simply overlook the pain you've caused me—and that you're causing me this very instant? I can't believe that last night I was thinking we could renew our love and make our relationship work, and this morning you're asking me to be the father to a child that isn't even mine. If this is the outcome of your foolish choices, what can I expect from you next?"

"Dylan, have faith in our relationship. You said you would love me for better or worse. I've always been honest with you. I'm sorry that I hurt you. I didn't realize you would get so upset. Truly, I only slept with someone else one time. It was an experiment that turned into a mistake and it didn't mean anything."

"I'm glad you're able to clear your conscience and

get your thoughts out in the open, Stella. And thanks for not lying."

Dylan couldn't put his clothes on fast enough. He ran out of his room, wanting nothing more than to be away from Stella. He couldn't believe the nightmare he was living. He left the apartment, slamming the door on his way out. As he walked down the stairs, his heart felt so heavy that it felt like it had dropped into a pit of misery. The fog in his mind loomed overhead like a blanket of doom as he walked down the sidewalk toward his car. He wanted to drive away, to flee his tortured emotions in hopes of finding some remnant of his departed sanity.

Stella sat as if paralyzed on Dylan's bed. Why hadn't her love spell worked? After paying the reputed real-deal bruja Naomi so much money, and lighting so many candles that she almost burned down her home while making the magic apple pie, she had expected Dylan's love to withstand this test of their commitment. As her assurance of Dylan's positive response waned, beads of sweat streamed down her face and her body began to shake.

Dylan didn't care what Stella was thinking. He wished he was on a sun-drenched island far, far away from the windy San Francisco Bay. Once in his car, he kicked over the engine, pulled out from the curb, and drove down the street like a reckless race-car driver. Sadly, he realized that he had lost all faith in Stella. How could he continue to allow himself to be manipulated by her painful choices for his future? He needed to make a change and would start making plans to walk off the stage of this drama in which he no longer saw himself playing a part.

Perhaps right now, if he focused on someone else's

problems, he could forget about his own. Remembering the touching poem Jodi had written him, he decided that once he got to the beach and could clear his mind, it would be a good time to use his Reiki skills and do a long-distance healing for her. As for his own healing, that would have to wait.

With every city block he drove past on the way to the ocean, he repeatedly told himself to breathe deeply and release his emotional stress. Once he got to the long stretch of beach that bordered the western edge of San Francisco, he parked and quietly willed himself not to cry. Trying to steady his shaken nerves, he made a vow to never let Stella make him feel this way again. And he had to stop feeling upset that Lisa hadn't called. Why was he being so stupid, to think that Lisa would be kind enough to say she was sorry for what had happened the other night?

He rolled down the car window to smell the fresh, salty air and tried to put his problems out of his mind. He needed to clear his head in order to do Jodi's long-distance healing. Jodi hadn't placed any demands on him at all, and knowing how her innocence had been victimized, she was one person who truly deserved help. She had always been straightforward with him and he respected that. It was a perfect opportunity to do an act of random kindness and use his energy to send Jodi a spiritual stream of healing energy.

After going into a concentrative meditation, he sat inwardly still and focused on sending healing thoughts and prayers to Jodi. Psychically, he envisioned sending angels of light to surround her with love and health-giving, ultraviolet rays of illumination to regenerate her ability to heal. But just as he was getting deeply into it, his phone rang and interrupted his train of thought. He saw from the caller ID display that it was Destiny. As soon as she spoke he could hear a tone of intense panic in her voice.

"I've talked with my dad about you coming over to visit with Angel," Destiny told him. "At first, he said no but then I told him that one time you rescued some woman who had been practicing Lobsang Rama's astral traveling techniques and had gotten stuck in the fourth dimension. You brought her back from near death. And if you could do that for a stranger, I'm sure you can help my sister, who's almost like your family. I need to warn you, though, that my dad said Angel isn't in her physical body and the ghoul inhabiting it is dangerously vicious. She's growling like a mad dog and trying to tear apart anyone who comes near her. Do you think you can help her?"

Dylan left the healing vibrations for Jodi to travel on their own for the moment. He was glad to do everything he could to take his mind away from his own problems, and often he felt more at home diving into the spirit realm than walking into his own apartment. It was one place he could get away from the worldly cares and complexities of his own life.

"Yes, I think I might be able to help her," he replied, wondering what had triggered her possession.

"Do you have time to visit with her today?" Destiny asked. "The sooner you can help, the better."

"Yes. I've got some free time and will be happy to try to help her. Are you going to be at your dad's house? I'll feel better around him if you're there too."

"Yes, I can be there. What time is good for you?"

"Can we meet there after lunch, around 1:30? I don't like involving myself in dark spirit activities on an empty stomach. I need physical strength to be as grounded as much as I can be to shut out the hubbub of logic."

He heard her grateful sigh. "Thank you ever so much, Dylan. I feel better just knowing that you're willing to help. I'll plan to arrive at my dad's before you get there."

Dylan ended the call and looked out the car window at the gray clouds floating by. *How much of what is happening with Angel is fact and how much is fiction?* he wondered while watching the surfers ride the waves. Then he returned his attention to sending healing energy to Jodi.

Before he left the beach to get some lunch, Dylan decided he wanted—or rather, *needed*—to pull a Tarot card and find out if the fates would offer any good advice. Without hesitation, he picked up his cell phone and called Carmella. Realizing that she was the last person who had made his heart smile, he felt relieved to hear her voice again.

"Carmella, will you do me a favor and pull a Tarot card for me? I just need a quick, one-card reading to help me understand what kind of joke the gods are playing on me."

"Dylan, are you OK? You sound a little shaky."

"I'm a little more stressed than normal but I'm OK," Dylan said, not wanting her to know how shredded and vulnerable he was feeling.

"Sure. I'll pull a card for you," Carmella answered. "Do you want to ask me a question?"

"No. Just pull one card for me."

"OK. I'm shuffling my cards right now," she told him. "Tell me when to stop shuffling and I'll pull the top card in the deck to represent what's happening with you."

Dylan closed his eyes and envisioned the spectrum of recent events in his life. When he thought about everything he had recently gone through, he felt lucky his head didn't explode. Was this really a good time to visit with Angel, who could be in seriously deep waters? Switching subjects, he tried to focus on Stella, then Lisa, then Angel, then his present commitment to make a change in his life. He imagined Carmella holding the cards.

"OK, stop shuffling and pull my card," he said.

"It's the Sun card. It indicates that positive vibrations will clear the storms of life and attachments to painful past memories. Whatever you're doing will turn out to be OK. Visualize yourself being healed by the radiance of the sun. Get in touch with a sunny attitude to adapt to evolving circumstances."

"Yes, you're right. Even though I'm not feeling very sunny, I need to be more in touch with positive energy…and I need to spend more time doing my magical work to connect with the invisible healing masters."

"Are you OK?" she asked again.

Without revealing his circumstance, Dylan replied, "I don't know but I appreciate your time and support, that's for sure."

"Do you want to come over?"

Dylan was silent for a minute before he replied. "If you want company, I think I'll be free tonight. I can call later to let you know what's happening. This afternoon I'm going to see if I can help a friend who I'm told is possessed."

"That sounds scary. How do you work with that?" Carmella asked.

"You just do it and see what happens."

"Oh, really? That makes me a little nervous. But since I pulled the Sun card for you and it symbolizes success, I won't worry. Please be careful and give me a call when you can to let me know how everything went and when you can come over. Bye, Dylan. And good luck!"

"Bye." He turned off his cell phone and started his engine. He was ready to find something to eat, then go over to Taylor's to meet with Angel and the spirit that had possessed her.

Chapter Twenty

Judgment
An Alternate Reality

Dylan was lost in his thoughts when Destiny opened Taylor's front door and greeted him. She looked like she had been crying. Dylan gave her a quick hug as he walked in, then his eyes settled on the pitiful sight of Taylor. The man was slouched over a table pouring himself a shot of rum. He was obviously in the middle of a disagreement with Destiny, and when he spoke, his words were slurred.

"We're not going to call 911! Just forget that stupid idea. Besides, your old boyfriend is here to save the day. Right, Dylan?" Taylor said sarcastically, looking at him with a crooked half-smile.

"Yes, sir," Dylan said respectfully to his old nemesis, remembering how much time they'd spent in the past arguing about the future of his dead relationship with Destiny.

In his present state, Taylor seemed less like the stubborn, bull-headed Taurus that Dylan knew him to be and more like a worn-down circus clown pretending to stay calm while losing control of untamed forces in the animal ring. *What a strange transformation*, Dylan thought, wondering if he would still have to endure the interrogations that were a typical part of Taylor's communications.

"I'm here because Destiny asked me to check on Angel," Dylan continued. He knew that in the past, Taylor had spread nasty rumors in the community about his manhood after he broke up with his daughter. Dylan had made a point of not being in the same room as Taylor ever since. Even now, Dylan didn't feel comfortable standing in front of him.

"I know why you're here," Taylor said spitting out his words. "You don't have to act so formal. I'm impressed that you've volunteered to help. Hopefully, the stories I've heard about how you can exorcize spirits are true. Your skills will need to be sharp if you're going to help our Angel."

Dylan tried not to respond to the intimidating look in Taylor's eyes or the dread he sensed in his words. He looked at Destiny, who was now wringing her hands with despair.

"Where's your sister?" he asked her. "Is she doing any better?"

"I'll let you make your own judgment call when you see her," Destiny responded, exhaling loudly.

"OK," Dylan answered, trying to diminish his growing sense of alarm. "Taylor, it's better for you to stay here. I'll let Destiny take me to see Angel. I know you're concerned about her but when I'm talking to her, I need the energy around her to be undisturbed so that I can do an unbiased reading of what's going on."

"*The energy around her to be undisturbed,*" Taylor mocked. "You're in for a big surprise, little man. I thought you had experience with possessions. How can you possibly think that the energy around her is undisturbed?"

Dylan held himself back from responding to Taylor's insult. He nodded and quietly said, "OK, I get your point but for now, I need you to trust me enough to be alone with her."

Destiny wanted to avoid any further banter between the two men. She hadn't forgotten how they could both argue endlessly about nothing, trying to prove who was smart enough to speak the last clever word, and she didn't want to waste a moment on a senseless power struggle.

"Dylan," she said, "let's go. I'll take you to Angel's room. Dad, you can wait here for us. If we need you, I'll call you."

Destiny led Dylan down the hall to Angel's bed-room.

"Do you need anything before I unlock the door?"

"No, I'm fine," Dylan answered. "Just don't act nervous once we're in the room with her. That's the worst thing either of us can do." He braced himself for the worst and steadied his nerves in an attempt to override his rising impulse to go in the opposite direc-tion.

After Destiny unlocked the door, he slowly pushed it open and peeked inside the dimly lit room.

"OK, let's go see your sister," he breathed.

Dylan went inside first and Destiny followed. There was an unpleasant odor that couldn't be masked by the cedar incense that was burning somewhere inside. Dylan looked around the room, which had been torn apart from floor to ceiling. It appeared as if a pack of jackals had run through it in a chaotic rampage. Uneaten dishes of food lay scattered everywhere. Shredded and soiled bedclothes lay in a tangled mess on the floor entwined in the cord of a shattered lamp.

Angel's head was at the foot of the bed covered in vomit and her hair looked like a matted nest. Dylan knew that Angel sensed their presence because she jumped up on the bed and began urinating on the torn mattress. Seconds later, Angel lunged at Dylan but he deftly moved out of her way and she fell to the floor, wailing as if someone was stabbing her.

Dylan quickly moved behind Angel, whose nose was now bleeding from the impact with the floor. He grabbed her arms from behind while she was disoriented from her fall, turned her, and threw her back up onto the mattress.

"Do you want to fuck me?" Angel snarled.

"No, Angel. Try not to move," Dylan commanded, his adrenaline surging. "Just stay in bed. We'll be leaving and won't bother you anymore."

Angel hissed and then spat at Dylan. She turned to Destiny and said with a smirk, "Sister, pretty sister, do you want to get in bed with me? We can cuddle together and I'll make you feel so fine."

Dylan reached for Destiny's shaking hand and pulled her toward the door. "Don't answer her. Let's go. We can't do anything for her right now."

"I love you, Angel," Destiny whimpered as Dylan pulled her from the room.

Once outside, Dylan closed the door, looked at Destiny, and held her close to stop her from trembling. "It will be OK. Don't worry. That's not really your sister in there," Dylan said, trying to reassure her.

Destiny spoke through her tears. "How is any of this going to be OK? Did you see what was going on in that room? She scares me!"

"Listen to me. Don't give any energy to that ghoul by reacting so strongly. Obviously, it wants to tear everyone apart and it will do a good job of it if you give it any power. You must appear strong, calm, and self-controlled when you go into Angel's room," Dylan asserted.

"That sounds easy when you say it but I've been in that room enough to know that I can't be calm, cool, and collected when I'm in there," Destiny answered.

Dylan noticed her fingers trembling as she relocked the double bolt on Angel's door.

"OK, OK. Just do your best." Dylan stepped back to breathe some fresh air. "If I'm going to visit Angel, it's not going to be in her room. Right now, I need to go somewhere quiet where I can be undisturbed for a short while. Then I can astral travel to find Angel and find out what is happening to her from another dimension." He consciously slowed his breathing as the first step in calming his mind to prepare for going into an altered state of consciousness.

Destiny took his hand and led him down the hall to her old bedroom, which had been transformed into an office. The door was wide open, welcoming them into a normal world. Dylan sat down in a comfortable chair and smiled, remembering their youthful romance and the memories of their past lovemaking, which soon became as visible as the paintings on the wall. He looked at Destiny, who was still upset.

"You've got to leave me in here by myself," he told her. "I need to be alone. Completely alone. I'm going to go into a trance and I don't want you watching and worrying about me. If I'm going to help your sister, you and your dad can't bother me while I'm in here.

Promise me that once you leave this room, you won't open the door until I say it's OK."

"Are you sure about what you're doing?" Destiny questioned with a note of alarm.

"No guarantees. I'm going to try to contact your sister from within the astral plane. I'm not sure what will happen but if she was astral traveling when this happened, her spirit has to be out flying around somewhere. I might be able to find her." Dylan gestured toward the door. "And you promise not to open the closed door, right?"

"Yes, I promise not to disturb you as long as you come out of this room before it gets too late."

"OK, fair enough. Now, go." He watched Destiny slip out of the room like a gentle wind and close the door behind her.

Dylan lit a candle on the desk. He stood up, shook the tension out of his body, then sat back down on the soft cushioned chair and closed his eyes. He started humming. His humming turned into a chant that was as low and quiet as the murmur of a well-oiled wheel spinning down the highway. His magical sound grew louder and louder until it was like a beating drum. Then he was silent.

In the total quiet, all Dylan could hear was his breath going in and out, in and out. His mind slowed, going deeper and deeper into inner space. From within his mind, he saw his subtle body rise and float above him. His inner spirit began to speak.

"I call on St. Germaine; Michael the Archangel; Thoth the Mighty; Mercury, bearer of the Caduceus; and all the other healing masters to accompany me on my journey. Soul of my soul, fire of my mind, beating heart of the seventh ray, answer my prayers, hear my chants, protect my spirit, and merge our collective dreams to raise God's window for Angel's healing. Let my spirit be a channel for your work."

Dylan felt energy rushing through him. He heard a voice calling somewhere in deep space, beyond the threshold of time.

"Call on your soul guide to help you find her," the voice said.

Dylan felt his spirit detach from his body and float away, still tied to an umbilical cord of light attached to his body. He started to fly through the clouds of mist in the inner heavens, in a space without time. He felt himself being lifted by a magnetic force that he was powerless to resist, and his spirit soared in spirals through cosmic windstorms. His movement suddenly came to a halt. He was without control over his own motion. He dropped downward until he landed on a soft, receptive, surging wave of solid matter. He opened his eyes wide to look through the pervasive, unfamiliar hues of light.

In the distance, sand dunes glimmered. Were they near or were they far? Mesmerized by their beauty, he couldn't tell whether they were a mirage or real.

Just looking at the fluorescent sun, which glistened like volcanic fire, made Dylan feel parched but he couldn't take time to think about that. Pulled solely by the will of his stubborn determination, he began searching for Angel, knowing that the longer he lingered in this peculiar place, the more difficult it would be to locate her. He called out to her in the echoing emptiness. He scanned the distance but the sand dissolved and mysteriously reappeared in a more distant place, leaving him disoriented. He willed himself to continue his search but as he went along, he realized he was in an endless maze of shifting, cliff-like sandbanks and his hope began to dwindle.

Again, his eyes swept the horizon, searching the volatile dunes that appeared and disappeared in the blink of an eye. He refocused his vision and summoned his courage to move forward. The ubiquitous, ethereal heat that moved within the multihued clouds of his dream-like state made him sweat until he was drenched. He saw shadows in veiled shapes dancing in the otherworldly desert landscape. These shadows took the seductive forms of Lisa and Stella, and Dylan watched them play their parts in the drama of his life.

Dylan remembered his promise to find Angel but at this dreary moment, his aloneness in this godforsaken place seemed foreboding. His heart ached from an overwhelming sense of betrayal by these two women he had trusted with his love. In his mind, he could see Lisa's face laughing at him, which made his heart beat in a rhythmic madness that drove his consciousness toward the point of snapping. He screamed in anguish, his cries echoing through endless chambers in his mind, making him even more aware of being lost in an unfamiliar astral space. He wasn't sure whether he was going forward or backward or standing still, and he desperately needed water to quench his thirst.

As if his scream had swung open a new doorway in his altered awareness, he saw Angel standing in the near distance, confined in a circular ring of molten fire. His hopes soared. Renewed by the sight of her, he quickened his steps to reach her but suddenly she seemed much farther away. What was that looming shadow that stood near her? The moments that it took to reach her seemed like hours, making him more conscious of the burning heat enshrouding him.

From somewhere in the distance he heard devious laughter.

"She is mine," a voice thundered all around him. "My sweet innocent belongs to me and me alone!"

Dylan refused to acknowledge the bellowing voice. He knew better than to activate a power struggle with an invisible force. With an intensified sense of urgency, he held on to the purpose of his quest and willed his spirit to move forward.

Light conquers darkness, he repeated over and over in his mind as he sensed that he was trespassing in an unknown predator's domain.

After what seemed an eternity, Dylan moved through the illusion and delusion of superficial space to reach Angel, who was now chained to a stake buried deep within a mountain of metallic stone. Using his hands as a tool, he began pulling on the chain, attempting to remove it from her wrist.

"Angel, what happened? Who did this to you?" he asked her.

"I don't know," Angel responded. "The last thing I remember is taking part in dad's ritual and starting to astral travel. Then I saw these large, red, slanted eyes. Soon I was immobilized and tied with these heavy chains. Dylan, I'm so afraid. Can you get me out of here?" Angel pleaded.

"Yes," Dylan replied, "but you must free your mind from your fear. Completely ignore every command from whoever has been speaking to you. You must be strong-willed to free yourself from this subterranean plane. I'm certain that we must be in the lower astral planes where inharmonic forces fight to reign. If you give your power to dark forces, they will use it against you. Don't let them have your power and they won't have it to use."

Angel started crying. "I don't know how I arrived here or how long I've been here, and I don't know how to set myself free. How do I keep my power when this force already took it?"

"We don't have time to waste talking. You have to trust me—" Dylan started to say, but was startled into silence by the sound of rattling chains coming from behind Angel. He jumped back as he heard a high-pitched screech that echoed in reverberating circles and penetrated the rational walls of his sanity.

A bodiless voice began to speak. "And what do you think *you're* doing? No one invited you here. Innocent pure is staying with me. I've seen enough of you in Norman's parking lot to know I don't like you and right now, I'm not the least bit amused. However, since you've crossed over to my side of reality, I might as well make your visit useful. Perhaps you won't mind letting me eat your heart for dinner. Your poor, betrayed, worthless heart."

If the situation wasn't already strange enough, Dylan might have been taken aback at facing the Seega head-on. He already knew that between the extreme heat in this place and the chains molded to Angel's wrist, they were both in severe danger. But knowing that he faced a powerful threat, his mind went into survival mode.

"You don't scare me," he replied, willing his voice to sound calm. "This is the inner plane and the experience of reality is only a delusion. You're not really of this moment."

"Oh, really?" the voice answered. "Then experience this reality, you dimwit."

Immediately, Dylan felt himself being lifted into

the air, turned upside down, and shaken like a rattle. He started to scream from a pressure inside his head that made his mind want to explode. Then he heard the shattering of glass and felt a glass-like shard penetrate his heart. Dylan gasped from the pain and frantically tried to free himself but the Seega's grip became tighter and tighter, intensifying the pain.

"Put me down!" Dylan yelled as he pulled his torso upward and started punching the invisible hands that held his ankles.

Suddenly, the colors of the surrounding mists changed. In an instant, the extreme heat cooled and Dylan felt his spirit being gently lifted and placed next to Angel. A commanding feminine voice spoke to him.

"OK Dylan, do what you need to do....and get the two of you out of here," the voice told him.

Dylan could hardly believe it. It sounded like, of all people...Jodi!

"Is that you, Jodi? It can't be you."

"Why can't it? I heard you screaming. At first, I thought the sound was coming from hell and I was having a bad dream but then I recognized your voice. I started looking for you and you quickly came into view. I knew you needed help so I came to help you deal with the spook. But you obviously shouldn't be here." Jodi spoke with a strong tone of authority. "In this place, nothing is predictable and the hot wind never goes away."

"I need to free Angel so she can go home," Dylan announced, trying to see Jodi's form in the mists surrounding them.

"It looks like you gave your power over to the spook you saw in Norman's driveway. Anyway, he's not as bad as he wants you to believe. He enjoys giving you a hard time. Since I've been here a while, I've had some time to figure out how to deal with his ghoulish outbursts and we've become friends. You know I don't put up with shit from anyone and I didn't let any headless spook tell me what to do either. His name isn't Seega. He likes to be called Zakar or Zak for short. You clearly haven't had as much magical training as you make out, or you would have been controlling Zak instead of him controlling you. I always suspected you were just full of hot air. Anyway, now is a good time to take your friend and make your way out of this timeless warp. You can't exist here for too long without it getting the best of you."

"But what about you, Jodi?" Dylan asked. "Can't we all get out of here, the three of us? And I don't know how to free Angel. Can you help undo those etheric chains?"

"Easy said and easy done. It's mind over matter. I thought you knew that. You need me to tell you how to work in the astral planes? This is hysterical!" Jodi laughed.

"It's not funny," Angel yelled. "Please get me out of these chains!"

"Yeah, yeah, I know it's not funny," the voice of Jodi said. "OK. On the count of three, I want to see your hands hanging free. On the count of three, your chains are gone!" Jodi ordered.

As invisible Jodi spoke, Dylan began to see the transparency of her thoughts turn into astral actions. He saw Angel's chains dissolve and turn into butterflies. He sighed with relief. He had just witnessed an imprisoned soul being miraculously released from bondage.

"Jodi," he said quickly, "if we can leave, so can you.

Come back with us."

"I don't think so. Except for occasional swarms of black holes, I like it here just fine. By the way, the spirit that's moved into Angel's physical body and is now living in her bedroom murdered children when he was alive. He's one mean bastard. He makes Zak, who captured her astral body, look like a saint in comparison. You have to make him leave her body or she'll be vulnerable to his possession forever," Jodi warned.

Dylan couldn't believe that Jodi was so knowledgeable.

"Thanks for telling us all of this. And you need to come back too," he repeated.

"I don't have anywhere to go," Jodi answered.

Dylan felt Angel move close to him.

"My hands are free! Jodi, you've rescued me!" Angel said into the ether. "You're welcome to stay with me. We have an extra room in my home. You don't want to stay here. Please come with us. We can hang out together."

"That's a nice thought. But I don't want to leave this world. And you need to hurry and get rid of the spook who is haunting your body," Jodi advised.

Dylan moved to where he could feel Jodi's electric heat. From his heart, he sent a telepathic thought telling her spirit that he would do whatever he could to help her.

"Stop sending those thoughts. You know I can hear them," Jodi replied boldly.

Dylan wanted her to know that he cared. "You've got to come back. You don't want to leave your body half-dead with cords plugged into your arms while you lay in a cold hospital room."

"No matter what you say to me, I'll do what I want," she answered.

"Yes, I know. I just want you to know that it's important to leave this place of shadows and illusions," Dylan said, rubbing his chest where not too long ago it felt like it had been pierced.

"I'll think about it," Jodi replied as her voice got fainter and fainter, until Dylan could no longer hear it.

"Jodi...Jodi, are you still here?" Dylan cried.

"Where did she go?" Angel asked.

"I don't know but what I do know is that you and I need to leave. We've got to get back and you have to be strong enough to force the entity to leave your body. Your body belongs to you. Even your DNA will help you reclaim it. You need to keep pulling your astral umbilical cord. As you start pulling on it, keep chanting for God's grace to help you move back into the center of your body."

"Aren't you going to help me?" Angel asked, sounding unsure.

Dylan knew that if they were going to be able to leave, he needed to open her mind to using its innate power and to summon the strength of her inner spirit. He spoke silently through his intuitive voice with a gentle, yet dominating tone. *If we keep in fear, it weakens our spirit and diminishes the power of our thought-forms. Whatever we think expands, so you need to see your strength. You don't have to let the negative play out in your life. And I'll help you even if I have to engage in telepathic Aikido.*

"Well," Angel said, "I want to go home and I want my body back."

"Yes, we both need to go home," Dylan answered as he began to chant his protective mantra.

He reached out to touch Angel's hand and together they floated through a spiraling universe toward home. Soon their astral bodies were hovering over Angel's bruised, unkempt, and misshapen physical form.

"It's time to reenter," Dylan reassured Angel. "Remember, I'll be helping you rid the entity from above your body. Don't give in to fear. Ask your guides to manifest love and healing and tell the entity to go to the Light."

Dylan watched Angel's spirit hover motionless for a few minutes, then dive toward her physical form. From where he was positioned, he drew an imaginary Star of David in the air and used it like a fly fisherman casting his fishing line. Soon the six-pointed star was being used like a hook to catch the darkness and yank the entity out of its new home. Beady, red, slanted eyes of fire floated from Angel's body and slowly rose to look Dylan directly in the eyes. Dylan psychically drew back and used his finger to draw an aerial image of a Celtic knotted dragon. Instantly, the entity dissolved in the air and Dylan could hear it screaming angrily as it drifted farther and farther away.

He looked down from above and watched Angel's physical body transform from hard and rigid to soft, supple peacefulness. Once he knew Angel was safe and back in her body, Dylan willed his astral spirit to go down the hall and return to his own physical body.

"Anyone in there?" he yelled to his body before diving into its welcoming form.

∽

Dylan woke up to Destiny and Taylor standing

over him, covering him with blankets.

"Dylan, are you all right?" Destiny asked with obvious concern.

"Breathe, Dylan, come on, breathe deep, come back to us," Taylor chanted.

"What happened?" Dylan asked, coming out of his sleep-like haze.

"Well, it looks like you went to the Illuminati's playground," Taylor answered. "What a trip you must have been on. The mirrors in our house were breaking and you were screaming so loud that I thought the neighbors would be calling the police. We came into the room and your body was frozen like ice."

"Wow," Dylan said, squirming under the blankets. "There're enough blankets on me now to cook me to death. You need to go check on Angel," Dylan sputtered, trying to get his mind back into earthly time and space. "She didn't know her way out of the fourth dimension so I had to show her the way. She's back in her body now."

Destiny and Taylor looked at each other, then ran out of the room, leaving Dylan to take care of himself. Trying to steady himself, Dylan sat up and looked around. He shuddered when he saw a shattered mirror and took a deep breath. Doubts about his recent sojourn flooded his mind and he started to worry about Angel. Just then, down the hall, he heard Destiny and Taylor talking excitedly with Angel. Dylan relaxed as it became more and more apparent that Angel had safely returned. *A happy family reunion,* he thought, not wanting to intrude.

Although he felt groggy, he happily remembered his commitment to call Carmella. Willing his mind to jump back into normal reality, he slowly pulled his cell phone out of his pocket to dial her number.

"Carmella, do you still want company tonight?" Dylan asked when she answered the phone.

"Yes, I'd love for you to come over," Carmella told him. "But I've got to tell you, Norman's father bailed him out of jail and he's coming here tonight." Her voice was filled with uncertainty. "I'd really like you to be here to give me some support. When I last saw him in jail, he was acting strange."

"He can't be acting any more strange than the people I've talked with lately," Dylan said with a laugh. "I have a lot to tell you. If you want my company, I'll be happy to come over."

"Good! I'll order some North Beach Pizza for our dinner. See you soon," Carmella replied enthusiastically.

Chapter Twenty-One

The World
Magic and Mayhem

*A*s Dylan drove across town, he could hardly believe it was still daylight. His mind was occupied with the shadows of darkness he had recently encountered during his sojourn into the astral planes and he had completely lost all awareness of time. His most immediate reminder that it would soon be evening was his stomach growling. Thank goodness Carmella had invited him for pizza. His favorite! Happily, he drove across town, relieved that he had found Angel even though she had been trapped in a fiery well of negativity in the astral planes. And even now the gods were obviously looking out for him, as he had no trouble finding a parking place on Green Street. His car fit perfectly in the space right in front of Carmella's apartment building with several inches to spare. He turned off the motor, looked at himself in the rearview mirror, and tried to smooth his wild-looking hair. Before opening his door, he took a deep breath and mentally released the stress that had accumulated earlier in the day. Diving into his inner calmness, he felt the cool ocean air revive his senses as he stepped out onto the curb and began the short walk to Carmella's.

Knocking on her apartment door felt strangely comforting, as if he was going to be united with a long-lost friend. Even before she opened the door, Dylan intuited her sense of welcome.

"Hi," Carmella said, opening the door. "I'm so glad you're here. Come on in. The pizza just arrived. Norman's already here."

Dylan walked into the living room and couldn't believe his eyes. Norman was sitting on the couch in a near fetal position, sucking on his bong as if he were a baby with a bottle.

"Hey, buddy," Norman said, blowing puffs of smoke through a crooked smile. "It's been a while since I've heard from you. Looks like you and Carmella have been getting along pretty well."

Dylan tried to sound nonchalant. "Life keeps going on, even when you're in the pokey," he told Norman. "I've been working really hard today and luckily Carmella invited me for dinner. She told me you'd be here. I hope I'm not disturbing your plans."

"Heck no, you're not in my way. Not now, anyway. I just stopped by on my way downtown. I've got to get something to help with my headaches before my old man makes me go to rehab again. So, I've got my man in the Tenderloin picking me up a 'prescription' of my favorite drugs. Once he calls to let me know that he's got what I want, I'm out of here."

"Dylan, have a seat," Carmella suggested, giving him a welcoming look.

"Thanks. I hope you don't mind that I didn't pick up anything to help with dinner. I'm so spaced out." He sensed something different in the tone of her voice and looked deeply into Carmella's eyes.

"What?" Norman said gruffly. "Don't you two sound lovey-dovey? I'm locked out of sight for a week and you two have become best friends."

"Norman, you're out of line," Carmella said with a frown.

"Oh, really? And now you're even talking for him. Something smells like dead fish around here."

"Norman, you're acting paranoid," Dylan said defensively. "Maybe you can thank Carmella for making us dinner instead of insulting her with your insinuations."

"And maybe you're full of shit. I may be a stoner but I'm not blind."

"Nothing's going on between us," Carmella replied with fire in her voice. "We're becoming better friends. But to keep our communication channels clear, I need to tell you that whoever I invite to my home is my concern, not yours."

"I don't need to listen to this bull crap," Norman spat. "I've got better things to do. I'm getting out of here to do what's really important. Besides, I don't have time to socialize. I've got business to take care of."

"Norman, what about the charges against you?" Dylan asked, trying to stay calm and undisturbed by Norman's aggressive words. "If you get caught buying drugs, you're going to have bigger problems to deal with."

"Don't worry, buddy," Norman said coyly. "I'll beat any drug-related charges. And this Jodi mess is on hold. I've been told that she could come out of her coma at any time and when that happens, I'll be free from charges of her endangerment. Besides, I know that her old pimp is still looking for her to get back some of the investment he put into building her career. I can prove that Jodi ain't so innocent. She's a hooker!"

Dylan tightened his arms and clenched his teeth to hold his emotions in check. He felt like grabbing Norman by the neck but he willed his body not to move and remained motionless.

"OK, if you've got to go and get your drugs, then just leave," Carmella said with obvious disgust. "I can't handle that you're fresh out of jail and you're in my home calling your buddies to get you high."

"Aren't you sweet? I get the message. I guess you won't want to be getting high with me later on tonight, right?" Norman replied, visibly annoyed.

"No, I don't want to be getting high with you and you shouldn't be getting high either. Your drug habit makes you look like you're sinking in quicksand."

"OK, *Mom*. You and Dad have a good night watching the telly and eating pizza. I'm going out to have some fun," Norman said sourly as he got up and went to the door. "Bye, my friends. I'll catch ya soon but not too soon," he said as he walked out and slammed the door behind him.

"Dylan, are you all right?" Carmella asked.

Dylan realized that he had been holding his breath and loudly exhaled. "Don't worry about me. I've got more important things to worry about than Norman." He smiled. "Like, when can I have some pizza?" He'd had enough stress that afternoon to last him a long time. He was more than ready to focus on something lighthearted.

Carmella returned his smile. She grabbed Dylan's hand and pulled him along with her to the kitchen, where the table was already set.

"You must be psychic. You set the table for two."

"I had a strange feeling we would be the only two people sitting down for dinner. I just knew."

"Well, next time I'm not sure what might happen I'll call you to get your intuitive scoop," Dylan said as he pulled out a chair and sat down. "If you're still looking for work, you can call a psychic hotline and ask if they need any extra help."

"You're funny. But it's been so stressful lately that I would like to pull a card right now. Let's ask the Tarot muses about our fate. We can just pull one card." Carmella pulled out her deck of cards from an antique chest sitting next to the table and fanned them out face-down. "OK, Dylan, pick one card to represent our future direction."

Smiling, Dylan closed his eyes and let his hand float over her cards until he felt intuitively drawn to pick one. After pulling it from her deck, he looked to see the name of the card he had chosen.

"It's the World card," he said. "Crowley calls it the Universe, the birth of the daughter of Babylon, 'the Virgin of Eternity.'" He studied the picture for a moment before handing it to Carmella.

"You sound as if you're reading from Crowley's *Book of Thoth*," Carmella said as she gathered the cards together and put them away. "But if I look at the card in relation to what's happening now, I see it as a sign to trust in the richness of life. Let's hope it means that we'll find resolutions to our challenges. That would surely be good." She turned back to Dylan. "By the way, can you tell me what happened to you this afternoon?"

"I had to take a little trip into the astral planes. A longtime friend had been separated from her body by a phantom who had moved into it while she was out and about flying around in her astral form. I had no recourse except to dive into interdimensional space to try to find her. The young girl had vanished beyond worldly existence but thankfully, I found her and brought her spirit back to reconnect her with her body. She wasn't mentally strong enough to get the phantom out of her body so I helped get him out and her back in."

"Wow...you can really do that?" Carmella asked incredulously.

"There's infinite power in your thoughts if you link them to the right energy. To help her, I had to surround myself with faith in overcoming the dark forces that blocked her return. Even when I thought I might fail, and in spite of my runaway doubts, my unseen guides helped me stay on course. It was like finding a missing child in the dark. In all honesty, if I hadn't found her, she might never have made her way back home and into her body."

"OK, now I know who to call when I'm lost in space," Carmella joked.

"While I was out of my body, I lost complete sense of myself. I lacked any awareness of time and place. Much to my surprise, when I thought I was doomed because of hostile forces, Jodi unexpectedly came from out of nowhere to rescue me. Just like we have weird energy in this world, there's so much strange, unpredictable energy in that invisible, nonmaterial realm."

"You saw Jodi! She was there?" Carmella was obviously taken aback.

"I don't know how she found me but she did. But I didn't see her. I sensed and heard her inner spirit as she was journeying through the etheric realms. She rescued us and defeated our hostile rival."

"I wonder how she's doing?" Carmella said. She was silent for a moment, then moved closer to Dylan before speaking again. "How did you learn to astral travel? Do you think you can teach me so that I can go where you went and find Jodi?"

"I learned in an occult school, and no, I won't teach you. Let's change the subject. I'm so glad to be here right now. I don't want to think about that strange world anymore today. Where's the pizza? I'm hungry," Dylan said with a childlike pout.

Carmella walked to the oven and took out a steaming pizza. Humming, she cut it and brought it to the table, then poured them both a glass of wine. She lit a candle and gave thanks to the Cosmic Mother. "I'm so happy you're here," she said to Dylan. "For some reason, I didn't want to be alone with Norman."

"No wonder. Norman looks like he's on a bad trip. I can understand why his intensity is a bit of a challenge. And you've been his lover."

"Yes, he loves me so much that when I overwatered and killed his peyote plants, he went into a fiery rage. I was afraid he was going to kill me."

"That is an odd brand of love and it doesn't sound too pleasant. Maybe our meal will taste better if we don't talk about him anymore."

"I agree. What would you like to talk about?" Carmella took a sip of her wine.

"Has anyone called you about Rambo yet?" Dylan asked with a frown.

"No. But this afternoon Luna came over and we practiced some magic that her coven suggested I do to find him. I'm hoping her spell really works because so far, trying to find Rambo by putting up 'lost dog' signs hasn't been very helpful. I feel so sad and violated that someone would trick me and just walk away with him."

"What kind of magic did you do?" Dylan said, looking slightly uncomfortable.

"We faced the noonday sun and put a mirror with a spiked collar on his pillow where he sleeps to reflect the light of some all-knowing Sun god, Amun-Ra. Then we sprinkled some dust on it that Luna said came from a hidden temple chamber in an ancient Egyptian pyramid," Carmella replied with an air of confidence.

"It might be simpler to walk around the site where you lost him and call his name," Dylan said with a chuckle.

"I did that most of yesterday and the day before, too. Actually, I know this sounds crazy but I think I saw Rambo being groomed on the movie set where I went to do my interview. But the dog had most of his hair shaved off and was taken away before I could get close enough to be sure of his identity. Despite all the weirdness, I had some good luck while I was looking for him at the studio. I had an unexpected chance to talk with the producer and he hired me as an extra to work on a documentary he's filming about the Inquisition. Tomorrow, I'm going back to the set to star as a witch who's about to be burned at the stake. But the main reason I want to go back is to have more time to look for Rambo."

"Maybe you should call Luna and get some tips on how to be a witch," Dylan said in a sarcastic tone.

"What? You're joking, right?" Carmella asked with obvious disbelief.

"Well, I remember how she looked at you when we met her. I'm sure she'd be happy to have an excuse to talk to you again."

"Dylan, you're sounding like a jealous boyfriend. But if you want to know about Luna and myself, she's already opened the door for me to join her coven."

"Wow...she wants you to join her coven?" Dylan asked, remembering the howling of aspirant she-wolves he'd heard when they first met Luna.

"Yes, but she's offered me more than what I can honestly accept. Her group is doing a private ritual and she asked if I would take a priestess role and play the part of the goddess Persephone. She told me there would be some surprises and she couldn't tell me all the details of her group's secret workings. Since she said they were doing sex magic, I was afraid I might be encouraged to have sex with Hades. I wasn't sure how I could set personal boundaries in a magic circle. I just can't put myself into a situation where I'm totally unsure of what's expected of me. I'm not so open-minded."

Dylan looked at Carmella with disbelief. For someone who was supposed to be a straight-laced, uptown writer, she certainly had more than her fair share of interactions with the occult underworld. Dylan took a bite of his pizza and chewed slowly while looking at his friend and trying to get a better sense of who she really was. After a long silence, he asked, "You didn't accept Luna's invitation?"

"No, but if I change my mind, I don't think it will be a problem joining her moon circle."

Dylan felt surprised at his emotional reaction to Carmella's story. He was relieved that she had said no to Luna. He wasn't sure exactly why but he'd felt a little uneasy when he met Luna. Perhaps it was because he had an uncanny sense that she was a little moonstruck over Carmella.

"Well, I'm happy you're here with me instead of dancing around a circle with a group of goddess-obsessed women," he told her. "Besides, you're already a Tarot reader and that's considered by many to be witchy. And tomorrow you'll be acting the role of a witch for a movie. How much more practice do you need before you become one? You'd better be careful or you might find yourself cooking your meals in a cauldron," Dylan cautioned with a smile.

Carmella laughed. "Yes, you're right. But you're forgetting the most important thing—hanging around you automatically makes me a witch's apprentice."

"I'm not a witch. Maybe a wizard but definitely not a witch. Did you know that when angels lose their wings, they fly on brooms?"

"No, I didn't know that. But I'm glad to have that very valuable piece of information," Carmella replied with a coy smile. She reached for his hand. "Also, I need to tell you that I showed Luna my magical stone. She sensed that it's an enchanted shaman's stone and told me I need to return it to where I found it as soon as possible. She compared its energy to that of a witch's injured familiar that suffered from being forced to do too much magic."

Dylan nodded thoughtfully. "Can I see the stone?"

"No. I don't want to take it out of its bag. It makes me feel strong yet renders me weak, and it's beginning to freak me out." She let go of his hand. "But I want you to take me to the old house so I can return it. I'm too afraid to go there on my own."

"Sure. I'll take you back to the old house. The other day I talked with a realtor about that place and it turns out that it was built over an Indian burial ground."

"Oh, great," Carmella said, showing tension in her expression.

Dylan couldn't help but feel empathy when he saw the look on her face. "It has an unpleasant history. No one has ever been known to be able to live in the house for very long. The last man who lived there committed suicide in the room upstairs where we felt the presence of departed spirits. For adventure's sake, I'm happy to have an excuse to go back inside." He was quiet for a moment. "Honestly, it's more of a treat that you invited me to be here with you tonight," he added.

"For me too," she answered.

Even though she spoke in earnest, Carmella didn't tell Dylan the complete story about her afternoon with Luna. In spite of her mind instinctively closing to Luna's invitation, her curiosity was attracted to the idea of playing the role of a goddess in a ritual. When she had refused Luna's invitation, Luna had laughed and told Carmella to stop holding herself in check like a shy schoolgirl. The energy around her seemed to be electrically charged as Luna said, "Let me teach you how to intensify your senses. I can initiate you into the mystery of the phoenix and the dragon and show you how to use alchemical formulas to tap into celestial power. With more knowledge, your psychic abilities can become keenly developed and you can harness the power in your stone for your own benefit."

Perhaps if I hadn't lost my dog, I wouldn't feel attracted by her invitation, Carmella reflected while looking at Dylan's beautiful eyes, which seemed to pierce the veil of her soul. She smiled at him and started to reach for his hand...but reached for another piece of pizza instead.

"It's funny," Dylan confessed. "Sometimes people

say I'm hard to talk to but it feels easy to talk with you. What do you think?"

Carmella was thoughtful for a moment as she chewed her pizza. "It feels like we've known each other for a long time and I'm really comfortable being here with you. But your life and my life are so complicated."

"Yeah, I know. I do my best to explain things to Stella but we don't seem to be able to hear one another. She thinks on a different wavelength. I'm seriously asking myself whether I can be married to her anymore. I've been willing to work on our relationship but she keeps driving me crazy with her unilateral choices for our life."

"Maybe we should ask Luna to do a spell to help your relationship," Carmella said in earnest. "Honestly, I know how painful it is to separate from someone and I wouldn't wish it on anyone."

"Oh, no, thank you very much. That's already being taken care of. I found out from my friend Destiny that her mother, the 'Wise Witch of the West' Naomi-Know-Me, was hired by my beloved wife to do a spell to weave our lives back together. If the spell worked at all, its magic backfired because Stella's pregnant with some other man's baby. I just have no idea how to be with her at this point in our relationship. I've lost all positive feelings toward her. Reconciling with her doesn't feel like it's in the cards."

"Oh, dear, that does sound a bit challenging to deal with. But whatever you decide to do, I'll support your decision and help you in any way I can."

"I appreciate that. A lot," Dylan said. As he looked at her, he couldn't ignore his feelings. Made more confident by the wine, he asked, "And what about us, Carmella? In what direction is our relationship going?"

"I don't know and honestly, I'm surprised to hear your question," Carmella answered. "You've been enormous support for me. I appreciate you as a friend. I know you've been having a difficult time in your relationship with your wife, so I've been trying to be respectful and not take your time away from your marriage. I've been learning from you. You know more about magic than anyone else I've ever met. Well, except for Luna, who also seems to know more than most people."

As Dylan thought about how to respond, his cell phone rang. He pulled it out of his pocket and glanced at the number. "I need to answer this," he told Carmella. "It's my mom and I haven't been able to get a hold of her for a while. She's been in the woods up north without phone reception."

He pushed a button on his phone and answered it.

"Hi, Mom," he said, getting up and walking to the living room so he could talk in private. "You left a message on my phone telling me that you're on your way to the rainforest in Brazil? What's happening? I thought you were fighting to save the redwoods in Sonoma County."

"Dylan, I don't have time to explain everything but in this world, this global village, everything's connected," Rowan said. "Yes, I'm still supporting our mission to stop the loggers but things are happening with the new man I met. He wants me to go with him to Brazil next week. He's so cool and he's helping me become more aware of my higher purpose, something I feel really good doing. I want to give my life to protect Mother Nature. The Amazon is the lungs of our planet. If they keep cutting down the forest, we won't have any air to breathe."

Dylan thought she sounded like she needed more air to breathe at that moment.

"Mom, what about your pregnant daughter?"

"I'm on a mission to become more alive than I've ever been in my past. Julie is old enough to handle her own life. If she can get pregnant, she can learn to be an adult and take care of herself. Besides, she's moving in with your father and he can watch over her."

"Mom, if you're going to the Amazon, who's going to look after your house?" Dylan asked.

"Why do you ask?"

"Because I'm going through a rough time with Stella right now. I'd love to have someplace to get away and clear my head so I can figure out what I want in my life in relation to my marriage. That woman is driving me crazy," Dylan confessed.

"Sorry about you and Stella. Right now there seems to be an epidemic of troubled relationships. My friend Moe refuses to talk to me. Last time I spoke to him, he mumbled something about my lack of integrity before he said he never wanted to see me again. After that, I had the surprise of my life when your father called me crying about his problems. He said he'd crawl on his knees and beg me to come back into his life if I would have him. He sounds like he's half crazy."

"Yes, I know. Dad's under scrutiny with his secret fraternity. He might be sued by an initiate who got hurt during some ceremony that went out of control."

"Well, his group has enough lawyers in it to sink the *Titanic*. Your father won't have any trouble doing some countersuit or mediating his way into being the helpless victim. Like they do for everyone in their group, his buddies will help him find a way to squirm out of trouble."

"How can you sound so cold-hearted about Dad?"

"Oh, right! I forgot," Rowan said with obvious sarcasm. "I'm not supposed to say anything bad to you about your father. OK, well in answer to your earlier question...if you want to make my home your home, that will actually help me out because I was wondering who I could find to feed my animals and water my plants. You'll have to walk my dog and get her groomed as part of the deal. Oh, and obviously keep an eye on your sister," Rowan said, quickly changing her tone.

"No problem. I'll be glad to do all that. How long are you going to be gone?"

"We'll stay as long as we can to fulfill our mission to help save the trees in the Amazon. I'm told that we might be gone as long as two or three months. Would you be able to stay that long?"

"Yes, Mom, I think that will work out well for both of us. I'll take good care of everything for you. Are you going to be home tonight? I can come by and get instructions."

"Yes, I should be home in about an hour. Come on over. But I'm frantic about needing to pack and get everything in order. I have so much to do."

"Don't worry. I promise not to take too much of your time. I'll be over later. Bye, Mom," Dylan said and hung up.

As he walked back to the kitchen, Dylan realized that one of the stresses on his mind had eased. He had made the decision to move out of his apartment. Now he had a plan and an easy escape from his life with Stella. His thoughts were disrupted when he saw Carmella putting a piece of pie onto his plate. Her inner beauty shined through her eyes but he couldn't help but sadly remember Stella's apple pie and her betrayal.

"My worldly mom," he said as he gathered his thoughts. "She's becoming a tree hugger with a vengeance. She's getting ready to go to Brazil to help save the rainforest. I'm going to house-sit for her while she's gone. Just the thought of having a different space to live in makes me feel relieved."

"Darn. I was hoping you'd ask to move in with me," Carmella said with a chuckle. It was obvious that she had continued drinking wine while Dylan was in the other room.

Dylan laughed. "Sure, that sounds good too. It wouldn't complicate things much, would it?" He felt his heart lighten at hearing her suggest such a possibility.

He was about to reach for Carmella's hand again when he was jolted by an unexpected noise. Someone was pounding on the door like thunder. They both jumped up and ran to the front room. Carmella looked through the door's peephole.

"It's Norman," she said.

She opened the door slightly.

"Hi, Carmella," Norman said, obviously in a daze. "I thought I'd come over and see if you were missing me. I need you to come over to my house 'cause I'm going to have a party tonight. I've invited this totally cool Jewish shaman with connections to the otherworld to come over and play drums to send the ghost in my driveway back to wherever it came from. Dylan, you can come over too. Maybe you and my shaman friend can drum together and get the boogieman out of my space. I'm hoping if I get rid of the ghosts, things won't be so weird around my house. Can you let me in? It's cold out here."

Carmella opened the door a bit wider and Norman walked in. His eyes looked wild and wasted at the same time. Dylan watched him walk and realized that he was so stoned, his feet didn't seem to move. Norman got to the couch and fell down. Dylan looked at Carmella and shook his head.

"Are you going to be OK?" he whispered so that Norman wouldn't hear.

She sighed. "Yes. It isn't like I haven't seen him like this before. I know what to expect." She turned to Norman. "Do you want me to drive you home? You look like you need a chauffeur."

"Yes, baby, that'll be great. But I'm not wanting to move right now. Maybe I can just sit here with you till my head clears enough to get in my car and go home," Norman answered with a slur.

"Well, if you've invited a shaman to your house, you should be going home soon to meet him," Dylan interjected.

"Don't worry, my man. I've already given him permission to be in my space and do his thing. You jealous? I've got my woman by my side and a shaman who knows how to get rid of boogies instead of run from them…like some people around here do. If you're lucky, you might learn a few lessons from this dude," Norman said in a condescending tone.

"Sure, maybe I'll come by to meet him," Dylan answered, feeling his blood begin to boil. "Carmella, it's time for me to go. I've got some errands to run before I can come to Norman's later. Thanks for the great pizza."

Dylan wasn't happy to see Norman grabbing at

Carmella and was even less happy to hear that he was getting her to drive him back to his home for the night. He decided it would be best to visit Norman's place later in the evening to check on her safety.

"Carmella," Dylan said, "I've got to get going but it sounds like I'll be seeing you at Norman's later. By the way, if you hear anything about Rambo, call me. I've got a gut instinct that he's coming home."

"Thanks. I hope you're right," Carmella said, opening the door for Dylan so he could leave. She walked him outside to say good-bye. "Thanks for being here with me. I feel happy spending time with you."

Dylan looked at her. She appeared vulnerable and strong at the same time. He was becoming more aware of his attraction for her and felt a soulful sense of longing. He leaned over and gave her an awkward kiss. "I'll see you soon," he said. "But it feels completely wrong to be leaving you with a crackhead. He's like an erupting volcano."

"I'll take him home. He's had a rough week. You don't have to worry," Carmella said.

"And what if I do worry?"

"It will be a waste of your time. Besides, I thought you said you were coming to his place later. I'll be waiting for you there. I'll even bring your slice of pie that you're leaving behind," she said, giving him a quick kiss on the cheek and a gentle push toward his car.

"I've sworn off of pie lately but I'll be happy to have a little more of you."

"Only a *little* more?" Carmella said playfully.

"OK…*a lot* more of you." Dylan looked at her and felt an unfamiliar sense of joy.

Chapter Twenty-Two

The Fool
The Cauldron of Consciousness

Surrounded by darkness, Jodi kept searching through the veil of shadows, trying to find the source of the voices she heard calling her name. For a fleeting moment, she glimpsed a ray of light. Then it vanished as suddenly as it had appeared. From challenging mishaps during her out-of-body journey and her accidental arrival at the crossroads of Alpha and Omega, she had been tested to the point where she knew the sound of truth from lies. She recognized the voices of the light from those lost in darkness. No spirit or worldly presence would ever be able to lie to her again without her hearing the falsehood.

Submerged in subconscious vortexes, she floated through timeless space. It had been a struggle to learn to decipher the differences between illusion and reality in the fourth dimension, and to make sense of what she was witnessing, especially since the reality she knew did not exist here and the strange world around her was constantly shifting like sand in windblown dunes. Through trial and error, Jodi came to understand that for her own survival, she had to make a choice between forming an alliance with her higher self and her light-body consciousness, or stumbling and tumbling into alignment with fear and terror. Like opening an unexpected gift, she used her intuition to play her part well in what she called the "Fool's Theater of Karma." She had learned to recognize the magical forces that existed beyond reason.

Jodi felt the pulse of her life force and realized she was near physical death. In vain, she tried to do away with the foreboding sense of her own demise. With every turn, her awareness told her that she needed to balance her perspective, find the center of her spiritual gravity, and make peace with the transformative forces of death and rebirth.

Somewhere on her journey—she didn't remember when or where—she made a pledge never to let anyone talk her into following a path that led away from her true self. But now that distant voices were calling to her, her spirit wanted to follow them to hear what they were saying. She listened with her heart to understand the meaning behind the words echoing off the canyons beyond the reaches of her mind and continued to search the emptiness to find where the voices were loudest.

"Jodi, please come to us, please..." she heard someone say.

Electric shivers ran through her. She hadn't heard anyone call her name for so long, it was shocking to hear a voice calling her now.

"We see you in the light and we want you to come home to us. Call on your angels to guide and protect you..."

Jodi looked around and didn't see any angels but

the pinpoint of light she had seen earlier was gradually becoming larger and brighter. The angel she had watched falter and fall into a trap set by Zak's fiendish strength wouldn't be able to help her, she was certain of that. But now she was afraid that she was losing her sense of what was left of her own power.

Oh my, God, am I going to die?

She tried to consciously hold on to what remained of her astral form and willed it to stop moving, but it was as if she was in a whirlpool being twirled in a flurry of dazzling electrical currents. Then, in the distance, she saw a tunnel of ghostly shadows and felt herself being hurled toward its light by some invisible force.

"I'm scared," she cried out in a loud voice. "I don't want to die!"

Another voice answered her and she knew it to be the soothing, familiar voice of her mother.

"Don't let your heart be troubled," her mother said. "Your spirit is pure and protected by the light. Please forgive me for the harm I've caused you. Fear not, for I am always with you as I am in God's house."

Now Jodi knew for sure that she was dying. Her spirit was caught in a whirlpool of motion beyond happiness or sadness that carried her to realms unknown. She stopped trying to speak. *So...this is what death is like*, she thought as she struggled to open her eyes.

Everything was blurry and she couldn't quite make out the forms that were slowly coming into focus. *Where am I?* she wondered.

She heard someone excitedly say, "She's opened her eyes! She's come back to us!"

Jodi felt herself in her physical body—the pain

frozen in her head, the annoying vibration of loud voices, and the shock of being in a bed in a hospital room with tubes running into her veins. She saw Dylan and Carmella standing next to the bed. Carmella spun on her heels and ran out of the room to call for a nurse.

Dylan held her hand and bent over to give her a gentle kiss on the cheek. "I'm here for you, Jodi. I'm going to make sure that your life gets better." He squeezed her hand.

His voice, appearing as light waves entering her mind, spoke silently with a gentle, humble tone.

"Do you remember rescuing me and Angel while we were stuck in the inner dimensions? One good turn deserves another. When you get out of here, it's my turn to rescue you and make sure you're safe. My mom is giving me her house while she's out of town. You can stay there, in my sister's empty room. It's comfy and secure, and this time, I promise not to let you down."

The shock was too much for Jodi. Was this real? The sharp pain in her head prevented her from speaking, even though she wanted to answer her friend. Just then, Carmella and a nurse entered the room. Jodi closed her eyes and pretended she was asleep.

"It's better to let Jodi rest. You both need to leave now," the nurse told Dylan and Carmella as she checked Jodi's vitals. "You can come back tomorrow to see how she's doing."

Carmella and Dylan each gave Jodi a kiss on the forehead before they left her side. As they walked to the parking lot, Dylan wanted to hold Carmella's hand but stopped himself. Even though he was drawn to her, he had made a silent commitment not to disrespect her relationship with Norman, and he would keep that commitment, even if it was becoming more difficult to do with each passing day.

They reached the hospital parking lot and climbed into Dylan's car. Dylan looked at his cell phone messages and was surprised to see that Lisa had called and left a message. *I'll never again listen to anything that woman has to say*, he thought as he erased her message without listening to it. Focusing his attention on Carmella, he said, "I'm glad you agreed to meet me here today after our crazy night at Norman's last night. I'm looking forward to his rehab treatment. Hopefully, I won't feel the need to check on your safety after he becomes clean and sober." Even as he heard himself say this, he wasn't sure he believed it. His heart would always be happy to see her, whatever the reason.

"You don't have to worry about me," Carmella answered. "Norman is a friend and nothing more. If I did have any lingering doubts about our relationship, Norman doomed any chance for it last night when he took out a syringe, pulled down his pants, and gave himself a shot of speed in the vein next to his balls. He's too crazy for me."

"Yikes! Maybe it's better not to think about Norman. My ears are still ringing from listening to his mojo friend drumming in the parking lot last night to scare away the Seega. Perhaps it wouldn't have been so hard on the ears if that guy would have taken a drum lesson somewhere along his shamanic path. But when I'm here, right now, in this moment, everything improves. Today's a brand-new day, the weather's great, and we get to drive up the coast together. I'm feeling good."

"Yes, I'm happy too, and glad to leave thoughts of Norman behind in the parking lot," Carmella agreed.

"And I'm feeling so much better after seeing Jodi open her eyes. My raven guides came to me last night in a dream and soared in a serene, unbroken circular pattern. When I looked past them I could see the turning of the earth and a bright light coming from a dark cave in the distance. When I woke up, I hoped that my dream symbolized that Jodi would be coming out of her unconscious state." Dylan looked at Carmella, then turned his ignition key and began to drive. He couldn't help but smile when he glanced at Carmella in the soft afternoon light.

"I wish you had seen Rambo in your dream and you could tell me that he's going to be all right."

"Have faith in miracles, Carmella. Maybe you'll find him roaming around somewhere today." Dylan reached over to squeeze her hand for support. "And your good fortune is that you've been offered an acting role in a movie."

"I'm not so sure about becoming a character actress," she said. "All my life I've been a writer and an introvert. Getting into the acting guild and jumping center stage in front of a camera is a little overwhelming."

"Life always presents new opportunities. My crystal ball tells me that you're perfect for the role because inside your soul lives a magnificent witch wearing a black cloak of invisibility."

"Thanks a lot for your vote of confidence. I don't know about this witch stuff, and I don't own a black cape or broomstick. And strangely enough, my shoot was canceled today. The secretary called me to say that

Mr. Stalsburg had an emergency and had to rush to the hospital, and most likely will be rescheduling my work this coming week."

"I wonder if he's suffering from a dog bite..." Dylan mused.

Carmella smiled. "If my dog is shaved bare naked with a henna tattoo on his butt, that might be the case. But then again, maybe you have an overactive imagination."

Dylan laughed. "And maybe I believe in magic."

"That's obvious, Mr. Magic Man," Carmella said with a grin.

"It's not a joke, really. It's just that my mind stays open to possibilities and the inner connectedness of all things."

"Really?" she asked. "Well, I believe in magic too. It's very magical that I'm here with you right now. I was so certain that your relationship with Stella would prevent us from spending time together and I was one hundred percent sure that I would never go to that haunted house again, and yet we're going there now."

"*Never* is a fleeting concept. For instance, my supposed lifelong bond with Stella is broken. Luckily, when she told her estranged lover that she was pregnant with his child, he was ecstatic and invited her to become part of his polyamorous tribal family. Its seven members swap partners within their own group but shy away from allowing new partners to join their intimate family. Because Stella's pregnant with the patriarch's child, she's being invited into their private circle. It's her good karma that she can explore love with the real father of the child and has an extended family to help with her baby. Her choice sets me free of my commitment to her. As of today, I'm moving out of my apartment and into my mom's home to take care of it while she goes to South America."

"This is beginning to sound like a romance novel. Are you sure about all these changes?"

"I don't know. I'm still a bit confused. Ever since several months ago, when Stella decided to change the terms of our relationship, I've been looking at the Fool card in the Tarot. I've been trying so hard to not let myself be the fool. Not having clarity about my feelings made it almost impossible to make decisions about what to do. Love is so complex."

Carmella gripped Dylan's hand tightly and took a deep breath. "I'm sure you're making the right choices. You're following your heart."

"I hope so. We'll find out, I'm sure. But for now, I'm feeling relieved. And as far as going back to the haunted house, I'm glad you're willing to return your mysterious rock to where you found it. It's good karma to return magical tools to their rightful owners, even if the owner might be a ghost."

"That house is scary but if you feel OK going there again, I'm willing to follow you. I'm hoping that when I return the stone, maybe my luck will improve. Besides, the energy in that stone keeps letting me know that it wants to be somewhere else and that it's unlucky for me. Since I've been carrying it, I've had one misfortune after another...the car accident with Norman, my ankle nearly breaking, and my dog disappearing, not to mention what happened with Norman and Jodi. When I think that the energy in the stone may have something to do with all those things, I feel a bit frightened."

"I'm not surprised. You probably have the invisible legions of the underworld knocking on your door to retrieve their precious rock." When Dylan saw the panicked expression on Carmella's face, he said, "I'm kidding, I'm kidding! Don't worry. Hopefully, everything's getting better."

Even though he was driving, he turned to look at Carmella, and for a brief moment, their eyes met. Lost in a growing sense of enthusiasm for his newfound freedom and the potential direction his relationship with Carmella might be heading, Dylan had to swiftly return his focus to the road and slam on the breaks to avoid passing the driveway that led to their destination. He turned the steering wheel and slowly drove down the bumpy driveway, parked the car facing the road in order to make an easy exit, and shut off the engine. He looked at Carmella and saw her face turn pale.

"We'll be OK. All we have to do is walk inside and return the rock. I won't try to communicate with any ghosts, so don't worry. We'll make it quick."

"I'm scared. I can't help it."

Dylan reached over to hold her hand again. "We'll be safe. Our thought-forms are connected to emotion. If we keep focused on fear, it feeds our thoughts and makes the negative grow. As our negative thinking expands, it attracts bad energy and we get trapped into believing that our fears have more power over us than they really do. Thank goodness we don't have to let negative forces rule our lives."

Carmella took off her seatbelt. "But why am I so afraid? This place freaks me out."

"Fears can be past-life memories or subconscious phantoms. You can ask your higher self, your spirit guides, or your angels to illuminate your path with protective light."

"So...you're not scared?"

"Truthfully, I'm just really thirsty," Dylan complained.

"Do you want to go back to town to get something to drink?" Carmella asked hopefully.

"It took us so long to get out here, let's just do what we came to do. But I really wish I had some water."

"We'll be quick. As soon as we leave, we'll make a stop and get some water for you," Carmella said reassuringly.

"OK, let's go in, return the stone, and get out of here," Dylan said as he got out of the car.

Soon he was leading them up the familiar path to the old dwelling. The wind had blown the door off of one hinge so that the door hung partly open. He gave it a little push and they entered the house. The smell of mold and decay assaulted their nostrils.

"Do you want me to help you? I don't want you to worry about being here," Dylan asked.

"You don't have to worry about me."

"Yes, I know, but I don't mind helping."

"I need to return the stone myself." Carmella went to the broken chest of drawers, opened the top drawer defiantly, and began to set the stone inside. At that moment, something caught her attention and she turned to gaze out a nearby broken window, the stone still in her hand. "Look outside, Dylan. It seems like this house is being woven with brilliant green moss to become one with the Tree of Life. It's so beautiful! I'm so happy to be here, where I can see something so out of the ordinary...so special. I feel like I'm walking on sacred ground where the energy is flying like sparkling jewels falling from a star. There's so much magic here. It makes me feel so empowered."

"No..." Dylan countered. "You're in an abandoned old house that is falling down and in complete ruin. There's only collapse and destruction here. If there was a tree outside, it would be the Tree of Death. There must be a spell within the stone that is keeping you from opening your eyes to the truth of what is in front of us. You've got to release your attachment to that stone or its enchantment will hold you captive to these crazy thoughts."

"No, Dylan, that can't be true..."

"I'm sure there's some kind of strange magic tied to that stone. Be present inside the reality you are in. There's enchantment here but it has a different intelligence than you or I. You must be true to who you are to be safe."

At that moment, Dylan saw an old lady with long, knotted white hair float across the room and disappear into a nearby wall. He muffled his unexpected screech of dread and with stressed composure, continued, "You must listen to what your heart is saying and see through this crazy mirage. That stone is gripping you as if you're a genie in a bottle. If you continue holding it, it will keep you captive in its ghostly demands and will most likely drain your life force. *You're* not seeing reality."

"There's so much heat. Look outside, Dylan, the roof is on fire...run...Dylan...run... You've got to leave right now or you're going to die. Hurry! You've barely got time to get to the door. I feel it in my heart. You're the one not seeing the world! You're in danger!"

"Carmella, because you've fallen in love with that rock, it's taking control of your mind. Let it go!"

As soon as Dylan had spoken these words, he

started to choke uncontrollably. A river of water began cascading from his mouth as if it were shooting out of a culvert after a rainstorm.

"Well, it doesn't look like you're thirsty anymore," Carmella said incredulously as Dylan began to wipe the flowing water from his chin. "I can't believe I just saw that."

With an increasing sense of panic, Dylan continued, "Let the stone go, now! It only has bad energy. Put up protective boundaries around your heart so that it can't control you. Think about where you want to go. This is the perfect time to fulfill your higher purpose, complete your writing, and activate your inner high priestess who wants to heal the world. Trust that the magic in the universe will give you what you need. You don't want this stone. You're a powerful woman without it."

Dylan started to feel an electric fire flowing through his veins. He knew that he too was becoming a victim of the stone's magical will. With all his might, he reached to grab Carmella's hand and tried to take the stone from her.

"Don't touch my stone!" she screamed, pulling her hand away.

"Let it go! Give it up! It's taking over your will and wants to take over your mind."

"You can't take it from me!" Carmella cried loudly while attempting to bite his hand as he again reached for hers.

Dylan quickly pulled his hand away and knocked her to the ground. They began to wrestle and the old house began to shake as if it were weathering a storm. Rolling on the dirty, wet floor, Carmella kicked fiercely while screaming like a hyena. Feeling an unknown strength, she punched Dylan as if he were a mere paper doll.

Writhing in unexpected pain from her strike to the crown of his head, Dylan realized he was wrestling with a force much larger than his slender friend. "You don't need whatever enchantment this stone is offering you. There's too much unknown, strange power in it," he said while gathering his strength and putting her in a leg lock. He then grabbed her wrist and began hitting her hand against the floorboards in an attempt to get her to release the stone.

Fearing that Dylan was about to break her hand, Carmella was brought back to a painful present reality. She unwillingly let the stone drop from her grip. Quick to react, Dylan kicked it across the floor to the other side of the room. Carmella started to cry.

"I'm sorry," he stated with sadness. "I would never hurt you. But if you didn't release the stone, it would never let go of its hold on you. You were in serious danger because it was merging with your life force and you didn't realize that you were under its illusion. Please know I would never intentionally make you feel bad. I'm only looking out for you." Dylan began to hold her and tenderly kissed her hand.

"I'm sorry too. I don't know what happened to me. I came here to return the stone."

"Magic isn't always logical," he replied, looking into her eyes for any hints of lingering supernatural energy. For a brief moment, he saw the symbol of the Eye of Horus as if it was a tattoo drawn on the center of her forehead, but it dissolved almost as quickly as it appeared.

Carmella turned her hand to hold his. She appeared to be waking from a bad dream.

"Come on. We've got to hurry and get out of here before something else strange happens," Dylan said, pulling her to her feet.

She looked at him. "I just felt something brush past my ankle and I'm getting scared again. Maybe it's the owner of the rock."

Holding hands, they fled outside into the sunlight. Even though they were both covered with dirt from head to toe, Carmella smiled. She was happy that she would never have to go back into the old house again.

"I'm glad to see your ankle has mostly healed," Dylan commented, noticing how fast Carmella had left the house.

"Yes...but that place feels so creepy that even if my ankle was broken in three places, I would have run out of there."

"Well, here we are," he said as they reached the car. "And it's a warm, sunny day." Dylan opened her car door. As he did, he glanced back at the house and was sure he saw a shadow move across the door. He decided not to mention it to Carmella.

Dylan got into his car, started the engine, and looked in his rearview mirror.

"Zak, get out of the car. You're not invited to come with us." He turned off the engine.

"What?" Carmella jumped and turned around to look behind her. She saw nothing but felt a large kiss on the top of her head.

Dylan felt the sense of a traversing power brush past him. He didn't move. After a couple of minutes of stressed silence, Dylan started the car again.

"We're out of here. I'll drive you back to your car."

"What did you see, Dylan? For a moment I felt like I was in a sci-fi movie."

"An old acquaintance. Don't worry. He's gone."

At that moment, Carmella's cell phone rang.

"Hello," she answered and was silent for a moment. Then she squealed with excitement. "You have Rambo? Thank you, yes, I'll be there as soon as possible!" She talked for several more minutes, then turned off the phone and screamed with joy.

"Someone found your dog?" Dylan asked.

"Yes, someone with a bandaged arm brought him to the secretary in the production office. She's sure its Rambo because his name tag is on his collar, and she recognizes him from the other day when she saw him with me. I'm so excited!"

"Does she know the person who brought him to her office?"

"She said a man she didn't recognize dropped him off and left quickly. She said he was polite but wouldn't say anything about where he found him. I don't care. I'm so happy!"

"So far, today is a day to celebrate. I'm very happy for you," Dylan said. "And I'm happy for Rambo that he isn't sporting a rainbow Mohawk."

Carmella laughed. She couldn't contain her excitement and repeatedly asked Dylan to drive faster, even though he was already going over the speed limit as he zipped around the curves and weaved in and out of the busy traffic.

"Will I see you later this evening?" Carmella asked when they arrived at her car.

"I was hoping you'd ask. I'll come by after dinner. Right now I'm going home to start packing for my move."

Carmella felt her heart smile as she opened the door to leave.

❧

Later that evening, Dylan found himself feeling anxious as he knocked on Carmella's door. He made a mental commitment to accept whatever happened between them with a positive attitude. Good or bad, right or wrong, he would welcome whatever this experience might bring.

Invited in like a long-lost friend, Dylan enjoyed the warm embrace and easy connection that Carmella offered him. After having watched her anxiously fret over her lost dog, it was a relief to see Carmella and Rambo back together again.

"I knew you'd find him. My gut instinct told me that he would be found."

"Yes. I'm so excited. And he has all his fur," Carmella said. "You were also right when you said things would be getting better. When I went online after I got home I had an email telling me that my 'Revolving Wheel of the Sacred Circle' magazine article sold and is going to be published next month. I'm getting paid enough for my writing and for my little acting role that I'll be able to pay my bills for a couple of months. And I feel so much better about myself knowing that someone appreciates my writing. It was so hard getting fired from my editorial position. I didn't know if I'd ever recover."

"You look like you're recovering just fine," Dylan replied with an expression of unswerving enchantment. "In fact, you're showing signs of doing better than if you had stayed on with your job in New York. And do you know how many people wish they could get hired at the production studio? Lots! Fortune is obviously on your side. And now you have genuine proof that you're one gorgeous witch."

Carmella laughed. Dylan felt irresistibly attracted to her. Her natural warmth touched his heart in a way that made him want to sing a song of gratitude to the gods.

A good sign, Dylan thought, but he didn't want to look too deeply into her eyes in case he was deluding himself and might wake up from this dream of happiness. Still, he couldn't deny that his longing for her grew stronger every time they were together. But what if she didn't feel the same way?

His uncertainty turned to excitement as he watched her kiss Rambo good night and put him into his doggie bed. She smiled with her bright, beautiful eyes, walked to Dylan's side, and pulled him close to her. Holding him tightly, she gave him a kiss that merged their bodies in an unspoken bond of trust. Together they turned and started to walk past the flickering candles toward her bedroom.

As Dylan took it all in, he began to experience something that had been missing in his life for a long time. His heart felt the peace and serenity of being welcomed home.

About the Author

Kooch N. Daniels, M.A., is a professional intuitive living in the San Francisco North Bay Area. She has spent her life doing readings and helping people develop their psychic abilities. Early in her life she traveled to India to study palmistry, and this experience, mixed with obtaining her degree in psychology, was a turning point in becoming a reader. By learning to listen to the silent voice of intuition, her professional journey has taken her from reading beer foam in bars to reading cards in Fortune 500 executive suites. For twenty-five years she has worked at California Renaissance Fairs, where she has given many thousands of readings. She has been the keynote speaker at Readers Studio in N.Y. and has given Tarot workshops in California, Europe, and Mexico. Her fascination with what lies hidden behind the veil has inspired a lifelong study of Eastern mysticism with many teachers, most significantly, Tantric scholar Harish Johari and the hugging saint from India, Sri Mata Amritanandamayi.

Website: www.cybermystic.com

Other Books by Kooch Daniels

The Art & Magic of Palmistry
The Sacred Wisdom of the Planets (eBook)

Books by Kooch Daniels and her partner, Victor Daniels

Sacred Mysteries, The Chakra Oracle
Awakening The Chakras
Tarot At A Crossroads
Tarot D'Amour
Matrix Meditations